Elizabeth Bankes, n
England and emigrat
family as a young child. In the 1970's and 80's she
moved between New Zealand, England, and
Australia, travelling widely in the following years.

Elizabeth is currently a tutor of English at the
University of New South Wales while previously
teaching in a number of secondary schools. Her
teaching career was interrupted by a few year's break
to work at SBS Television.

The Body in the Boarding House is her first novel
although she has written two screen plays and in
2014 completed her Master of Creative Writing
(Merit) at the University of Sydney.

She lives in Sydney with her second husband, has two
grownup children and currently has three
grandchildren.

Credits

I would really like to thank the following family and friends who read the various versions of this book, offered suggestions, and corrected my punctuation.

It has been a slow process as working fulltime only allows a few hours per week to write but we got there in the end.

I've listed everyone in first name alphabetical order – easier that way.

Alicia Jacenko
Catherine Charles
Christina Austron
David Whitehouse
Dinah Rawlinson
Julia Morgan
Lea Barker
Lucy Burke
Narelle Hassell
Pat Chamberlain
Steve Bankes
Sue Fullwood

THE SCHOOL

The road is an ugly gash through the school grounds. It divides the area into the traditional and modern. One side of the road contains 1960's bland rectangular blocks of brick, while the other side is sandstone, imperious with a mock medieval turret jutting from the roof. This side was built in the 1800s. No school, even with the amount of money this private one has, can afford to construct in sandstone anymore.

The original three-storey sandstone building is large and dominates the oval. The balcony off the staffroom has views over Sydney Harbour as do a number of the classrooms.

Boarding houses, like stately homes, are dotted on the periphery of the extensive school grounds which contain tennis courts, rugby fields, cricket pitches and nets, and even an old Fives court.

There are no lifts in the old part of the school. Stairs zig zag their way up from the ground floor which contains the Art Department, to the classrooms, the staffroom and to offices for select members of staff on the floors above. Stone and wood are the predominant materials.

Along the corridors are glass cases filled with memorabilia: the World Wars, House Colours, sporting victories, historical artefacts, and photographs of past and present students. In the gaps between the cases are the gold engraved boards listing the names of past pupils and masters who died fighting for their country.

In contrast to the melancholy of the past, modern metal lockers are placed in discreet corners of the corridors to house the boys' academic and sporting paraphernalia. They are the heart of the school. It's where friendships are forged, enemies are fought, gossip is spread, and secrets are kept.

The school is a place of privilege.

A RUGBY MATCH

The mirror smirked back.

Bentley Shute stood turning his face from side to side. He leant in closer to the mirror, squinting as he studied his nose. Were there any problem areas? A facial was due soon. Maybe he should bring the appointment forward. The mirror began to fog with the steam from his breath. He rubbed a section of the glass for one last look. Not bad. But, a facial and a touch up of the roots definitely wouldn't go astray. Bentley folded his towel over the rail and wandered naked into his bedroom. The noise of a crowd gathering on the playing fields outside his apartment drew him to the window.

   The boarding master could see that it was another sparkling autumn Sydney afternoon with the sea in the distance reflecting the bright sunlight. Boys, some with parents, and clusters of Old Boys were starting to line the perimeter of the rugby field. Many of the spectators wore the school scarf, the fathers wearing cream chinos, navy blue jumpers thrown with careless precision around shoulders, the mothers in Country Road skirts and jackets, in preparation for when the sun had dimmed and the air chilled. Parents from the opposing school were also wearing similar attire, the uniform of the middle class.

The game, soon to start, was especially important. Last season St Cuthbert's had narrowly lost the Greater Public Schools' Rugby Union Shield to Ignatius College, but this year, 1986, would hopefully see the return of the Shield to St Cuthbert's, believed by the school to be its rightful owners. Tension was mounting around the ground and the spectators eagerly awaited the kickoff.

Turning away from the window, Bentley slid open the wardrobe and pulled out a neatly ironed dark blue shirt and pulled a pair of cream trousers off their hanger. His choice of dress was classic. He had no time for the current tasteless fashion. *Miami Vice* had a lot to answer for. He chose some burnished tan brogues from a collection neatly paired at the bottom of the wardrobe, then from a chest of drawers took out a selection of underwear which he laid carefully on the bed. Boxers or Y fronts? He wanted to be comfortable, but he also wanted to be prepared for whatever may eventuate this Saturday night. He chose the Y fronts. They showed him off to better advantage than comfy boxers.

After a subtle spray of Davidoff's *Cool Water*, the teacher swung the school scarf nonchalantly around his neck and left the flat. The boarding house was empty of boys. Bentley walked slowly down to the playing fields to mingle amongst the swelling crowd. Boys stood aside as he walked past, some calling out,

'Afternoon, Sir' while a number of the fathers shook his hand. He stopped to chat with parents about the pending game and its likely winner, then moved on, spreading his benevolence papal-like to his admiring flock.

Among the throng of parents, boys and spectators, a couple stood, slightly removed from the rest of the spectators. Occasionally, a parent or teacher would go up to them and shake the man's hand or kiss the woman on the cheek. Bentley too, wended his way through the crowd to pay his respects, shaking hands and murmuring consoling words to the pair. After the brief exchange, he continued his walk towards St Cuthbert's oldest sandstone building which towered over the Oval, where the tall goal posts stood at either end ready for the game.

On the hallowed turf of the rugby pitch a mob of Sulphur-crested cockatoos pecked at the cropped grass, oblivious of the crowd standing at its perimeters. Suddenly, without warning, the cloud of white flew into the air as one, screeching like banshees as they made their way over the school to settle in the tall eucalyptus trees which shaded the cricket nets on the other side of the road. Conversations stopped as heads turned upwards to watch the spectacle. Bentley frowned as he glanced skyward. Stupid noisy creatures.

The three storey building had a view which encompassed the wealthy Eastern suburbs with their private jetties and the exclusive inlets in the not far distance. The school, like many of the other private institutions, was positioned on some of the most valuable real estate in the city.

A group of teachers had gathered on the staffroom balcony. The game was about to start, and they could see Bentley making his way through the crowd.

'Bentley. Bentley,' one called out. 'Come up here. Better view.'

Bentley acknowledged the request with a slight nod of his head, but before venturing up the stairs to join the group, walked over to another cluster of parents and boys to share his predictions. The boys smiled with gratitude at his presence, and a couple of the mothers giggled appreciatively on hearing his hope that the other team would be thrashed. One mother observed to him and those hovering in her immediate circle, that it was nice to see the Sinclairs at the game after the sad loss of their son. Such a shame, as he was in Year 11 with a bright future ahead of him and he would have been playing today.

And it was hard to believe that it was only last year when that other poor boy had that dreadful accident on the excursion to New Zealand. Heads nodded vigorously in agreement and sympathy while another mother whispered to the group that perhaps excursions should be stopped. For a seventeen-year-old boy to end up in a wheelchair was just too awful to think about. Such a waste. Bentley agreed with the mothers' observations, and with seeming reluctance, left the group and walked upstairs to the staffroom and out onto the balcony to join the teachers awaiting his arrival.

'About time,' scolded Ian Walsh possessively, in an attempt to reinforce himself as an established member of Bentley's inner sanctum.

Bentley smiled with his brilliant white teeth. 'Well, at least one of us has a sense of duty.'

The sound of cheering made the teachers turn their attention to the action on the field. It was 3.15 at last, and The First XV ran out, lining up to welcome the opposition. The team, along with the spectators, clapped the arrival of the rival Greater Public School rugby team. This match would decide the finalists for the Shield. The teachers on the balcony watched with interest.

'Do you think we'll win?' Marlene asked eagerly; the only woman in the group surrounding Bentley.

Bentley slowly turned his head to stare at her. 'I have absolutely no idea, my dear. Nor do I care. Rugby is such a brutish game.'

'I thought you liked it?' she asked peevishly, shocked at what seemed such a contradictory attitude.

'Oh, but I do. It brings kudos to the school if we win the Shield. But the game itself means nothing to me,' he stated derisively.

Marlene was about to speak then stopped. It didn't pay to query Bentley.

A TEACHER IS MISSING

The knocking on the door to Mr. Shute's apartment was tentative, timid. There was a pause, an expectant wait, nothing. The next knock was louder. More insistent.

'Sir. Sir. It's Matthews, Sir. Mr Pritchard wants to see you, Sir.''
He aimed his voice at the crack between the door and the jamb then pressed his ear up against the door and held his breath, listening for movement in the flat.
Silence.

James Matthews, a Year 11 boarder stood and waited. His hair was wet from a shower after footy practice, his khaki uniform hastily put on. Should he keep knocking and risk the wrath of Mr Shute or do as he was told by Mr Pritchard? It wasn't always easy to know what mood Benty would be in, especially early on a Monday morning.

'Matthews. Be a good lad and tell Mr Shute I need to see him urgently. Ask him to come straight to my office,' the headmaster had instructed the boarder after waiting on the sideline for him to finish footy practice. Aware that Mr Shute's mercurial nature could be both appealing and frightening, made the head put his hand affectionately on the boy's shoulder to reassure him that his assistance was much appreciated.

'Yes, Sir,' Matthews answered as if on army parade, happy to please and to be given responsibility, even if it meant interrupting Mr Shute's morning routine.

As he raised his hand to knock again, a boy emerged from a dormitory wearing only boxer shorts and carrying a towel. He wandered up to Matthews and stopped inquisitively.

'Gidday, Matto. What'cha doin'?'

'Trying to wake Benty up. Mr Pritchard wants to see him.'

'Oooooh. Benty in trouble?' Stuart asked hopefully.

'How would I know?' Matthews protested. 'But he won't answer the door.'

'Knock again. Maybe he's having a shower.'

Stuart threw the towel over his shoulder and hammered on the door.

'Jesus, Stu. Take it easy. You'll bloody wake the dead,' Matthews whispered desperately.

The two boys stood looking at the door then at each other. Suddenly a bell rang from across the playing fields.

'Bugger. That's breakfast. Gotta have a shower. Sorry, mate, gotta go. Keep trying,' Stuart yelled as he ran off down the corridor to the boarders' bathroom.

The bell soon rang again warning the boarders that there were only five minutes to reach the dining room before breakfast was served. Doors opened from the dorms. Boys emerged putting on ties, tucking in shirts and pulling up socks, eager to appease the hunger, which was rarely satisfied with the institutionalised food of a boarding school.

Matthews stayed where he was, hoping that the bell would jolt Mr Shute into action. As a boarding master, Mr Shute attended breakfast with his house and he was one for carrying out the duties of a master diligently. He stood by the traditions of the school with great devotion, especially as this school was one of the most expensive and oldest private schools in Sydney, possibly Australia.

Matthews knocked again but his attempt lacked his previous urgency as he now knew there would be no answer.

'Jonesy. Have you seen Benty?' Matthews asked as Peter Jones hurried past on his way to the dining hall, yanking up his tie while attempting to button his shirt

'No. And I don't want to. Bloody pillow biter,' Jones replied.

'Mate. Keep your voice down. You don't want him to hear you.'

'I don't care. He threatened to give me the cane in prep yesterday. And I'd done nothing.' Jones looked around quickly, his voice having risen in protest at the perceived injustice.   'Anyway, why do you want him?'

'Pritchy wants to see him.'

'Hope he's in trouble. Serve him right. Bloody sadist,' Jones complained as he ran to catch up with the stragglers.

Matthews took one last look at the door to Mr Shute's flat, shrugged and walked down the stairs to the entrance hall then made his way across the Oval and up the stone steps to the headmaster's office.

This time his knock was answered, and he regretfully told Mr Pritchard that Mr Shute wasn't in his rooms. Mr Pritchard, irritated by the information, clicked on his intercom, and asked his secretary if she could call for Mr Shute over the school's PA system. A minute later Daphne rang the headmaster to inform him that Shute was not at breakfast in the dining hall.

'That's odd. He never misses his breakfast. Oh well, perhaps he's a bit under the weather.' Pritchard hung up the phone slowly and turned his attention back to the student. 'Anyway, Matthews, thanks for trying. Hurry on to breakfast now.'
Pritchard picked up the phone again once Matthews had left the office and tapped four digits. It was answered immediately.

'Jim. It's Robert. Can you pop into my office?' Pritchard asked, then as an afterthought, added, 'Better bring Bill as well.' His face was a mixture of puzzlement and anxiety. Where on earth was Shute? This was his school and as he frequently told Daphne, it had to run like a well-oiled machine.

Within a few minutes, Jim Cameron, the Deputy Headmaster knocked at the headmaster's door and walked in without waiting for an answer. Jim, a man in his forties, had an aura of authority which his position required, but at the same time his open and regular features made him seem personable and approachable. According to Daphne, many women would have found him attractive.

He was soon followed by the entrance of Bill MacGregor, the School Sergeant. Both were surprised and a little annoyed by the request to see the head at this time of the morning when classes were about to begin. Normally the two men would be doing their rounds of the school to make sure that all boys were heading straight to class, that no-one was mucking up and that uniforms were being worn correctly.

Mr Pritchard, at his desk, looked up gratefully. 'Thanks for coming so quickly but I'm a bit concerned about Mr Shute. I asked Matthews to tell him to come and see me before breakfast, but according to Matthews he didn't answer the door and he didn't attend breakfast either. It seems a bit odd. I wondered if the two of you could go to his flat and see if he's okay. It's not like him to miss breakfast with his boys.' Pritchard scratched his head. 'It's probably nothing, but just want to make sure.'

'He may have slept in,' Jim Cameron suggested, wondering why Pritchard needed the two of them to locate the boarding master.

'Possibly. But anyway, would you mind going to the boarding house to check on him?'

'Of course not, Robert,' Jim replied, trying to keep the sigh out of his voice and with a nod at Bill, they left the headmaster's office.

'What is it about bloody Shute that has everyone running around after him?' Bill asked rhetorically as the men walked briskly across the Oval to the boarding house. 'God knows why we both have to go.'

THE BODY

Bill MacGregor, the school disciplinarian, and the monitor of school security, reached into his pocket and pulled out a bundle of keys. He quickly selected the master key to all the boarding houses and their private apartments and inserted it into the lock of Mr Shute's door. MacGregor, like a few of the men on the staff sported a military style moustache, a brylcremed head of hair and wore his family tartan kilt on special school occasions with great pride. He administered his punishments with both humour and relish.

As Bill pushed the door open, Jim waited cautiously before entering the rooms. He knew he was being ridiculous to think there could be a booby-trap in a boarding master's living quarters but his experience during his tour of duty in Vietnam had taught him to always expect the worst. He peered into the room then signalled for the Sergeant to follow him in. There was no sound of any movement in the flat although somewhere a radio could be heard playing quietly.

They stood in the lounge feeling like intruders but noting the décor. The carpeted floor was covered with a large oriental rug on which stood a glass coffee table decorated with miniature boxes painted with scenes of jagged trees and rock formations. Wall hangings, hinting at geishas performing sexual activities on seemingly satisfied customers, covered the crisp white walls, and on the kitchen-divide was a Japanese-style teapot surrounded by five small handle-less cups. Placed above the fireplace were three curved samurai swords with delicate carving on the blades.

Bill frowned with disapproval at the effeminate quality of the apartment. 'Bloody poofter,' he muttered under his breath, then peered around guiltily in case he'd been heard by Jim or the occupant. He knew that Jim had an Asian wife so probably wouldn't find the stuff in Bentley's lounge odd. They walked through the lounge, past the open kitchen towards what they assumed to be the bathroom. They cautiously opened the door. The bathroom was extremely neat, and the two men could see hair gels, moisturisers among the usual toiletries. Bill held his tongue.

Closing the door, they paused in front of the door to the last room which could only be the bedroom. Bill hung back and let Jim tap on the door.

Neither men had been in Shute's apartment before. They moved in different circles among the staff even though many of them, including Bill and Jim, lived on the school grounds. Shute had a coterie of teachers and older students who paid him homage. His tongue could strip a person bare and although Bill MacGregor was tough, he found the camp overtones to the vitriol most unsettling. The thought of sex between two queers was disgusting. His body gave an involuntary shudder.

Jim, had no such reaction to the possible homosexual clues in the apartment. His philosophy was each to their own. He'd seen too much of man's inhumanity to man. His face was impassive as he waited for a reply to his knock.

The radio in the kitchen continued playing a song that neither recognised.

Jim knocked again this time louder but as before there was no answer. He turned the knob on the door which opened easily but he did not enter. MacGregor also hesitated in the doorway. Would they find sex objects, piles of male magazines or Shute still in bed handcuffed to the bedpost? MacGregor was surprising himself with his own imagination. Jim Cameron had no such thoughts. He was back in his army days, carefully predicting what he might find and how to approach a potential crime scene.

He held up his hand for Bill to wait by the door, putting his finger to his lips and tiptoed carefully into the room. The thin white blinds were still down, and the room was striped with rays of light. Jim thought he could make out a shape under the quilt cover or was it merely the elaborate pattern of a samurai warrior about to strike the enemy with his sword? He crept closer. He could now see Shute's blond hair poking out from under the cover. The normally carefully gelled Nazi-esque coif was askew. 'Mr Shute. Bentley. Are you awake?' Jim whispered urgently as Bill edged closer to the bed to watch.

The deputy head lent over and pulled back the quilt. Shute, still fully dressed, lay with his face in the pillows. Bill stepped backwards in horror as Jim slowly replaced the quilt on the body's torso after he'd noted the back of Shute's head, neck and shoulders were covered in slashes. One was deep enough to show bone and bloodied flesh. Blood had seeped out of his shirt and onto the pillows and a large stain had spread onto the sheet covering the mattress.

Jim, pushing up his jacket sleeve, carefully pressed his fingers under Shute's ear. There was no pulse. Not that he'd expected one. No-one could survive such a loss of blood.

'Are you alright, Bill?' Jim asked, seeing him pull out a handkerchief and gag into it.

'Yes. Yes,' the Sergeant exclaimed quickly, embarrassed at his own queasiness. 'What do we do now?'

'There must be a phone here. We need to ring an ambulance. And the police.' Jim walked around the bedroom then into the lounge searching for a telephone. He found it hidden behind a small Japanese screen as if its presence was offensive, an ugly practical object in the middle of delicacy and beauty.

21

Dialling 000, Jim gave the address to the service operator, with a brief description of the state of the dead teacher.

'Bill, can you contact Daphne and tell her to ring the police and inform Robert what has happened,' Jim said as he handed him the receiver and hurried back into the bedroom.

MacGregor, glad to have something to do, pressed the numbers for the extension and was quickly answered.

'Mr Pritchard's office. Daphne speaking,' Daphne answered in her secretarial tone.

'Where's the headmaster? It's an emergency,' demanded MacGregor who normally spoke to Daphne in what he hoped was a winning way. Despite the blood and gore in the bedroom, he was still able to picture her wearing the tight black jumper, black stockings, high heels and the knee length check pencil skirt. Daphne's fashion preference leant back to Mary Quant of the 1960s, much classier than the current trend of frizzy dry hair, shoulder pads and high waisted baggy jeans.

'Oh. Hello, Mr MacGregor,' she replied with exaggerated patience. Bill could be very demanding when he wanted to be. He needed to be kept in his place or he'd have her running around like she was his secretary. 'Mr Pritchard is interviewing parents and cannot be disturbed.'

'Sorry, Daphne, but you'll have to get him. It's Shute,' he paused. 'I can't say why. But it's urgent.'

'Mr MacGregor. I'm sorry but I can't interrupt him.'

'Daphne. There's been a terrible accident. Get the headmaster and call the police.'

'Oh, my God, Bill. What's happened?' Daphne capitulated; her voice full of concern.

'I can't say now. But tell him to come quickly to Shute's apartment,' MacGregor instructed. 'And the boys can't be allowed back in the house.'

'I'll go and tell him now, Bill. I'll ring the police once I've told him,' Daphne said. 'Can I do anything? Is Bentley okay?'

MacGregor ignored the questions and hung up the phone. He couldn't be doing with Daphne's concern at this moment. He walked quickly back into the bedroom to join Jim, his eyes avoiding the body, but he didn't want to be alone. MacGregor looked around the room in the vague hope that he would see a clue as to what had happened. Nothing seemed out of place but how would he know? He'd have to leave the detective work up to the police. Jim seemed to be taking the whole drama in his stride. He too stood by the bed, his eyes moving from the body to the furniture, to the window and the floor. Like Bill, Jim had not been in the flat before, but Bentley's taste did not surprise him. Bentley had often held forth on the high quality of Japanese art and furniture.

The alarm clock on the Japanese cabinet next to the bed, jarred. Its functionality seemed out of place. Shute's clothes were hung neatly over the back of a wicker chair and his polished shoes were placed under it. A Japanese kimono was draped over the end of the bed. His school brief case sat next to the cabinet, its brown leather shiny, with his initials B.S. embossed in gold on the front below the lock.

He must love all things Asian, thought MacGregor as he took in the room. What's wrong with being a bloody Australian? He shook his head and returned to the lounge. It was all too disturbing. The lounge was no better as Bill noticed the books of Japanese eroticism which lined the slim bookshelves and the small lithographs of men in various sexual positions dotted above the shelves.

Bloody pervert. Unbelievable the way they carry on. Hope the boys don't see any of this stuff. MacGregor, caught up in his disapproval, was surprised by the sudden appearance of the headmaster in the lounge.

'Bill. What on earth is going on? Where's Jim?' Pritchard asked, walking urgently up to Mr MacGregor as if wanting reassurance.

'He's in the bedroom. Still in bed. Looks like he's dead. Actually, he *is* dead. Not Jim. Shute,' he corrected. 'There's a lot of blood. The ambulance is on its way.'

Pritchard was shocked into silence by the description.

'Sir? Robert?'

'Oh, yes.' Pritchard reflected for a moment, staring at MacGregor as if puzzled as to why they were in Shute's apartment. 'Daphne's rung the police,' he said absently. He stopped speaking as it dawned on him the magnitude of the situation. His hands fumbled at his tie and he pulled at the Windsor knot.

'How did he die? Has he had a heart attack?' Pritchard asked as Jim joined them in the lounge.

'No!' Jim and Bill answered in unison.

'A young man like that wouldn't die in his sleep. Would he?' asked Pritchard, his face full of concern as he clutched at straws.

'He didn't die in his sleep. It looks like someone attacked him with a knife, or maybe an axe. I think he's been murdered,' MacGregor admitted. Jim stood back letting Bill have his moment in the sun.

'Oh, my God,' Pritchard said, his voice trembling with shock. 'This is a disaster for the school. Our reputation. Are you sure he's dead?' he pleaded, turning to Jim.

'Unfortunately, yes. Very much so.'

Jim led the headmaster into Shute's bedroom and indicated the body partially hidden underneath the stained colourful quilt. Pritchard moved a little closer and went to touch him but then pulled back his hand as he saw the gashes and the blood. The stillness of the man repelled him.

Pritchard turned to his deputy. The ramifications of the situation were all too obvious. Police. Media. Publicity of the worst kind. A death could result in a loss of enrolments. The parents of future boarders might think twice about sending their sons to a school if it were linked to danger.

'Bloody hell, Jim, we've only just got over the last disaster.'

'And the media loved it. Fed the public the usual snobby rubbish about private schools,' Bill butted in to confirm Pritchard's fear that the school would receive negative publicity.

'Oh God, we'll just have to deal with it. Where on earth are the police?' Pritchard asked desperately.

'An ambulance is on its way and the police should be here soon,' Jim stated calmly. Robert would need to keep his head and wits about him in such a situation.

THE POLICE ARRIVE

The three men stood silently in the lounge, all aware of the body in the bedroom and all wishing for the ambulance and the police to arrive. Jim could sense Robert and Bill's discomfort so said nothing as they all turned to leave the flat and wait in the corridor of the boarding house, but their departure was stopped when they heard an urgent knock on the door. Jim opened the door to find a flustered Daphne who led two policemen into the living room. Pritchard and MacGregor walked eagerly up to them, relieved that help was at hand and the situation was no longer their responsibility.

The younger policeman dressed in a sergeant's uniform followed slightly behind his superior, a detective in civilian clothes, a dark suit, white shirt, and neutral tie.

The latter put out his hand to Bill MacGregor, mistaking him for the headmaster and introduced himself and his colleague, 'Good morning. I'm Detective Alan Stone and this is Sergeant Raymond O'Shea.'

'Good of you to come so quickly. This is the headmaster, Mr Robert Pritchard, and Mr James Cameron, the deputy headmaster,' MacGregor explained, conscious of the mix up as Pritchard and

Jim reached out and pumped hands with the policemen.

'Yes, gentlemen, thank you both for coming. This is Mr MacGregor, the School Sergeant,' the headmaster introduced, seemingly unaware of the mistaken identity.

The two policemen glanced at each other.

'The school disciplinarian,' the headmaster explained. 'Bill and Mr Cameron found Mr Shute. And you've met Daphne, my secretary.'

Daphne nodded, unsure what to do now that she had fulfilled her role, but curiosity kept her lingering and with luck she may be needed. The two policemen took it in turns to shake her hand, her face trying not to show surprise that she was included in the greeting. Their handshake somehow completed her feeling she was a player in the action. It was just as well that she couldn't hear what they were thinking.

'We're still waiting for the ambulance,' Jim said. 'So, you've made good time.' As he spoke, he looked closely at the detective. There was something about him that seemed familiar. While Jim had dark hair that had a tinge of grey at the edges, Stone was sandy haired. Jim thought he detected an accent that wasn't Australian.

'Actually, we're just up the road at Waverley so it didn't take long to get here,' Detective Stone explained, then asked, 'Can you point us in the direction of the accident? It's better if you all stay in here. We don't want to disturb anything.'

'Of course. Of course. Mr Shute's bedroom is through that door,' Mr Pritchard said pointing.

The policemen made their way to the door of the bedroom, peered in, and then stepped carefully up to the bed. Daphne followed as far as the open door, peering in, torn by what horror she might see but drawn to the drama of the scene. She gasped, her hands covering her face. The sight of Bentley lying there with his face buried in a bloody pillow was appalling. How could anyone do such a thing? No wonder Robert and Bill didn't want to go back into the bedroom.

Jim joined Daphne in the doorway and seeing the police standing over the bed, said, 'I pulled the quilt cover back to check on Mr Shute, thinking he may have been asleep. Originally, it nearly covered his head. Once I saw what had happened to Mr Shute, I laid the cover back down. I also tried to feel for a pulse.' He was aware that he had tampered with the crime scene. Stone subtly raised an eyebrow to his sergeant and made a note in a small pad he'd taken out of his pocket.

'But the room is as it was when you entered?'

'Yes. Nothing appeared disturbed. No sign of a struggle.'

'Thank you, Mr. Um, Cameron?' Stone queried.

'Cameron. Jim Cameron,' Jim reinforced as they both puzzled about where they'd seen each other before.

'Right.'

29

Unable to drag herself away, Daphne watched as Detective Stone slid his hand under Shute's chin and with his index and second finger on the dead man's throat, felt for a pulse although it was obviously a futile gesture. He withdrew his hand and wiped it on the handkerchief he'd taken out of his suit pocket.

The detective remained standing by the bed. He looked over the dead man at the contents of the room and then walked around to the other side of the bed and again peered over the dead man. Then he knelt down and lifting the valance, peered under the bed.

'Sergeant, can you get me a big plastic bag. There must be one in the kitchen,' Stone called out as he lay face-down on the carpet. Everyone rushed towards the kitchen area but stopped as they reached the other side of the kitchen divide. On the floor were shattered shards of crockery.

'Could everyone please go back into the lounge area,' Sergeant O'Shea directed. 'Boss, there's some broken stuff. Looks like a cup or dish on the floor of the kitchen,' he called out.

'Okay. But leave that for the moment. Can you get me a towel from the bathroom.'

O'Shea hurried into the bathroom and from a tidy pile of towels stacked on a rack near the shower, took one and returned to the bedroom.

Stone wriggled his way under the bed. Using both hands he managed to lift up the object and worm his way back without his find touching the carpet. It was a sword.

The sergeant lay the bath towel down on the carpet as if he were about to sunbathe. The detective delicately spun his body towards the towel and placed the sword on it. The two men picked up either end of the towel and carried it and its prize into the lounge and placed them onto the kitchen divide.

Everyone crowded around to stare at the discovery. Blood, strands of hair and what looked like small bits of uncooked chicken were stuck to the sword. No-one said a word. It must have been the murder weapon but the murderer had made no real attempt to hide it.

'Mr Pritchard, it's best that you all leave now while we gather up the evidence and then we can meet in your office to continue after the ambulance has come. Does that suit?' Stone asked.

'Of course. Of course. Daphne, we can't be disturbed. Please change my appointments.'

'Yes, Mr Pritchard.'

In the distance a siren could be heard coming closer.

WHO IS BENTLEY SHUTE?

After the others had left, the quiet of Bentley Shute's flat was shattered as Sergeant O'Shea ushered the ambulance men into the flat. It was going to be difficult removing the body as the building had no lifts. Luckily, there were no students in their dorms as returning to the boarding house was banned during school hours.

'Don't worry, mate. We're used to buildings like this,' the ambo said glancing at his colleague who shrugged knowingly.

'He's in here,' O'Shea told them as he led the way through the lounge and into the bedroom. Stone was waiting by the bed.

'Bloody hell. Someone didn't like him,' the second ambo exclaimed as he lent over the bed to take a look at the body. 'What the hell was he killed with?'

'A sword,' Stone replied.

'Fuck me. A sword. In this day and age,' the ambo exclaimed.

'One of his own by the looks of things. We found it under the bed.'

'Right,' the ambo stated with disbelief.

At that moment Forensics arrived. The ambulance men, Stone and O'Shea stepped to one side as photographs were taken, swabs, hair samples and bodily fluids were placed in test tubes and sealed. Efficiently, the team fulfilled their duties and hurried their evidence, plus the sword, back to the laboratory. It was obvious how the man had died but the police would have to work out why.

With the departure of the Forensic team, Alan Stone returned to the body. Where would the attacker have stood and delivered the blows? Why was Shute lying in such a position? Why was he so passive?

There was no sight of a fight in any of the rooms except for the smashed cup. What was it about this apartment that seemed wrong, if that was the right word? Unusual? It was very tidy, almost obsessively so. Stone knew he was making a subjective judgement, but the tidiness *was* unusual for a man. Also, the fixation with Japanese items seemed over the top. But, would any of these qualities make him a murder victim?

Stone bent over to look closely at Bentley's head. The colour of his hair was golden yet his eyebrows were very dark. Was his hair dyed? Again, Stone knew he was making judgements but he didn't know any man who dyed his hair. It would have been considered vain and effeminate to do such a thing.

The detective walked back into the lounge and checked the titles on the bookshelves. Some were Japanese erotica and some were art books. There were no novels. On the coffee table was a small pile of magazines. He picked them up and flicked through them. The one at the bottom proved the most informative. It contained pictures of buffed men in positions which showed off their bodies to the best advantage.

Ah. Perhaps Mr Shute was homosexual. Perhaps he was attacked by a body building gay man.

'Sergeant, have a look at this.' O'Shea stepped across the room to join his colleague.

'I think our man here may have been a homosexual. I found this magazine under the others on the coffee table.' Stone handed over the magazine. O'Shea flicked through the pages, frowning with every turn of the page.

'Do you think he was killed by a queer?' the sergeant asked.

'It's a possibility. Assuming Mr Shute was a homo, that adds another route to go down.'

Both men glanced at each other, trying not to grin. Stone had not intended the pun. He turned to the ambulance men instructing them to take the body and then walked over to the radio and switched it off. 'Getting a bit sick of that bland noise.'

THE SWORD

Not long after the bell rang to indicate lunch time had ended, the police returned to Mr Pritchard's office where Bill, Jim and Daphne were waiting. They were keen to question those who had discovered the body. The longer they left it, the more likely it was that their memories would become unreliable.

Stone had detected that Bill MacGregor was somewhat prejudiced in his views and could embellish his answers to make himself seem important.

'Mr MacGregor. Can you think of any reason why someone would have wanted to murder Mr Shute?' Stone asked, focusing all his attention on the School Sergeant. MacGregor shuffled his feet a little and folded his arms as if to put a barrier between him and the detective.

After rubbing his chin thoughtfully, MacGregor answered, 'Can't say I can think of anyone. Didn't mix with Shute's crowd. Not that I wanted to. He had his followers, but they certainly weren't my cup of tea. He could be rather, how can I put it? Bitchy. But not enough to warrant being murdered. Well, not as far as I'd know.'

'Fair enough,' Stone replied. 'And it was one of the boarders who alerted the headmaster to the fact that Mr Shute did not answer the door?'

'Yes. Yes it was. Matto. James Matthews. He was the boarder who'd been told to fetch Mr Shute but as he didn't answer the door, Matthews reported this to the headmaster and when Bentley, um, Mr Shute, didn't go to breakfast Mr Pritchard asked me and Jim to go over to investigate.'

'Bentley? Was that Mr Shute's Christian name?' Detective Stone asked, not quite able to keep a hint of disapproval out of his voice.

Bill MacGregor, picking up the tone, nodded his head in agreement and informed the detective that yes it was indeed Mr Shute's name, although the staff and boys sometimes called him Benty. Not that Mr Shute would ever answer to his nick name. Jim remained silent. He'd let Bill continue to have his moment.

Detective Stone jotted this information in his notepad then continued his questioning.

'Was the door open when you went in?'

'No. But I have a master key to the boarding houses,' MacGregor replied authoritatively.

Stone turned to Pritchard, 'Do many have access to these keys?'

'Yes. All the boarding masters have sets in case there's a problem in one of the houses. And of course, Mr Cameron.'

'So, nothing is ever really securely locked?'

'I suppose not. We have to be able to get into any of the dorms, or the boarding masters' apartments in case of accident or trouble. We have a duty of care at all times,' the headmaster emphasised.

'And by boarding houses, you mean, the accommodation for the students?' Stone asked.

'Yes. But we have day boys as well. The ones who live at home. The majority are day boys, although there are about 150 boarders.'

'Right. So, what was Mr Shute's role?'

Mr Pritchard, assuming that not everyone knew the intricacies of a boarding school, explained that each of their boarding houses had a master who ran the house, its staff, and the boys. All the boarding masters lived in private rooms in each of the four houses, like the one Mr Shute occupied. Warming to his topic, and relieved to be on safe ground, Pritchard went on to inform Stone and Sergeant O'Shea that there were day boy houses as well. Every boy was assigned a house when they started school and each house had a house master who was a teacher on the staff.

Detective Stone acknowledged the information then returned to his questioning of the school sergeant. Stone was fully aware of the intricacies of a boarding school, having been to one himself in Auckland, but he thought it better to play dumb. Also, he doubted that Sergeant O'Shea was familiar with this type of school and he needed to know how they were run.

'Mr MacGregor, as you and Mr Cameron were first on the scene, did you notice anything odd? Anything out of place?'

'No. But I've never been in here before, so I wouldn't really know.'

'Did you touch anything?'

'Definitely not. I've seen enough detective shows to know not to interfere with the scene of the crime,' MacGregor answered firmly.

Detective Stone smiled at this cliché then turned his attention to Mr Cameron. He was aware of the deputy headmaster standing quietly in the background of Mr Pritchard's office. Unlike Mr Macgregor, Cameron seemed reluctant to be in the limelight. He was sure he'd met this man before, but perhaps he looked familiar because of the area. The Waverley Police station had many schools in its vicinity.

'Mr Cameron, is there anything you want to add?' Stone asked.

'Well, yes. We've met before, Detective. I thought I recognised you, but it's been a few years,' Jim said, pleased that he'd finally worked out how he knew Stone. 'And no, I wasn't in trouble with the police,' he explained to the curious audience.

'James Cameron? Jim?' Stone asked in surprise. 'I didn't twig when Mr Pritchard mentioned your name. But I did wonder when I met you. And you certainly weren't wearing a, what's it called, a gown back then.'

'Well, it was a while ago now, back in the '70s,' Jim excused. 'And you weren't a detective then.'

He grinned at the detective with pleasure as he realised Alan was an old mate.

The detective laughed. 'No, I was merely a shit kicker.'

He reddened. 'Sorry about the language, Mrs Withers.' Daphne shrugged and smiled her forgiveness. She'd heard worse.

Sergeant O'Shea was also following the conversation intently, eager to know how the men knew each other.

Jim sensing their curiosity, explained, 'Alan and I were both in the Cook Islands a number of years ago. Maybe ten or more. We were a lot younger then.' He laughed. 'I'd taken a school rugby team to Rarotonga and he was working over there. On secondment from the New Zealand Police, if I remember correctly.' Jim looked at Stone for confirmation. Stone nodded, grinning broadly.

'Exciting times, eh Jim?' Alan Stone said, grabbing Jim's hand and shaking it hard. 'We sorted it out in the end, didn't we? Good to have the old team ride again.'

Jim scoffed, 'Don't know how much I did. You did most of the work. And now you're a detective in Sydney. How long have you been here? Did you bring your 'chully bun' with you?' Jim's attempt at a Kiwi accent caused a wry laugh from Stone.

'God, don't you start. The number of times I've been told to say 'fush and chups'.'

Daphne's curiosity couldn't be contained. 'What happened?' she asked eagerly. Mr Cameron certainly was a bit of a dark horse. A man of mystery.

'It's a long story,' the detective deflected. 'More pressing problems at the moment.'

Jim agreed. Now wasn't the time to talk about the past.

'Well, great to see you again, Jim, but we'd better get down to the current business,' Stone said and returned his attention to Mr Pritchard, 'When did you go to Mr Shute's flat, Mr Pritchard?'

'After Mr MacGregor contacted Daphne, rather, Mrs Withers,' Pritchard corrected himself. 'She told me what Bill had said. He, and of course, Jim, realised something was very wrong as soon as they saw Shute.'

Stone made another note in his little book. 'Were any of you aware of how many swords Mr Shute had on his wall?'

They all shook their heads. Earlier that morning, in Shute's rooms they had watched the detective walk over to the fireplace and stare at the display of samurai swords above the mantle-piece. His hand had outlined the curved outline of the absent sword, although he took care not to touch the wall. However, it seemed obvious that the sword found under the bed, was the one taken off the wall.

'And the radio was playing when you went in?' Stone asked. Bill replied that it was and neither of them had touched it. 'Anything you recognised?'

'No. Well. He was a poof...' MacGregor began then realising the implications of his words, stopped abruptly.

'A what?' Stone asked.

'Ah. No. It was just that he was a bit odd in his hobbies.'

'Mr MacGregor,' warned Pritchard. 'It's not our place to comment on the social...,' he paused, desperately trying to think of a word which would not sound judgmental, '...activities or leanings of other members of staff.'

'No. No. Of course not, Headmaster.'

Stone, aware of the prejudice against homosexuals, stared at Bill MacGregor then glanced around the room at the others. 'We're going to have to interview staff and students. How many members of staff are there?'

'Well over one hundred. And there are nearly a thousand boys,' Pritchard despaired. 'Do the boys have to be interviewed? Surely they'd have nothing to do with this. In fact, why would anyone do such a dreadful thing?'

He looked at both policemen. 'We've already been through a couple of disasters when we lost a student on an excursion and that other terrible accident. Now this. Will it be made public?'

'Hopefully not yet, Sir. But things have a way of spreading. Especially with such a large number of people. It's hard to keep a murder out of the papers,' Stone said.

'Oh God. A death on the school grounds is the last thing we need.' Pritchard removed his glasses and

41

rubbed his eyes. 'It certainly looks like murder, doesn't it?'

'It does. But we'll keep you informed.' Stone looked at Pritchard. 'In the meantime, keep everything running as normal. However, the flat is now a crime scene. Even though Mr Shute's body has been removed, no-one can enter.'

'Will the police be here all the time?' Pritchard asked anxiously.

'As I said, it's a crime scene. The boys mustn't be allowed entry. Not for a while. Nor any of the staff.'

'My God. The boys. They'll know something's wrong when they see the police. We'll have to warn them,' Pritchard panicked. 'Can they go back to the boarding house?' he asked Detective Stone.

'Not yet. The house will have to be searched. The boys need to stay somewhere else until the search is over.'

Mr Pritchard turned to Daphne whose nod indicated that she would take care of it.

'But what will we tell the boys, Jim?' Pritchard asked. Jim pursed his lips before saying, 'We can tell them that there are problems with the plumbing.'

'Yes. Good idea,' replied the head. Thank God. Easy.

Stone nodded. 'But say as little as possible. No need to mention anything about Mr Shute. That will all come out in the fullness of time. Oh, by the way, Mr Pritchard, why did you want to see him?'

The headmaster looked again to Daphne then to Jim then back to Stone. 'A parent. Um, parents had asked to talk to Mr Shute about their son. Their son is in the boarding house. It's normal to be in touch with the boarding master. Their second home,' Pritchard rambled.

'Yes, yes of course,' Stone confirmed.

PREJUDICE

The police had departed, and classes were over for the day.

Daphne handed a cup of tea to the headmaster, who was perched on the edge of his chair as if about to stand up. Bill MacGregor sat on the Chesterfield couch with his legs stretched out in front of him, ankles crossed. Daphne's face showing concern, looked anxiously from Mr Pritchard to Jim who stood near the door. Despite the headmaster's dithering he was a kind man who did not have the patronising behaviour that many of those on the staff had towards women.

'Come in and sit down, Jim. For Heaven's sake,' demanded the headmaster as he settled in his chair, then softened his tone. 'We've got to sort this mess out quickly. I can't have the school go through another scandal. Those bloody tabloids will have a field day. Any excuse to criticise what they see as privilege.'

'I know,' Daphne sympathised. 'Look at that recent article about government funding.' Pritchard nodded.

'If the government fixed up the state schools, we wouldn't cop such flak,' MacGregor interjected.

45

'That's a fairly simplistic view, Bill. But anyway, let's work out what we're going to do. I don't want police all over the place with the media following closely behind.'

Pritchard stood and strode over to his office window and stared at the Oval. 'I love this school and I'm not going to let it go down the gurgler because someone had it in for Bentley.'

'To think that someone could have mur… murdered him,' Daphne stammered, her hand going up to her mouth at the shock of the word. The sight of his body and hacked neck was a vision she wasn't going to forget easily.

'It certainly looks like that. Someone had a right good go at him,' MacGregor responded emphatically.

'All right, Bill. Anyway, however he died, he's certainly dead,' the head answered.

'The poor man. How awful,' Daphne sympathised.

MacGregor raised his eyebrows to Pritchard and shook his head. 'He mixed with some very dodgy people.'

'Did he? How do you know? I thought you didn't socialise with him?' Daphne questioned. Bill was fond of sweeping statements.

'Well, I can't understand why his cronies here have never twigged that he's a poofter,' Bill said, staring at Daphne. Bloody woman. She should keep herself out of this.

'Bill. That's enough. This is a boys' school. It can't be public knowledge that some members of staff are homosexual,' Pritchard protested as he returned to his seat.

'I don't see why not,' said Daphne. 'I have homosexual friends and they're not out to have sex with every man or boy they meet.'

'Yes, well...' doubted MacGregor, not noticing the withering stare Jim gave him. To Jim, Bill was old school. Stuck in an era where a woman's place was in the home and men were 'men'. Bill voiced such clichéd views. Jim wondered if Bill ever questioned his own views or did he take comfort in the familiarity of them.

'What are we to do? Let's stay on track,' Pritchard urged them. 'We want to keep this to ourselves as much as possible. Is there another way of finding out what happened before the police do and the media get hold of it?'

'We need our own Miss Marple or Hercules Poirot,' Daphne suggested, smiling.

Pritchard stared at her in surprise. 'That's not a bad idea, Daphne.'

'But how can another person do police business?' MacGregor asked sceptically.

'I have to say I agree with Bill,' Jim said with reluctance. 'We need to support the police in their enquiries. If this can be solved quickly, it would lessen the amount of publicity. It's a bit like politics. People forget easily. In a month or so, there will be another drama somewhere else to take the place of Bentley's death.'

'My God, I hope you're right Jim. So, we offer them all our assistance,' Pritchard suggested before adding, 'The fact that you know Detective Stone may be useful for us. That's a bit of a coincidence.'

'It certainly is. But he's a good bloke and cluey. He'd know if we're trying to hide stuff from him,' Jim justified. He knew that Alan Stone was perceptive and unbiased.

MacGregor, obviously annoyed that the attention had shifted from him, interrupted, 'But can he be trusted not to be prejudiced against a school like ours?'

'I don't think he'd care either way. State or private. He just wants to get the job done.' Jim paused. 'Alan was very methodical and rational when I met him in Rarotonga.'

'Can you tell us what happened?' Daphne asked eagerly. 'You haven't mentioned going to Rarotonga before.'

'Another time, Daphne. It's a long story. Over a drink at the pub on a Friday,' Jim deflected.

Daphne frowned. Jim hardly ever told her anything about his life. She knew that he'd fought in Vietnam in the late 1960's or early '70's and his wife was Asian, possibly Vietnamese or Thai. It was hard to tell. Julie in the office had told her that Jim and his wife had met in Sydney, although she wasn't really sure. He had a couple of children, but he rarely brought them or his wife to the school.

'Anyway, back to the matter at hand,' Pritchard said. 'Obviously, Daphne can offer administrative assistance but Jim, how about you are the go-to man when the police are here, and you could do a little bit of investigating on your own. You help the police and they help us. Considering you have a relationship with Stone, he'll no doubt be willing to share information.'

'Maybe,' Jim doubted. Stone was a professional so how much would he give away?

'What can I do?' Bill asked peevishly.

'Bill, I'm sure there will be a lot you can do to help the investigation, especially when it comes to the boys,' Pritchard placated. Daphne rolled her eyes at Jim who pretended not to see. Bill could be a real pain when he wasn't the centre of attention.

THE GOSSIP

The following morning, Daphne arrived at work earlier than usual to find Detective Stone and his offsider, Sergeant O'Shea, waiting in the corridor outside her office. The school was almost deserted except for the cleaners and Bill whose job it was to open the school.

A few boys straggled in to attend early morning sport's practice. Bill had already shown Stone and O'Shea around parts of the school which he felt would be useful for them to see and had pointed out the different boarding houses dotted around the perimeter of the grounds.

Daphne had slept badly. Images of Bentley's head and the hideous gashes in his neck and shoulders had flashed into her dreams. She dreamed that Mr Pritchard held the sword over Bentley's head and was yelling about his ruining the school, then Pritchard transformed into Jim Cameron, who slashed angrily at the pot plant. She had woken up exhausted but with no desire to go back to sleep.

'Good morning, gentlemen,' she greeted, trying to sound perkier than she felt. 'Would you like a cup of tea or coffee? You're here bright and early.'

Daphne rummaged through her handbag and pulled out a set of keys. She opened the door to her office and indicated for them to come in.

'Tea, coffee?' she repeated once they had entered the room. Both declined. Daphne fiddled with the cover of her computer and pressed the on button. It was too early in the morning to be questioned by the police. They stood watching her, sensing her discomfort.

'Sorry to be so early, Mrs Withers, but we wanted to get cracking and just have a couple of questions for you,' Detective Stone explained pleasantly.

'For me? Of course. What do they say? A policeman's work is never done. Or am I mixing up my metaphors? And please call me Daphne. Mrs Withers makes me sound so old.'

The two men laughed a little, neither of them thinking that she was old. In fact, quite the opposite. Daphne stood still. 'How can I help you?'

Stone took the notebook from his jacket pocket and flipped over a couple of pages. 'We thought as you are at the centre of the school you may be able to point us in the right direction when it comes to those who associated with Mr Shute,' Stone flattered. 'We'd like to start with those who were friendly with him. Those closest to him on the staff.'

'His clique?' Daphne asked with a rise of well-defined eyebrows.

'Yes. Or anyone who didn't like him. Someone who may have had a grudge,' Stone encouraged. Daphne seemed more than willing to be of assistance.

'The women teachers didn't like him,' she said emphatically. It was easier for her to focus on the ones who had been victims of his vitriol. 'Especially, the newer ones. They have a life and don't, didn't need Mr Shute to,' she hesitated, 'to give them a sense of meaning or purpose. Not like some of the other teachers.'

'Why didn't they like him?' Stone asked.

'Gossip,' Daphne answered. 'He spread gossip. Some of it true, some not. It turned teachers against each other. Only the strong ones could resist the temptation to toe the line.'

'So, Mr Shute was a divisive figure,' Detective Stone said, paraphrasing her words.

'Very,' Daphne said firmly. 'He didn't like the threat that the young, attractive women posed to his popularity. He was reasonably young too, but that little group really upset him.'

'How could they threaten his popularity?' Sergeant O'Shea questioned while wondering if Daphne too had been a threat to Shute?

Daphne looked at him closely. Lovely eyes, she thought. 'Um. Mr Shute always had to be the star, the centre of attention and because there haven't been many women on the staff until recently, he didn't really have any competition.'

Both men nodded. 'Do any of the other men feel the same?' Stone asked.

'Some, but not as much as Mr Shute did. The ones who are more traditional have found it hard to be working closely with women. This school is pretty old fashioned, although Mr Pritchard is trying to bring it into the 20th century.'

'I hope you don't mind my asking, Mrs With… Daphne. But how did you feel about Mr Shute?' Stone asked.

Daphne hesitated. She didn't want to speak ill of the dead, but she was no fan of Bentley Shute. 'I can see why he was popular with some of the staff as he could be very entertaining, but he had a nasty streak and caused a lot of hurt.'

'Through his gossip?' O'Shea asked quickly.

'Definitely.'

'What about his 'clique' as you call it? Who was in his group? Teachers? Boys? People from outside the school?' the detective continued with his questioning. Daphne was proving to be a great source of information.

Daphne twisted her watch as she thought about his questions, although the noise of students arriving and walking in the corridor was a slight distraction.

'Let me think. Funnily enough, Marlene Bates, obviously a female, was one. Brian Taylor in Science, Rodney Addington in History. Gary Powell, also in Science. Ian Walsh, Economics, and Don who helps out with sport.'

'Not a particularly large group,' Stone observed.

'I suppose not, but somehow they seemed to hold a lot of power. Or perhaps it was just Bentley who did, and they benefitted.'

Stone added the names to his book.

'Daphne, we don't want to hold you up too much longer, but who do you think Mr Shute picked on? If I can use a rather adolescent term?' Stone asked quickly, aware of the sound of students in the corridor and that Daphne may soon be needed by the headmaster.

'Gosh. Where do I start?' Daphne asked rhetorically, twisting her hair into a curl. 'Sue, Mrs Armstrong. She was a favourite topic for Bentley. She's pretty and the boys like her. Some of them have crushes, even a few of the teachers, but Bentley doesn't, didn't, like that. He spread some pretty alarming stories about her private life and her relationships.' The men could almost see the inverted commas around the word relationships.

'Is she married?' O'Shea asked.

'Yes, she is, but that didn't stop Bentley implying affairs and all sorts of goings on.'

'Is there any truth in what he said?' Stone interjected.

Daphne considered the question. 'I don't think so. I've met her husband and children. They seem a happy family. Bentley was malicious, and he certainly wouldn't let the truth get in the way of a good story.'

Stone made another note. 'Anyone else you can think of? How was he with you?'

'With me?' Daphne asked as she pushed her hair behind her ears. 'We-ell... He was okay with me. I suppose being Mr Pritchard's secretary, I had some protection. Or maybe I wasn't a threat as I'm not a teacher.'

The detective nodded at her logic and glanced at his notes. 'So, can you think of anyone else, apart from Mrs Armstrong, who could have had a grudge against him?'

'The female teachers in general but particularly Jenny Bartoli and Lillian Cutler. They started at the same time as Mrs Armstrong,' Daphne said with a sigh. 'He didn't seem to like women much, which is a bit unusual for a gay man. He was friendly with Marlene though. I don't think she was much of a threat as she isn't....' She was about to add that Marlene wasn't very attractive, but she couldn't bring herself to say it. Daphne mentally scrambled for something to add. 'Oh, and she's friends with Julie in the office so she could pass on any juicy information she'd heard.'

'Thank you, Daphne. You've been a great help. We won't take up any more of your time,' Stone said as he and Sergeant O'Shea prepared to leave. 'If there's anything else you can think of, please don't hesitate to contact us. No matter how insignificant it may seem.'

The detective shook her hand before she tripped pertly in her stilettos to open the door but she stopped suddenly and swivelled around. 'Just a thought. Bentley and Rodney Addington seemed to have had a falling out. Things were pretty frosty between them. Not quite sure why. Maybe it was the excursion. But they certainly weren't as close as they had been, although I think Rodney still joined in some of their get togethers.'

'Right. Thanks again,' Stone reiterated. 'Sorry. One more question. Could you point us in Mr Cameron's direction and I promise you, we'll leave you in peace.'

'Please don't apologise. Anything I can do to help,' she offered with a small pout of her lips, while glancing from one man to the other. 'Jim is just down the corridor next to Mr Pritchard's office. On the left.'

The policemen mumbled their thanks and set off to find Jim.

Jim was not surprised by the knock on his door. He'd noticed a car parked out the front of the building when he arrived. It looked like a regulation police Holden.

'Come in,' he called out and stood up as Stone and O'Shea entered his office.

'We can't keep meeting like this,' Stone joked as he shook Jim's hand.

'People will start to talk,' Jim responded sotto voce and greeted the sergeant with a quick gidday.

Jim indicated for them to sit and went back to his chair behind the desk. Stone gazed around the room. 'Feel like I'm on detention, Jim.'

The deputy laughed. 'How's it going? How can I be of assistance?'

'We've just been talking to Daphne. Getting feedback about some of the staff and we're wondering if you can enlighten us as well. Judging from the ferocity of Mr Shute's injuries, he was attacked with a lot of passion. If that's the right word? Someone clearly had something against him.'

Jim sat silently, his eyes staring into the distance as he listened. Stone continued. 'Forensics have been busy fingerprinting and the pathologist is doing his business as we speak so should find out more shortly. Time of death etcetera, so meanwhile, we want to get a picture of Shute's life here at the school. His friends. His enemies.'

Jim pushed his thick hair back off his forehead, leant forward to place his elbows on the desk and joined his hands in a pose of contemplation. He knew the police would want to know as much as possible about the victim. He'd watched the military police in action in Saigon. Squeezing information out of a suspect with apparent passivity and nonchalance, then brutality. He appreciated that Alan had to solve this case, but he knew the damage that could be done to people's lives and the school.

'We gather from Daphne, that Mr Shute had a group of followers but that a number of women teachers were not his biggest fans,' Stone began.

Jim agreed with this summation and stated the names of those who were part of Shute's inner circle. His list matched Daphne's.

'Daphne also implied that Shute and the chap, Rodney Addington may have had a falling out. Were you aware of this? Do you know what may have caused it?' Stone asked.

The deputy head thought before answering. Having to expose the behaviour of teachers and events that had occurred did not sit well with him, but the truth had to be told.

'Daphne's right. Things were tense between Rodney and Mr Shute. They were the teachers in charge on a recent school excursion and unfortunately, a boy died. Drowned. Obviously, there was an investigation into the accident and neither of them were blamed but it seemed to cause bad blood between them. Rodney is ex-army and does everything by the book. It's only my opinion, but I think that he felt that Shute gave the boys too much leeway and the result was the drowning.'

Stone made notes while waiting for Jim to continue. 'However, I don't think Rodney wanted to be on the outer. Knowing Shute's propensity to gossip they kept up the appearance of still being mates.'

'Did Mr Shute really have such power over his colleagues?' Sergeant O'Shea asked, surprised.

Jim faced him. 'Yes. Unfortunately he did. A school such as this, is a microcosm of society. There are factions. Those who are 'in' and those who are 'out'. And of course, there are those who want to climb up the career ladder. Bentley wasn't popular with everybody, but many were scared of him because of his knowledge and his gossip.'

'So, there would have been a number of people on the staff who may have disliked him. Enough to kill him?' Stone asked eagerly.

'That's a bit strong, Alan. But I suppose you're right, as someone has killed him.' Jim was reminded of the war. He'd seen soldiers do things out of fear

59

that in civilian life would have been unthinkable. He remembered the bully in his unit. What was his name? Something unusual. Perhaps that was why he became a bully. Leatherbarrow? He typically picked on those whom he thought were weak. But one night when they were involved in the Battle of Kham Duc, two of Leatherbarrow's victims crept into his bivouac wearing Vietcong uniforms and pissed on his face. He stopped his bullying after that.

'What about the women on the staff? Daphne mentioned that there were a number of women who were on the receiving end of Mr Shute's gossip,' the detective prompted.

'Sorry? Ah yes. From what I gather the younger and newer members of staff copped a lot of flak.'

'Who in particular?'

'To be fair, Alan, I think you should interview all the women teachers. If you single a few out, it will be obvious that you have suspicions about them,' Jim suggested. He didn't want the female teachers to suffer because of Bentley's penchant for vitriol.

'I agree. We'll make it clear that we have to interview everyone. But if you could tell us who Shute had it in for.'

'You realise that my ideas are based on gossip? Mr Shute didn't talk to me but word has a way of spreading,' Jim explained, his reluctance to name names was clear.

Stone nodded. He knew that Jim would not like to be party to salacious rumours, but he needed to make a start and the women who were the victims of Shute's tongue may shine light on possible motives.

Jim coughed before answering, 'Jenny Bartoli. Lillian Cutler and Sue Armstrong are the three most recent arrivals. Marlene Bates and Mrs Goldman have been here a lot longer. Of the three new ones, Sue Armstrong is the one who was talked about the most. This is hearsay, of course, but Shute was spreading the rumour that she was 'friendly' with students. I gather that Shute was a bit put out by the attention Sue and the other two received.'

'So, there's no truth in the rumour?'

'Not that I'm aware of. Be highly unlikely. She'd lose her job if it were true. Plus, she's married.'

Stone raised an eyebrow. Being married didn't stop people from having affairs and from what he'd seen, many of the boys were big enough and old enough to make advances.

'On another note,' Stone continued. 'I've got the feeling, that Mr Shute could have been homosexual. Is that the case?'

Jim didn't answer immediately. He was aware of the prejudice against homosexuals and he had no desire to reinforce this attitude. He didn't like Shute because of his behaviour towards others, not because he was gay.

'Does it matter if he were?' Jim asked. He hoped that Alan Stone was liberal in his views and thinking back to Rarotonga had the feeling that he was not as biased as many.

'It might. There are still those who are anti-gay, despite it no longer being a criminal offence,' Stone justified. 'It seems that some men find the thought of a mate or colleague being gay threatening to their own sexuality. God knows why.' He didn't want Jim to lump him in with the many men who had antiquated attitudes to homosexuality.

'Do you think he could have been attacked because he was gay?' Sergeant O'Shea asked bluntly, staring at Jim.

'We have to think of all possibilities, Sergeant,' Stone answered for Jim. 'Some men, and the odd woman are very prejudiced. As I said it can threaten their own sexual identity. And some men are married despite being gay so they might be worried about being connected to another gay man. Their secret could be blown so to speak.'

Jim was impressed by Alan's analysis. Human beings were an odd lot.

'Yeah. Maybe Shute made advances to a member of staff and was killed because of it?' the sergeant hypothosised. The two men couldn't help but agree with his summation.

'Possibly. We need to think of all motives.' Stone turned to Jim. 'So, we have women who were the victims of his gossip, and men who may have been anti-gay. Or it may be someone with another motive altogether.'

THE SCHOOL ASSEMBLES

Mr Pritchard, a black academic gown over his dark grey suit, stood at the lectern on the stage facing the auditorium full of boys. Behind him in rows, sat the teaching staff also attired in academic gowns.

The Lord's Prayer led by the school vicar, had reached its conclusion and Mr Pritchard was about to tell the whole school that one of its members was dead. His face was solemn and to keep composure, he focused on the rows of Year 7 boys seated in front of him. There was an atmosphere of expectation.

The assembly and memorial service for the student who'd died while on a field trip was the last time the whole school had met as one. Normally, assemblies were divided into the junior, middle and senior years. The fact that all students were included, and on a Tuesday afternoon when assemblies did not normally take place, added anticipation and excitement to the event.

Voices were muted, and boys watched the staff eagerly to see if their faces would give them a clue as to why they were there. Was it connected to the sudden arrival of police cars yesterday?

Matthews sat towards the back of the auditorium with his friends, analysing the events of the last couple of days. He knew that this assembly had something to do with Mr Shute. Benty hadn't been at prep the night before and hadn't come to the dining hall at all. The boarders under Mr Shute's care were told by Mr MacGregor that the master was unwell and must not be disturbed. And they had to take their clothes and books and sleep in the other houses. It all sounded a bit of a bullshit story.

'Good afternoon, gentlemen. Good afternoon, fellow staff. I have called this assembly today to tell you of a very serious and sad accident that has occurred to the boarding master, Mr Shute.' Mr Pritchard peered down at his notes then swivelled his head to take in the full auditorium. 'Mr Shute has passed away.' He paused to let this news sink in. There was a collective intake of breath from teachers and students.

Matthews turned to his neighbour and whispered, 'Shit. I knew something was wrong. That's why we had to move out last night.'

Another boy in the row behind him leant forward stating under his breath, 'Not surprised. Bloody prick.'

Matthews shifted uncomfortably but a couple of the boys nearby muttered in agreement. 'Benty was an arsehole. Tried to touch me up once,' said a Year 10 student.

'In your dreams, Daniels. Ya big poof,' Peter Jones scoffed to the amusement of his audience.

'Shut up, Jonesy. Mr Kendall's watching,' warned Matthews while looking around furtively to see if the master on duty had noticed their talking.

The boys went quiet and stared at the stage. The staff sat stunned, enveloped in their black gowns, some wrapping the voluminous sleeves protectively around their arms while waiting for Mr Pritchard to continue.

'Gentlemen. Teachers. I want you to be aware that the police are involved so if you see any policemen or their vehicles around the school that is to be expected. Those of you who board in Mr Shute's house may be questioned by the police as well as those who had him as a teacher.'

The headmaster stopped speaking. It occurred to him that some of the boys may be upset. He'd been so busy thinking about the negative impact on the school, he hadn't thought that the boys could be distressed by the news of Shute's death. He was a popular teacher after all.

'Boys. I want you to know that if this unfortunate situation has caused any distress to any of you, you can contact my secretary, Mrs Withers, and she will arrange counselling for you.'

There was a murmur around the auditorium. What wuss wants counselling? Who cares that Benty is dead? The boys who did care kept their mouths shut.

'The boys from Churchill will be able to return to their house very soon,' the headmaster resumed, aware of the mixed reaction to his suggestion about counselling. Talking about emotions and feelings wasn't normally encouraged.

Mr Pritchard removed his glasses, rubbed them with a corner of his gown and with relief instructed,

'Now let us bow our heads and listen to Reverend Thompson's words of comfort.'

Reverend Thompson stood up and walked solemnly back to the lectern, on which he carefully placed his Bible and bowed his head, 'Lord God, we beseech you in this time of sadness to comfort ….'

His words filtered around the auditorium; boys and teachers lost in thought about how Mr Shute could have died. Was he ill? Did he have that new disease which was creeping through the homosexual community? Did he kill himself? Maybe someone killed him?

The teachers on the stage listened with bent heads as Reverend Thompson's words meandered on. Sue Armstrong nudged Bruce Hardy, a fellow History teacher who sat with his head bowed, staring at his shoes.

'Do you think he committed suicide?' she whispered.

'No,' Bruce reflected behind his hand. 'Loved himself too much. He'd think the world wouldn't survive without him.'

Sue couldn't help but elbow him gently in agreement then guilt, as it has its way, took over and she kept quiet. The man *was* dead after all. A sniffle could be heard from the row behind. Sue quickly turned to see who it was. It was Marlene. Of course, she would be upset, she was part of Benty's inner circle. He must have seen something of value in her even though she didn't seem quite his class. Perhaps Bentley surrounded himself with followers whom he could easily feel superior to.

Sue remembered how Marlene hadn't extended the hand of friendship to the three of them who'd joined the school a couple of years ago when it was going through the transition phase from essentially men-only staff to employing more women as teachers. Marlene's position as a novelty on the staff was immediately undermined by their arrival. Who do they think they are? she had churlishly asked her male colleagues, but they didn't have the answer. They couldn't admit to her that secretly they were pleased to have more attractive women on the staff.

It didn't take long for the three new arrivals to realise that attempting to befriend Marlene was a waste of time. As the reverend's words continued soporifically, Sue thought back to the Christmas party held at the end of the first year she'd started at the school. Her heart sank when she saw that she'd been seated at Marlene's table in the function room of a local sporting club. Some bright spark had had the idea of mixing up the members from different departments to encourage bonding. The bottles of wine and beer on the tables were consumed rapidly, many thinking that they may as well drink as much as they could at the school's expense. Marlene was one of those and she was also enjoying Sue's discomfort at having to sit near her.

'What do you mean the boys are saying stuff about me?' Sue asked in response to a thinly veiled dig from Marlene.

'Oh, you must know there are some boys who love to gossip,' Marlene stated knowingly, as she poured herself another glass of Jacob's Creek Chardonnay.

'I don't think it's the boys. I think it's the teachers. What exactly have you heard about me?' Sue probed, trying not to sound annoyed at the inference but eager to hear the answer.

'Nothing really,' Marlene protested half-heartedly, her eyes flicking around the room.

'Well, there must be something otherwise you wouldn't have brought it up.'

Marlene feigning reluctance, finally said, 'It's just that Bentley said the boys think you are going out with one of the students.'

Sue drained her glass and faced Marlene directly, stating, 'Maybe it's Benty who's going out with a student? Not me.'

Marlene reached out and picked up her drink. She stared across the table at Gary, from the Science Department and shrugged her shoulders. Brian, also from Science, his face hidden behind a schooner glass, mouthed something to Marlene who put down her drink and walked off to the Ladies. Sue poured another glass and took a long swig. This was the moment to tackle Marlene. What a bitch.

Stepping carefully around the tables, Sue made her way to the restroom and waited for Marlene to emerge from her cubicle. Sue leaned against the row of sinks while pulling a cigarette out of a packet in her pocket and lit it hurriedly.

'What *is* your problem?' Sue asked Marlene after she finally emerged from the toilet cubicle to the noise of flushing.

'What problem?' Marlene answered dismissively as she tidied her hair in the mirror.

'I've done nothing against you,' Sue stated defensively. And at least I wash my hands after going to the toilet, she thought angrily.

Marlene's reflection showed her disbelief. 'Not according to Bentley.'

'Why is it always about Bentley?' Sue asked.

'The boys talk to him. He told me what you said about me.'

'About you? Who to?'

'The boys.'

'What?' Sue protested. 'I *never* talk about other teachers and I would *never* say anything about you. Why on earth did Bentley tell you that? What's he trying to do?'

'Don't ask me,' Marlene said shrugging as she walked towards the door.

'Shouldn't we women stick together in this chauvinistic environment?' Sue demanded.

'You can do whatever you like,' Marlene flung at her as she left the bathroom.

Sue stood uncertain of what to do next. The thought of facing the teachers at her table had no appeal and Jenny, her friend who'd started at the school at the same time, had refused to come to this end of year function in protest against the treatment of the female teachers.

'Why on earth are you going? I don't want to have a drink with that lot. Bunch of bloody chauvinist losers,' Jenny had said when Sue tried to persuade her to attend.

But if she left straight away it would appear that Marlene had won. And if she weren't present, then she would be the object of gossip. Bentley was seated at a nearby table and he would love to see her squirm. Perhaps she should go and sit with him. That would set tongues wagging.

Schools, like politics, were full of factions. It was not only divided into subject departments but political alliances; those who were part of the inner circle, those on the outer and those who desperately wanted to be in the inside.

Sue ran her cigarette under the tap and threw the butt into the bin. She took a last look in the mirror and pushed her hair behind her ears. Seeing she had enough lipstick still on, Sue walked back into the noisy function room. Marlene, bent over whispering to Gary, stopped when she saw Sue re-emerge and make her way back to their table. Gary pushed his chair back and sauntered over to join Bentley. It was an unusual friendship. Gary was such a blokey bloke;

a leader of the cadets; his army uniform worn with enormous pride. He was the coach of the Second 15 and despite his protestations about how the school was being ruined by the arrival of women, was keenly pursuing Lillian Cutler, the third of the trio whom Bentley enjoyed bad-mouthing.

Gary grabbed a chair from a nearby table and forced his way between the other diners next to Bentley. The two sat huddled together, grinning in Sue's direction.

Sue grabbed her bag off the floor and ignoring Marlene's darting eyes, wended her way through the tables to join Bruce out on the balcony having a cigarette. She frantically ripped off the cellophane from a fresh packet and asked for a light.

'This place stinks,' she complained to Bruce after inhaling and almost spitting out the smoke.

'What? The rugby club?' he asked.

'*Nooo*. The school. That bloody Marlene was making cracks about me at the table and when I asked her about it, she said that Bentley had told her things I was meant to have said to the boys. God, she's a bitch and so is he.' She drew deeply on her cigarette. 'I wish I could have sat at your table. Whose stupid idea was it that we all got mixed up?'

'Mrs Goldman's. She's trying to stop us being cliquey,' Bruce explained wearily.

'She's another bloody pain. What is it with these women on the staff? Why is fucking, excuse my French, Bentley, such a bitch? I've got heaps of camp mates, so what's he got against me?'

'Darling. You know Benty. He hates competition. He wants to be the star with the boys and having gorgeous women around is a big threat. Take no notice. Marlene's a sad case, so don't worry about her. She's just jealous.'

'It's alright for you to say but I hate being talked about.'

'You've got nothing to worry about,' he paused. 'Have you?'

'No, I haven't,' Sue answered emphatically. She hesitated then stubbed out her cigarette. 'Think I'll get going. This is crap. See you tomorrow. Last day, thank God.'

Sue kissed Bruce on the cheek and hurriedly skirted around the edge of the room and without saying goodbye to anyone else walked to her car and drove home.

The noise of the boys getting to their feet for the departure of the staff off the stage brought Sue back to reality. She joined the procession of teachers as they shuffled past the chairs to the steps down to the auditorium. The boys stared at them as they solemnly made their way through the centre of the hall and back to the staffroom.

MATTO

A knock on the door to Jim Cameron's office interrupted his musings. His watch showed him it was a little after 8 am. He couldn't stop thinking about Bentley. It was odd how he was just lying there. Bentley wasn't a small man and could have easily put up a fight, but there was no sign of it. And why was the cup smashed? Bentley was so fastidious he wouldn't have been able to leave a mess like that.

He called out for whoever was at the door to enter. James Matthews cautiously opened the door and stood awkwardly, his school bag dangling heavily from his right hand.

'Hello, James. Come on in,' Jim greeted the boy warmly. 'Please sit down. How can I help you?' Jim asked as he positioned himself behind his desk.

The boy stood undecided whether to sit while the deputy head sat waiting silently. He stared at Mr Cameron then at the floor. His bag dangled heavily.

'James. Was there something you wanted to ask me? Why not sit down? We're very grateful for your quick thinking the other day.'

The student couldn't help but show his pleasure at the praise, especially from someone like Mr Cameron. He'd heard that Mr Cameron had fought in the Vietnam War and was given some award for bravery. James sat down on the edge of the hard wooden chair and deposited his bag on the floor. 'Mr Cameron,' he started. 'I, um, don't know how to, um, tell you...'

Jim leant back and tried not to look too interested. 'I'm assuming that you're here about Mr Shute.'

'Yes, Sir.' Matthews nudged his bag with his foot and stared at one of the pictures of the school on the wall.

'James. Let's have a chat. I won't be 'dobbing' you into anyone.'

Matthews smiled weakly at the deputy head's use of the adolescent term. 'Sir. It's just that some weird things have been happening here lately. And Bent... Mr Shute is dead.'

Jim waited.

'It's a bit hard to say and I don't want to get the other boys into trouble,' Matthews finally said, nibbling at a piece of rough cuticle on his thumb.

'I'm not going to tell anyone,' Jim reassured him, hoping that this were true.

'Well, we all know, knew, that Mr Shute was a, well you know, but it didn't matter. Well, until recently.' Matthews stopped. 'I saw the ambulance and we're not allowed in the boarding house.'

Jim nodded. 'That's because Mr Shute had died,' he explained.

'I know. But....' The boy began to chew at the cuticle again.

Jim kept his face as passive as possible. 'Do you think something suspicious has happened? He never did, 'er, try, um, anything with any of the boys, did he?' he asked hesitantly.

'No. No. Not at all. Not with me anyway.' Matthews' face flushed.

'Do you mean that he tried to do something with the others?' Oh, God. No, Jim thought. He really didn't want to hear about any sexual goings-on between the teacher and boys, even though it could be relevant to the investigation.

'No, not really. It's just that sometimes after footy practice I'd see a couple of the older boys going into his flat.'

'What's wrong with that?' Mr Cameron asked, hoping he didn't sound accusatory.

'Nothing, I suppose. But I saw them a few times and it was always quite late at night.'

'Didn't Mr Shute have homework sessions to help boys who were having trouble? Needed help with assignments?'

'Yes, but those guys weren't his students and some of the other guys reckon that they are, well you know.'

'Mmmm. Yes. You mean the boys who went into Mr Shute's flat?'

Matthews nodded. 'And they don't belong to Churchill. They're in Chamberlain.' He stopped.

'Maybe I shouldn't have said anything. It's probably nothing. Lots of the boys liked Benty. They thought he was good fun.'

Jim Cameron looked closely at Matthews. He was somewhat shocked by the admission that Bentley Shute was good fun. An acquired taste perhaps. 'Are you upset that these boys visited Mr Shute? Do you think they may have done something wrong?' He didn't know how to articulate the possibility of gay sex to an adolescent.

Matthews seemed alarmed by the questions. 'I don't care what the other boys do, Sir, but this is a boarding school. You know what it's like. It's just that those boys visited regularly and now Mr Shute is dead.'

'Quite,' Mr Cameron said. He was surprised by the maturity of Matthew's answers. 'Do you want to tell me who the boys are?'

Matthews peered down at his bag and then looked up at Mr Cameron, 'The guys who seemed to visit the most were... They're a couple of prefects... Phil Sutton and Dave Judd.'

Jim, taken aback, sat up. 'Sutton and Judd. Year 12,' he repeated, trying to keep his voice as neutral as possible. He leaned forward and placed his elbows on the desk. 'James, you've been very courageous coming to see me and telling me this. It's best if you don't say anything to anyone. Not even your best mates. Keep it under your hat. There's a good man.'

He stood up, quickly followed by Matthews, who now with bag in hand, followed him to the door. 'If you want to talk to me again, don't hesitate.' Jim Cameron patted Matthews on the back and watched him as he slung his school bag over his shoulder and headed out into the corridor.

That was a brave thing to do, thought Cameron.

He remembered that Matthews was a townie but as his parents had divorced when he was in Year 7 came to board at the school soon after. Rumour had it that Mr Matthews was searching for a wife to replace James's mother but so far had been unsuccessful. There were always a handful of boys who boarded despite having family homes in Sydney. The school did its best to provide a sense of belonging and security.

Am I being taken in by him though? Jim asked himself. Has he given me this information to put me off the scent? Jim grimaced at his use of such a cliché. But it might be true. Matthews had come to see him very quickly after hearing about Shute's death. Was it in reality, Matthews himself who used to visit Shute? They both lived in the same boarding house and Matthews would easily know Shute's comings and goings.

That comment about Bentley being good fun. That was not how he saw Bentley. Bentley entertained others with gossip, but he wasn't one for telling jokes or having a laugh. Had Matthews seen a different side to him?

However, why would he name those two boys out of the thousand who were at the school? Was it a random selection or had he really seen them go into Shute's rooms? Sutton and Judd had never struck him as being gay, but then he was no judge. Maybe this was *The Prime of Miss Jean Brodie* but in reverse gender. Some teachers loved having a circle of students they could mould and influence.

The bell rang for the first lesson of the day. The volume of chatter in the corridors decreasing as boys entered rooms and settled at their desks.

He wearily lent back in his chair and smoothed his hands over his hair then sat up. 'Well, this won't buy the baby a new bonnet,' Jim muttered to himself, remembering the expression his father had used many years ago.

MORE SUSPECTS

James Matthews had only been gone a few moments when there was another knock at the door. This time it was Daphne, who hardly gave Jim any time to answer. She walked briskly into his office with an aura of self-importance. Jim wasn't sure, but she looked a bit different. Had she changed her hair?

'Good morning, Mr Cameron. Detective Stone and Sergeant O'Shea are in my office and hope to have a meeting with you now and Mr Pritchard when he's free.' Her formal tone implied that he didn't have a choice. Jim gathered the folds of his black gown closely around him and without a word, walked after her.

The two policemen could be seen standing, waiting expressionless in her office. Jim couldn't help but wonder if they were taught that at police training. In his army days, he had learned not to show any emotion. Emotion was equated with weakness. But this wasn't war time.

As Jim entered, Stone smiled and held out his hand. Jim shook hands with the two men. 'Morning, gentlemen. How are you?' They assured him that they were fine before apologising for taking up more of his time.

'No problem,' he reassured them. 'I know I shouldn't really ask, but anything to report?' he questioned, cocking his head. He wondered when the time would be right to tell them about his visit from James Matthews.

Daphne who was pretending to busy herself at her desk, paused to hear the answer. Stone, aware of her interest, was about to suggest going to Cameron's office but changed his mind. Perhaps if she were party to certain information, she could fill in the gaps. She definitely had her finger on the pulse of the school.

'Yes. We know the time of death and how he was killed. That was pretty obvious, but it's been confirmed. Shute died on Saturday night, somewhere between 6 pm and 12 midnight from injuries inflicted by a sword. One of his own.'

'Not Sunday night?' Jim asked.

'No. Saturday,' Stone reiterated. 'It seems odd that no-one noticed that he wasn't around until Monday morning.'

'Not really. Boarding masters often have fewer duties on Sunday. And prefects can replace them for minor duties. The boarding houses have more than one master who could take over. Shute had a deputy as well,' Jim explained. 'They *do* have to have a life outside of the school.'

The expression on Sergeant O'Shea's face showed his scepticism at how boarding schools functioned.

Parents putting their faith in a school to look after their sons. Seemed rather risky.

'Bit like window leave for the boarders?' Stone asked Jim.

'Nothing slips past you, Alan,' Jim stated grinning.

Stone laughed. 'It's common knowledge that boarders go to the local pub. You must know that, Jim? The school would rather the police know where the boys are and for us to keep an eye on them.'

'Mmm. True. But it's not quite the same as a boarding master taking time off.'

'Suppose not. Anyway, we'll need to talk to the prefects and to the teacher who was on duty that night. And the boys in the house. Daphne, can you give me a list of the names of all the boys and staff who live in Mr Shute's house?'

Daphne stood up quickly and began to flick through her files in the filing cabinet behind her desk. She soon extracted some sheets of paper and handed them to Detective Stone who scanned the names.

'The other boarding master is Peter Charteris,' Stone stated, glancing at Jim for confirmation.

'That's right. He's been in the house about a year. Came to us from a boarding school in Bathurst. In the Art department. Gets on well with the boys.'

'How about with Mr Shute? Were they on good terms?'

'Reasonably. But I don't think he was part of Shute's gang,' Jim replied.

'Right,' said Stone jotting a note next to the man's name.

'Actually, while we're talking about who's in the house, I had a visit just before from one of the boarders from Churchill,' Jim began but couldn't continue. He felt caught in the middle. On one hand he felt obliged to tell the police of the information Matthews had supplied, but on the other, guilty for implying to Matthews that his naming of Judd and Sutton would be kept secret.

Jim raised his eyebrows to Stone and subtly inclined his head to indicate that he would prefer to speak elsewhere. Stone stood up and after telling Daphne, that they would leave her in peace, followed Jim and Sergeant O'Shea out of the office.

'Sorry about that, Alan,' Jim said. 'But didn't think it was wise to pass on information in front of Daphne. Not that she can't be trusted, but the boy who came to see me told me in confidence. I feel pretty bad telling you, but as it's a murder case, it may be relevant.'

The three entered Jim's office and sat down. The police could sense Jim's disquiet and waited patiently for him to begin. Stone admired Jim's sensitivity. He was an honourable man in the true sense of the word. There was no bathing in reflected glory or enjoying the misery of others when it came to Jim.

Finally, Jim explained, 'James Matthews is the boy who told Mr Pritchard that Shute wasn't answering his door. He's a boarder, in Year 11. He's always been a good student and has never caused any trouble. He came to see me because now he knows Bentley is dead and the police are involved. He felt that he might have seen something useful.'

'That's very responsible of him,' Stone observed. 'What has he seen?'

'It's more who he saw. James said he'd noticed that two boys in particular seemed to be regular visitors at Shute's flat. He's aware that Shute held study evenings, but these two boys are not boarders in that house and there were times when he saw them late at night.' Jim coughed uncomfortably.

'How was James able to see the boys?' Sergeant O'Shea asked, his voice rising at the intrigue of the situation.

'He sleeps in the dorm directly opposite Mr Shute's flat so if he were going to the bathroom, he could have seen them.'

'How often?'

'It sounded like quite a lot.'

'And this boy always happened to be in corridor. Seems a bit odd,' O'Shea said disapprovingly.

'What was he doing out there?'

'I have no idea, Sergeant. You'll have to ask him,' Jim replied, with a hint of sarcasm. Realising he was being a little judgmental, he grimaced apologetically at the sergeant.

'Okay. I know this is awkward for you, Jim,' Stone interrupted, 'but we will have to talk to James. Can you tell us the names of the boys he mentioned?

Jim took a deep breath before saying, 'The boys are David Judd and Phillip Sutton. They're both in

Year 12 and board in Chamberlain House. There's probably a very simple explanation.'

'What are they like? Do you think they're capable of ...?' Stone's question tailed off. He knew that it was impossible to judge whether someone was capable of murder. It was often the unlikeliest person who committed the crime.

Jim thought again of his time in Vietnam. The men who had seemed full of bravado were often the least brave, while the quieter ones could take you by surprise.

'Judd is a follower and does whatever Sutton tells him. But whether he'd be willing to attack Shute, it's hard to say. Sutton has a big opinion of himself, but again it's impossible to say if he'd be up to murder.'

The police listened intently to his description of the two boys. 'Well, we can't jump to any conclusions about anyone until we've spoken to them. Also, we don't want to make it obvious that we're singling them out, so they'll be interviewed along with others,' Stone said. 'You don't think that James is trying to get them into trouble?'

'I wouldn't think so, Alan. I can't see what he'd gain by making enemies.'

Stone thought for a few moments. It was a touchy area that he was about to bring up, although he knew that Jim was open minded.

'This is a tricky topic, but I have to ask. Do *you* think that Mr Shute's death could be linked to his homosexuality? No-one has said outright that he's gay, but it seems pretty obvious. Perhaps, the boys were in a tryst with Mr Shute and something went wrong.'

'It's possible, but to be honest, I have no idea. I didn't socialise with Shute. It was nothing to do with his being gay, but he just wasn't someone I identified with. Bit too much of a gossip for my liking.'

'That seems to be the impression we're getting. Jim, it's great getting your insight. Is there anyone else you can suggest we speak to?'

'Oh God, Alan. You'll have to speak to the whole school. I'm exaggerating, but it could have been anyone. And maybe with luck it has nothing to do with the school.'

'I sympathise, but we have to start here. Daphne mentioned that Shute seemed to, if I can use the word, victimise some of the women teachers. Do you agree?'

'Unfortunately, I do. Bentley seemed to be threatened by the arrival of the newer women teachers and went out of his way to undermine them,' Jim said.

'That's what we've gathered. Sue Armstrong has been mentioned.' Stone paused to check his notes. 'Along with Jenny Bartoli and Lillian Cutler. He glanced at Jim to see if he agreed. Jim nodded.

'Anyway, thanks Jim. We've taken up enough of your time again.'

'No, you haven't. I understand what you have to do. I'll have a word to Daphne and get her to organise a room for you both. Then you can talk to people in peace. It's not exactly the same as the police station, but better than being homeless while you're here,' Jim offered. In an odd way, despite the circumstances, it was good to be working with Alan again.

MORE QUESTIONS

After leaving Jim Cameron's office, Detective Stone and Sergeant O'Shea headed straight back to the boarding house and entered Mr Shute's private rooms.

They stood in the middle of the lounge, noting their surrounds. Neither of them voiced their opinion at the nature of the ornaments and decorations.

O'Shea's father had fought with the Australian army towards the end of the Second World War and seeing such a display of Japanese objet d'art bewildered the sergeant somewhat. They had been the enemy, yet this teacher appeared to idolise the Japs.

Stone was reminded of his own father who'd fought with the New Zealand army in North Africa against the Germans. He remembered how upset his dad had been when his own sister and brother-in-law had bought a Volkswagen soon after the war. That was a tactlessness that didn't gel.

'Is anything missing? Something out of place?' Stone asked rhetorically. 'Except for the broken cup,' he said, answering his own question.

'It's hard to tell. Nothing else seems disturbed,' O'Shea answered. 'And there'll be so many fingerprints because he had lots of students here. And colleagues.'

'Well, we know he was killed by blows to his neck and head by the sword. It would take some strength to hit him so hard. The fact that the perpetrator left the sword under the bed is a bit of a statement. No attempt to conceal the weapon. Bit like giving the finger. And why smash the cup?'

'Who's he giving the finger to?' O'Shea asked. 'Certainly not to Shute as he's dead.'

They stood staring at the samurai swords above the fireplace.

'An execution,' O'Shea said doubtfully. He thought about the war films he'd seen and samurai swords had featured in a number. The Japanese soldiers were always portrayed as having buck teeth, mean slanty eyes and were happy to lop off the head of an enemy prisoner.

'Well, we know that's where the fourth sword was. There's the screws to hold it onto the wall,' Stone said pointing at two screws a foot apart, with another two above them to hold the top of the sword.

'Does this mean the murder was spontaneous and the bloke just grabbed any weapon he could?' O'Shea asked.

'Possibly. But why leave it behind? Why not remove the evidence? Does he,' he paused, 'or she, want to be caught?'

'She?' O'Shea laughed sceptically. 'Really?'

'Stranger things have happened,' Alan Stone responded, tapping the side of his nose. 'We've got the weapon and the cup which with luck may provide fingerprints and there seems to be a number of people, staff and boys, who could have a motive, but I wouldn't mind another chat with the headmaster. Can you give him a call and ask him to join us.'

Sergeant O'Shea went over to the phone, which he now knew linked Shute directly to the headmaster's assistant. He picked up the receiver, unconsciously straightening his shoulders and tapped in a few numbers. Daphne answered immediately.

'Mrs Withers, would you mind asking Mr Pritchard to come to Mr Shute's rooms, please,' O'Shea asked politely, but in a tone he hoped sounded authoritative. He, like MacGregor, pictured Daphne's tight top encasing two large orbs. Daphne was more like Marilyn Monroe, soft and rounded, unlike Madonna with her sharp points.

'Thank you. We'll wait for him here,' he responded, his voice cracking slightly as he tried to compose himself.

Bentley's wardrobe, artfully arranged, revealed nothing of any real interest except that both men thought he left them for dead when it came to being orderly.

The bathroom, like the wardrobe was organised and contained a variety of hair and face products, piles of folded towels and cleaning items. Apart from a packet of Panadol, there were no drugs.

There was nothing in the kitchen area that stood out. The Japanese teapot still had the five cups placed around it and the oven and microwave were spotlessly clean.

The sergeant rifled through the material on the bookshelves. Shute's taste was not to his liking. There were no novels, not that the policeman was a reader, but a variety of arty books and antique catalogues. The Japanese drawings of explicit sexual acts hidden between the large art books were not titillating. A drawing was nothing like the real thing.

Their search was interrupted by Pritchard hurrying in, followed closely by Daphne.

'Morning gentlemen or is it afternoon?' greeted Pritchard, peering at his watch. 'You already know my secretary, Mrs Withers.'

'Hello again,' she said smiling, as Stone and O'Shea acknowledged that yes, they had met.

'Thanks for coming. We want to run a few ideas past you,' said Stone. He pointed at the three swords above the fireplace. 'Do you know if Mr Shute had many of these swords? We've found the one that we presume was used to kill him, but did he have any more?'

Daphne and Pritchard quickly looked at each other. Both went to speak at the same time, but Daphne deferred to her boss who informed the police that Bentley did have a penchant for Japanese objects, but he had no idea how many swords he had.

Daphne couldn't resist. 'Mr Pritchard. You should tell them about that incident.'

Stone and O'Shea waited.

Mr Pritchard, conflicted by his loyalty to the school but wanting to aid the police, thought for a moment. 'Ah. Yes. Well. There was an incident a while ago when Bentley, Mr Shute, was found on the Oval. Running around in a kim, what's it called? A kimono? It appeared that he'd had a bit of a breakdown.'

'A breakdown?' Stone queried, surprised.

'Well, either that or drugs,' Pritchard blurted out.

'What sort of drugs?' Stone quickly demanded seeing that Pritchard had spoken without thinking.

Pritchard, now aware his rashness could not be undone, unwillingly replied, 'Oh God. Um. What was it called? A letter or something.'

'An E? Ecstasy?' asked Stone. This new drug of choice had flooded the club circuit recently.

'Yes. Yes. I think that's what he was meant to have taken.' Pritchard's face reddened with embarrassment. He cringed, aware of how this information sounded. How could a school keep employing a staff member who had been caught running around the sports field acting like a lunatic.

He looked anxiously around the lounge as if its occupant could appear at any moment. Daphne too, was sensing the presence of the dead teacher. She didn't believe in ghosts but standing in this room surrounded by Bentley's collections, he was very real.

'Did he threaten anyone?' Stone asked.

'Definitely not,' Pritchard denied desperately. 'It was a momentary glitch in his mental state.'

'Did he take drugs often?' O'Shea asked, trying not to sound too eager to hear the gossip.

'No. No. That was just a rumour. You know what schools are…,' Daphne interrupted, realising how badly Shute's actions reflected on St Cuthbert's.

'He'd been under some pressure from the enquiry, so his behaviour was a little erratic for a while.'

'Enquiry?' O'Shea continued to question.

'A student drowned on an excursion which Mr Shute and another teacher supervised,' Pritchard told them reluctantly. 'It was a complete accident, and no one was responsible. But he took it very hard.'

'I read about it in the paper,' Stone said. 'I gather that private schools often take students on adventure type courses. Put them through their paces, so to speak. Out of their comfort zones.'

The inference that students at private schools needed to be put in challenging situations was not lost on Daphne or Pritchard.

'Just because some of the boys come from wealthy families does not mean they have no backbone,' Pritchard challenged. 'Also, there are many boys who come from families who have made great sacrifices to send them here.'

Stone attempted to look chastised. 'I suppose that's not really the issue anyway. We need to work out why Mr Shute was the focus of such an attack. Do you think it had something to do with the excursion?'

Mr Pritchard scratched his chin, frowning. 'Obviously, the parents, the Sinclairs, were terribly upset. Tim was their only child. But they've remained in touch with the school since the tragedy happened. Shute and Rodney Addington had to answer questions about whether they had behaved responsibly and followed the school's guidelines. Neither were blamed although it does seem to have caused a bit of ill feeling between the two of them, but surely not enough to cause such a dreadful act.'

Stone remained silent.

Sergeant O'Shea smiled at Daphne and asked, 'How long have you been at the school, Mrs Withers?'

Daphne who smiled in return said, 'About 10 years. It's Daphne, please. Only the boys call me Mrs Withers.

'O'Shea struggled to put his passive work face back on. 'Apart from the staff you've already mentioned, can you think of any other reason why someone would want to kill Mr Shute?'

Daphne dabbed at the corner of her mouth with her polished nail and suggested that Mr Pritchard should be the one to answer as he was the headmaster.

'It's alright, Daphne. You go right ahead. I'm sure you're more privy than me to the ins and outs of this place.' He turned to the policemen. 'The talking tends to stop when I walk into the room.'

Stone agreed that being a figure of authority could put one on the outer. 'Was Mr Shute visited by anyone from outside the school? Was he in a relationship?'

Daphne shook her head. 'I wasn't aware of anyone who wasn't connected to the school and I didn't know him well enough to know if he was in a relationship. You'd have to ask those closer to him about that.' She paused then said, 'I'm starting to feel guilty talking about Bentley. I didn't really like him, but he is dead after all.'

'Daphne. It's fine,' reassured Sergeant O'Shea, ignoring the rather quizzical stare from Detective Stone. 'Most people feel guilty talking about someone who's died.'

Waiting for Mr Pritchard's reassurance for her to continue she said, 'Well, as I told you before, Mr, er, Bentley, had a nasty tongue. He loved to gossip, and he was very good at spreading stories. Some of it true, some not.' Daphne thought for a few seconds.

'Many of his colleagues were, how can I put it? They were friendly to him because they were frightened of what he would say if they got on the wrong side of him. They didn't want to be the object of his tongue. But then some were good friends.'

'I gather you're not referring to the women teachers. Those you mentioned before?' Stone asked.

'No. They didn't want to be his friend. Except of course, Marlene Bates. She was very fond of him. But his other friends were all men.'

'Yes. I see.' Stone made another note in his book, then turning to the headmaster asked, 'Mr Pritchard, when was the last time you saw Mr Shute alive?'

'My God. Let me think. It would have been on Friday. We have a meeting of House Masters and Heads of Departments once a week. Mr Shute came to that.'

'Right. We know that Mr Shute was killed on Saturday night. But you didn't see him during the day?' The detective looked from Mr Pritchard to Daphne.

Daphne said no, while Mr Pritchard scratched his head. 'I didn't see him on Saturday because I was busy with other school business, but Bill said he was at the game. Apparently, he was with his usual colleagues,' Pritchard explained.

'Thank you. You've been extremely helpful,' Detective Stone said, closing his notebook but as a seeming afterthought asked, 'This is just a formality, but I do need to ask where you were on Saturday between 6pm and midnight. We can then tick the

95

two of you off. So to speak,' the detective said, trying to soften the question.

Daphne blushed. 'Gosh. Are we suspects?'

'We have to ask everyone their whereabouts on that night. It's normal procedure,' Stone explained.

'Oh. Of course. I...I was on a date with a gentleman. A friend of a friend. A blind date,' Daphne said, her blush increasing.

'That's nice,' Stone said. 'Where did you go?'

'We went for a drink at the Royal in Paddington, then to a French restaurant close by. I got home around 11.30.'

'And your friend can confirm this?'

'Yes. But it'll be a little awkward as it wasn't a successful date. I didn't want to see him again.'

'That's a shame,' Stone consoled. 'If you could write down his name for us. That would be very helpful.' He handed her his notebook open at a blank page.

He'd wondered about dating services for himself and whether that was how Daphne had met this man. Dating agencies were growing in popularity. It was hard meeting someone at work. There weren't many women in the police force and those who were at the station were either much younger, married or possibly lesbian.

Alan Stone wanted company, not just a one night stand. He felt lonely. Ngaire, his last girlfriend, had no desire to live in Australia. She didn't want to be one of the thousands of Kiwis who'd left New

Zealand in the late 1970s and now in the '80s. The long distance relationship hadn't lasted.

Daphne wrote down the name. She felt very awkward about exposing her private life. Stone then asked Mr Pritchard the same question. Pritchard didn't seem put out and told him that he, for once, had had a night off from social duties and spent the evening at home with his wife and that she would vouch for him.

Stone thanked them again and as he shook the headmaster's hand, Sergeant O'Shea reached out to shake Daphne's. She smiled gratefully as he thanked her for the assistance that both she and Mr Pritchard had offered.

'It's my pleasure,' she said blushing, but aware of the stock answer she had given, added, 'Well, it's not really a pleasure but we'll do what we can to help.' Daphne gushed, looking at both of the policemen.

Stone was more her age but there was something about Sergeant O'Shea that was rather appealing. The sergeant's hair was the opposite to hers, dark and cut short befitting his role as a policeman but his eyes were blue hinting at his Irish background.

'Daphne. Daphne. We'd better get on,' Pritchard reminded her. He'd noticed her blush when shaking O'Shea's hand. 'I think you might have an admirer,' he whispered once they were outside Shute's flat.

'Mr Pritchard, Robert. Really,' she protested. But he could see that the possibility had occurred to her as well.

'Man in uniform and all that,' Robert laughed.

'That'll do, Mr Pritchard,' she said primly.

97

'Yes. Quite,' Robert acquiesced, as he followed her out of the boarding house.

IN NEED OF A CUP OF TEA

Jim Cameron was in need of a cup of tea. His loyalty to the school was being challenged. He knew that Alan Stone had a job to do but exposing facts about the institution he loved didn't sit well with him.

Volunteering to fight with the Australian army in a war that the majority of the population was against, had led to ostracism and a number of his friends disagreed with his stance so much, that they were no longer friends. He accepted that. The war had proved very divisive and he wondered if he'd known at the time, what he learned later, whether he would still have volunteered. But Jim couldn't sit back and watch others dying. Having principles was hard.

As he made his tea in the staffroom, Gary Powell stood next to the open fridge, taking milk out of a compartment in the door. He poured some into a grubby looking mug, a relic from a sporting competition, stirred vigorously then put the milk back into the fridge.

'Afternoon, Gary. How're you?' Jim enquired.

'Gidday, Jim. Good thanks. Well, not so good, really. This whole situation with Bentley is bloody shocking.'

'Yes. It's very upsetting,' Jim sympathised as he opened the fridge and retrieved the milk.

'He wasn't old. To die so young. Dreadful. Do you know how he died?'

'Mr Pritchard will explain at the meeting this afternoon,' Jim replied, evading the question. He stirred the milk into his tea.

Gary was one of Bentley's inner circle. An unusual choice of friend. Jim wondered if Gary knew that Bentley was gay. He couldn't imagine the two of them having much in common and Gary had never seemed broadminded in his views. He wasn't as bad as Rodney Addington, but Oxford Street and its activities was definitely not his choice of venue. What did Shute have over Gary that made him loyal?

The final bell of the day was due to ring in a few minutes. Jim tipped out what was left of his tea, rinsed the cup then made his way to Mr Pritchard's office to accompany him to the staff meeting that had been called for the end of the school day. It was his duty to support the headmaster.

The 3.30 bell rang and soon after the staff filed into the staffroom. Some read the notice boards, which were always covered with the multitude of school minutiae; lists of sporting teams, detention rosters, playground duties, cover classes. Others checked their pigeonholes for messages and teaching materials, while a couple went into the phone cubicles to make calls. The small kitchen section was swamped with teachers eager to make tea or coffee in the limited time available.

The chatter diminished slightly when Mr Pritchard entered the staffroom followed by his deputy. They stood near the notice board and after a little a'hemming caught the attention of the staff.

'I'm sorry to keep you after school. I know how precious your time is,' Pritchard apologised. 'But I want to use this, er, moment to reinforce what I said at assembly yesterday and I'm sorry that I had to inform you then of the terrible news regarding our colleague, Bentley Shute, but there was no other suitable time.'

Pritchard could sense the disbelief from the staff. Why hadn't they been called into the staffroom prior to the assembly or first thing in the morning? Weren't they important enough?

The headmaster, doing his best to ignore the atmosphere of antagonism, continued speaking. 'Mr Shute's death has come as a shock to us all. Many of you knew him extremely well and his demise will affect you, and the boys.' He stopped as Jenny from the Language Department had put her hand up.

'Yes, Miss Bartoli?'

'It's been a few days since Bentley's,' she hesitated, 'death, and we're none the wiser. What are the police doing here?'

Inward drawing of breath could be heard. There had been a gradual realisation that the 'accident' may have been something else. That explained the police cars.

Mr Pritchard flinched slightly at the use of the word 'death' but then answered, 'It's exceedingly difficult for me to talk about Mr Shute. Something like this has never happened before at the school and I have never experienced anything like it in all my years of teaching, but it appears that Mr Shute was attacked and killed.'

Gasps of shock emanated from the staff. Teachers clutched at each other; hands went up to mouths. This was dreadful. At a school like this.

The headmaster waited till calm returned. 'The police are investigating, and we are assisting them in every possible way.'

His eyes took in all the teachers. 'They will, of course, want to speak to all of you and the boys. I'm sending a letter home to every parent and the boarding masters and school counsellors will assist the boys in Mr Shute's house and those boys in his classes.'

The head waited for this information to sink in, then continued. 'I don't want to hold you up any longer than necessary but obviously this is a very serious situation. I know this seems an impossible request, but if you value the school, I ask you to limit what you say to anyone from outside. Spreading gossip will only damage St Cuthbert's and we have to let the police do their job. Churchill House is a crime scene so none of the boys can go back there at the moment.'

'Something wrong with the plumbing. My foot,' was muttered by a couple of boarding masters who'd taken in the boarders from Shute's house.

Mr Pritchard, unwilling to answer any more questions, indicated that the meeting was over and left the room and the staff to their thoughts.

No-one was in a rush to leave. The thought that an actual murder had taken place was amazing. And for it to be Bentley. Some appeared upset while others raised eyebrows at each other as if they were not surprised. They could imagine Bentley making enemies. Heads huddled together. Jim could see Sue Armstrong talking earnestly with her female colleagues. She looked up and saw him watching them. She extricated herself from the group and made her way over to him.

'How are you, Mr Cameron?' Sue asked. 'This is a terrible situation, isn't it?' Jim could only agree. He was aware of how attractive she was and how that could be to her detriment. In such a very male environment, she attracted both positive and negative attention. As if it were her fault that she was pretty and young.

'It's been a huge shock. How are you going, Sue?' Jim asked, shifting the conversation. 'I haven't had a decent chat with you of late. Is the school treating you well?'

Sue thought for a second. 'Do you mean by the boys or the staff?'

'The staff, I suppose. It's a while ago now, but I seem to remember that your arrival, along with Miss Bartoli's and Mrs Cutler's, caused quite a ripple.'

Sue laughed tiredly. 'It certainly did. It was ghastly. So chauvinistic. The men mainly, not the boys. Hard to believe how old fashioned this place was,' she paused and leant closer to him. 'And still is.'

'Surely not all the men are still so old fashioned about having more women on the staff?' Jim asked, hoping that it didn't look as if he were fishing for information.

'No. But a few of them have certainly gone out of their way to make life hard for us.'

'How?'

Sue frowned at him doubting his need to ask. 'Well, put it this way. Gossip has a way of spreading around the school. It's amazing how many men I've slept with. Not counting the boys of course,' Sue stated, staring at the deputy intently and she raised her eyebrows as if challenging him to dispute her statement.

Jim had no reply. He glanced at her. He knew she was the butt of gossip. There was always that sort of talk. Boys had crushes and so did the teachers. However, Sue had really copped a lot of unfair criticism. Her promotion to being the first female housemaster of a dayboy house had not helped her cause.

'Mind you, my complaints are nothing compared to what happened to Bentley. Dreadful.' Sue took out a cigarette packet from her handbag then put it back remembering there was no smoking in the staffroom. Her eyes flicked around the room. She was about to say something then swallowed.

'What is it?' Jim asked quickly.

'I don't know. It's hard to say,' Sue flustered.

'Would it be better to talk somewhere else? You can always come and talk to me in private.'

Sue quickly glanced around the room again. 'Yes. It probably would be better to talk somewhere else. Walls have ears and all that.' She laughed at the old wartime saying her father had quoted frequently.

'Also, what about the police? Will everyone be talking to them?' she asked in a rush.

'I presume so. As the head said they're going to interview everyone, now they know the cause of death. Anyway, please don't hesitate to come for a chat.' Jim smiled. He didn't want to push Sue, but he believed that she would be aware of the social dynamics of the staffroom. She seemed perceptive and as one of the few females on the staff had suffered the slings and arrows from certain teachers, particularly those from Bentley and his cohort of supporters.

He'd noticed however, that some of the real old timers on the staff were more accepting of the women teachers and more benevolent towards them. Surprisingly, the prejudice and chauvinism came from the younger men. Perhaps they were threatened by the rise of feminism.

Pouring himself a glass of water at the sink, Jim could sense someone behind him, probably waiting to rinse a mug. He turned around and found Rodney Addington staring intently at the dishwashing liquid.

'Hello, Rodney. How are you?' Jim asked. This man was someone Jim had never warmed to. For a man who was a stickler for the rules, there was something about him that was underhand. He couldn't put his finger on what it was, but he always felt slightly uneasy in Rodney's company.

Rodney didn't reply immediately but finally disclosed that he was fine.

'I know you were good friends with Bentley. It must be a bit hard for you at the moment,' Jim said cautiously.

Rodney shook his head. 'I'm alright. You get used to anything being in the army. As you'd know, Jim.'

'True. True. Still, it's a big shock and he was a large part of many people's lives.'

'You've got to continue. Bentley upheld the values of the school and he wouldn't have wanted the boys or the staff to crumple.'

Jim nodded in agreement although deep down doubted Rodney's belief of carrying on regardless. His lack of sentiment at a friend's death seemed unconvincing.

The teacher was shortish in stature and erect in stance. He had entered the teaching world after being a professional soldier. He'd achieved the rank of Colonel although, unlike Jim, had not actually gone to Vietnam.

As a teacher he brought with him a strictness, a conservatism and military efficiency, which many boys professed not to like but in fact, did. They knew where they stood with him and if he ever caned, the boy accepted the punishment usually without question. However, his conservative attitudes put him at odds with the majority of female teachers. He, like Bill MacGregor, still believed that a woman's place was in the home and if they did have to work then it should be as a secretary or librarian. Men understood the boys, women didn't.

The vitriol that Rodney had expressed when Sue was promoted to housemaster was memorable. He made it very clear to those who would listen, that she must have slept with the headmaster to achieve such a position. He, and Bentley, had assumed that the position would be his once Ralph Jackson, the then Day Boy House Master retired.

However, it had been on the recommendation of Jackson, that Sue be his successor. A benign Kiwi, and as one of the older men on the staff, Jackson was not as biased in his thinking as some of his younger colleagues. He had seen in Sue the potential to nurture the boys in the house rather than only inflict punishment.

Rodney's bitterness at being overlooked bubbled and boiled and he'd had a willing audience in Bentley, Gary, Brian, Don, and Marlene to vent his anger. They too enjoyed the bile of his words against Sue. Of course, she must have slept with the headmaster. How else could she have risen so quickly up the career ladder? They knew deep down it was highly unlikely that Sue, married with two small children, would be attracted to a man like Pritchard.

However, they clung to this theory of sexual nepotism to soothe their own feelings of the perceived injustice of the situation. Rodney's strong belief in himself and the superiority of men, could not accept any other version. Sue must have beguiled Pritchard.

Bentley fed this theory like a chef adding spices to a curry and he found many willing tasters including students. The boys he entertained with intrigue, felt flattered to be party to such adult talk. The students, as well as some of the male teachers, believed that the head would have lusted after Sue, as they too fantasised about her and the other two new female arrivals. She'd found clumsily written notes shoved under her office door containing declarations of love in undisguised handwriting.

Jim Cameron had been aware of Rodney's anger and jealousy towards Sue as had Mr Pritchard. Both found the gossip unpleasant and unprofessional. It was completely against the philosophy of gentlemanly behaviour, which was the basis of the school. Mr Pritchard, in his addresses to the school assembly stressed the need to behave like a gentleman. To Jim the idea that Sue had received the master-ship of a house by sleeping with a decent man such as Pritchard was inconceivable.

Rodney Addington turned away from Jim, washed his mug and dried it thoroughly but disdainfully with a rather grubby tea towel. He placed the mug neatly in the cupboard above the sink where the staff stored their personal crockery, folded the tea towel in half, length ways and draped it over the cupboard door.

He walked primly across the staffroom to check his pigeonhole, as Sue, after finishing her cigarette on the balcony, was about to check hers. She stopped when she saw Rodney at the boxes. She waited for him to move away but he turned to face her.

'You for one, won't be sorry Bentley's dead,' he spat quietly. 'Got anything to tell us? Or maybe your friend has?' Addington managed to make the word friend sound menacing and the sneer on his face added to the threatening tone.

The teachers standing nearby gasped, uncomfortable at such a blatant accusation. They hovered waiting for Sue's reaction, pretending interest in the notices next to the boxes.

Sue, her face bright red with anger put one hand into the pigeonhole feeling at the back to see if she'd

109

missed any small pieces of paper. As Sue pulled the messages out of the small box, she could feel breath on her hair. She turned quickly, and Rodney Addington took a step backwards. Her look of shock at the challenging demeanour of this man changed to a mixture of dislike and concern.

'Mr Addington. You amaze me. Just because you have a nasty little mind, doesn't mean that we all do,' Sue said with quiet vehemence. As she began to walk away, he reached out and grabbed her arm.

'Excuse me,' she stressed, wrenching her arm out of his grip. 'How dare you touch me?'

'We all know that you hated Bentley,' he snarled.

'Oh, for God's sake,' Sue responded angrily. 'Get a life.'

'Come on, Rodney. Leave her alone,' demanded Steve, a bearded art teacher, as he sprang up from his chair. 'Don't be such a bully.'

Jim quickly strode over to intervene. 'I think we should all calm down. Rodney, there's no need to take your anger out on Mrs Armstrong.'

'That's right. Take her side. You're as bad as Pritchard,' Rodney whined. He appeared to be about to say more but the silence around him told him that everyone was listening, and he wasn't doing himself any favours.

He grabbed the material out of his pigeonhole and stormed across the staffroom. Heads swivelled to watch his departure and once the door was shut behind him, whispers began.

'Are you alright, Sue?' Jim asked, shepherding her away from the audience.

'Oh yes. I suppose so,' Sue answered despondently. 'He's such a horrible little man.'

'Don't take it personally. He's upset. Bentley was a good friend of his,' Jim tried to justify.

'It *is* personal,' she stressed. 'He hates the fact that I'm a housemaster and he's not. I know what they say about me.'

Jim reached out to comfort her but pulled his arm back. In an environment like this any show of affection or understanding could be misconstrued. He felt for her though. It wasn't easy being a young, pretty woman in such an environment. It would have been so much easier for her and the other two if they were plain and older.

He'd heard about the incident when one of the male teachers had asked Sue in front of a number of male staff members how her map of Tasmania was. What an oaf. The insensitive comment designed to get a laugh at Sue's expense was so typical of the attitudes of certain men. The Women's Liberation Movement had not yet impacted on the prejudices of many of the teachers.

Sue angrily grabbed her bag and left the staffroom. Heads turned away, not wanting to catch her eye nor for Sue to see the discomfort they felt at Rodney's outburst. Even the most hardened teacher had squirmed at such a display of aggression.

THE TEA GARDENS

The pub was busy for a late Wednesday afternoon. Its tiled toilet-like walls echoing the loud conversations and a punkah, a mimic of Britain's colonial past, wafted backwards and forwards above the drinkers, stirring up the smoky air.

Backpackers, mainly English and Irish, with a few Maoris, lined the bar wearing dusty shirts, trousers, and heavy boots. They worked on Sydney building sites, living around Bondi beach or the Junction.

Apart from the Maoris, most were on working holiday visas and hoped to get permanent residency, but if that didn't happen, stay one step ahead of the late-night knock on the door from the Department of Immigration.

Detective Stone and Sergeant O'Shea ordered a couple of schooners and wended their way through the crowd to a spare tall table against which to lean. O'Shea pulled out a packet of cigarettes and offered one to the detective. They both lit up, relishing the combination of a beer and a smoke.

'Wonder how many of them are over-stayers?' Ray O'Shea asked rhetorically.

'Not our problem. At the moment, anyway.'

'Suppose not. Bigger fish to fry.'

'What do you think, Ray?' Stone asked his colleague once they'd downed a few mouthfuls of beer.

'About the school?'

'Yeah.'

'Well, our Mr Shute certainly seemed to have it coming. Very unpopular with some of the staff.'

'True. But unpopular enough to kill him?' Alan Stone asked doubtfully. Most workplaces have trouble. Internal politics. Romances gone wrong. Horrible bosses.

'What about the girls on the staff?' Ray suggested.

'Girls? Ray. Really?'

'Wha'at?' Ray whinged.

'They're not girls. They're women.'

'Alright. Women. Anyway, most of them didn't seem to like Shute. And what about the teacher who went on the excursion with him? Then there's the two boys Jim Cameron mentioned. That looks dodgy. Plus, Shute appears to have been queer so maybe someone didn't like that. He was definitely bent.' Ray O'Shea chuckled at his pun.

Stone shook his head despairingly. He thought for a minute. 'We also need to interview Peter Charteris. He may have seen or heard something that night. He lives in the same boarding house and must have had a lot to do with Shute and the boys. We'll talk to him tomorrow. My God, there are so many people we're going to have to interview. Such a bloody big school.'

'What about Jim Cameron? Do we interview him? Bit of a coincidence that you know him,' Ray said slyly.

'Yeah. I suppose it is,' Alan agreed. 'Small world.'

'What actually happened?' Ray asked.

'Oh. It was ages ago. There was an incident in Rarotonga. He was there with the school rugby team. As Jim said.'

'How come you were there?'

'I was on secondment from the New Zealand police. New Zealand helped run the place. I went back home afterwards then came here a bit later,' Alan explained. 'Jim's a good bloke and it's useful for us that he can offer his knowledge of the school and the staff.'

Ray listened to his superior while looking around at the clientele. There were no women in the pub as it was too early for those in 9 to 5 jobs. It was mainly the tradies who finished at 3, the odd elderly man and a few unemployed.

'Have you ever been to Ireland, Alan?' Ray asked after hearing the chatter of nearby drinkers.

'I have. Went o.s. before I started my training. Like most Kiwis, it was almost compulsory to head to London and go from there. That's if you didn't get trapped working in a pub. Too easy to live and drink in the same place. Or, if you didn't stop over in Australia and get stuck here.'

Stone took a swig of his beer before continuing. 'Ireland was good value. England was too, 'specially up north. They all love a drink. You should go,' the detective suggested as he watched the punters draining their glasses, eager for the next beer.

They both peered through the smoky haze listening to the mocking humour of the drinkers but it was a struggle to understand exactly what was being said. The accents varied from the different Irish counties to Scouse from Liverpool and Cockney from London.

'Anyway, it's going to be a big job. So many people to interview,' the detective said tiredly. 'What do you really think of the headmaster, Pritchard?' he asked his sergeant, forcing himself to get back on track.

'What do I really think?' Ray asked, flattered by the attention his senior was giving him.

'Of course. You've seen and heard as much as me,' Alan said.

Ray dragged on his cigarette. 'I think the head is more worried about the school than the victim.'

'I agree,' Stone said, stubbing out his butt. 'What sort of school did you go to?'

'The local state high school out West. Nothing flash. Certainly not like St Cuthbert's. God. Just look at their grounds and facilities.'

'State schools are pretty good in New Zealand, so no real need to spend all that money,' Alan justified. He was reluctant to tell Ray that he too had been to a boarding school. His parents were dairy farmers and the area lacked a high school that was reasonably close to home. He felt it was better if he

115

appeared ignorant of the intricacies of such an environment.

Don't know if I'd have liked to have gone to a private school,' Ray stated.

'Come on. Who wouldn't want to go to somewhere prestigious? Old Boy network and all that. Foot in the door,' Alan argued.

'Yeah. Well. Can't all be born with a silver spoon.' Ray picked up his drink and gulped.

'Anyway. Putting your prejudices aside, we need to get this sorted out. Who is responsible and why.'

'Do you think Shute's homosexuality has anything to do with it? Being queer at a boys' school?' Ray asked, aware that he had sounded bitter about his working class origins.

'Definitely. Being a homosexual doesn't have the stigma it once had but it's still not fully accepted, and I doubt if many parents would want their sons taught by one.'

'But would someone go so far as to commit murder?'

Alan twirled the dregs of his beer. 'Probably not.' He drained the glass. 'Fancy another?'

'Yeah. Why not?'

Detective Stone walked over to the bar, carrying both glasses, and placed them on the counter.

The barmaid smiled at his thoughtfulness. 'Same again?'

Stone nodded, and she pulled out two more schooner glasses from under the bar. He watched her flick the tap into the tilted glass. 'Worked here long?' he inquired.

'A couple of months. At home I was a nurse but felt like a change,' she answered in what he thought was a Dublin accent.

'Lots of your compatriots in here,' Stone stated, staring around the pub as he handed her some coins.

'Certainly are. A home away from home,' she laughed.

'Well, it's nice to get good service for a change. Not many barmen, sorry, barmaids remember what you ordered,' Stone complimented, grinning.

She returned the smile, but another punter was waiting impatiently at the end of the bar waving a $2 note.

He wandered back to the table, careful not to spill any beer in the crush of drinkers.

'Thanks, mate,' O'Shea said as the beer was placed in front of him.

'Right. Let's recap.' Stone took a long drink and lit another cigarette. 'Whoever killed Shute got into the flat without breaking in which indicates that he had a key or Shute let him in. Or maybe Shute left the door open. Perhaps he was expecting someone.' He took another swig. 'MacGregor, the sergeant or whatever the hell he's called, had a key so it seems easy to get hold of a copy.'

'I can ask Daph.'... Mrs Withers, who had access to keys,' O'Shea suggested.

'Isn't she a bit old for you?' Stone asked with a grin.

'Nah. Rather like older women and she's not that old anyway. In her forties, maybe. Experienced,' Ray emphasised.

'Well, don't let her cloud your judgement,' Stone warned knowingly. 'Anyway, back to business. Why did the perpetrator leave the sword under the bed? Was it meant to be a message? Or a warning? Is Shute the first?' He took a gulp of beer. 'We now know he was killed somewhere between six pm and midnight on Saturday night. He was seen at the footy on Saturday afternoon.'

'But not seen since then,' O'Shea added.

'No. So someone went to his flat sometime on Saturday night and done him in,' Stone laughed at his attempt at Cockney.

'Wouldn't Shute have woken up if someone had come into his apartment? How come he was lying face down? Do you think the murderer forced him to lie in that position?' Ray wondered.

'But there was no sign of a struggle. No obvious footprints on the carpet.'

Ray looked puzzled at Stone's statement.

Stone continued while peering into his glass. 'You know what I mean. No one was dragged along the carpet into the bedroom. No blood anywhere except in the bed.'

'So was he drugged?' Ray queried.

'We'll find out soon enough. The results from forensics should come back soon,' Stone said, draining the drizzle left in his glass. 'The person who did it, didn't seem to know how to use a sword. It was all over the place. A hacking job.'

Ray stared at Stone as if for confirmation. 'Was it calculated? A crime of passion or something spontaneous?'

'Maybe,' Stone mused. 'The weapon was the sword so either the killer knew it was there and planned to use it while visiting or acted spontaneously. The killer had to be tall enough to reach the sword easily so that eliminates the very young, or dwarfs.' He grinned, scratching his hairline. 'Sorry, bad joke. Leaving the weapon under the bed makes me think that it wasn't planned.'

Both men were distracted by a sudden increase in the volume of noise. Two attractive girls had walked into the pub and their appearance was greatly appreciated by the male drinkers.

'Bloody hell. You'd think these men have never seen a female,' Stone complained.

Ray nodded and drained his glass. 'We'd better make tracks. I'll ring Daphne when we're back at the station and tell her we'll be there bright and early tomorrow morning.'

'You do that, Ray,' Alan smirked in reply. 'I'm sure she'd love to hear from you. Oh, and, just one more thing before we go,' the detective mysteriously. 'I did a check into Bentley Shute's background and he's not called Bentley. His real name is Ronald. Bit of a difference, eh? Ron Shute doesn't sound quite so flash, does it? Positively borstal. Wonder what else he's changed about himself?'

Pocketing their cigarettes and lighters, the two men worked their way through the bar to the outside world.

JIM V. JAMES

Jim Cameron peered closely at the school timetable pinned up on his office wall. He ran his finger along the lessons held on Thursdays.

Lunchtime was an hour or so away and he had decided to talk to the student, Matthews again. Jim believed that Matthews would be more relaxed talking to him than to the police. At least at the beginning of the investigation. He didn't want to go into the classroom and draw attention to him, so it was better to wait in the corridor until the class was dismissed. Matthews seemed to be very observant of Shute and his activities.

It was hard to believe that Bentley would risk his positions as teacher and housemaster of a boarding house by having a sexual relationship with a student but then, Jim thought, he was only human after all and boys in Years 11 and 12 were at their sexual peak according to current research. Or, maybe the boys were exerting their power over Bentley and he had no say in what went on. Blackmail? And maybe, Matthews was just an attention-seeking liar.

He shook his head. There was no point in jumping to conclusions. The whole thing was a jigsaw and one day, the final piece would fit into place.

The bell had not yet rung for the end of lesson as Jim wandered out into the corridor and climbed the stairs to the next level of classrooms. The school was always eerily quiet when the boys were in class.

His footsteps on the dark wooden floorboards echoed down the brick corridor while the faces of alumni and present pupils peered down from the walls. Could it be that one of these boys had murdered a master?

Jim found the classroom and stopped outside the door. He peeked quickly through the glass panel in the door and he could see the teacher was Sue Armstrong.

She was standing on the podium at the front of the room, talking animatedly to the students. Some of the boys listened attentively while others just seemed to be watching her. Matthews was near the back, staring out of the window, his chin on his hand, his eyes tired and droopy.

Sue's blonde hair was haloed by the sun that shone through the window and the outline of her legs was silhouetted through the flimsy material of her flowing skirt. He was reminded of the naive Princess Diana when the world was titillated by her see-through dress.

The class began to pack up and within a few seconds, the bell rang. Chairs were shoved back under desks and bags heaved over shoulders. Boys filed out of the room to make their way to the next class as Sue picked up her books and bag and walked towards Jim waiting by the opened door.

'Hello, Mr Cameron. Can I help you?' Sue asked.

'I'm just after one of your students, Mrs Armstrong.' He looked at the few remaining students as they left the room. Matthews was the last to leave.

Mr Cameron stepped forward to greet him, 'Hello, James. Can you spare me a minute? Perhaps we could go to my office. That might be easier.'

The boy dithered but not one to disobey authority, especially Mr Cameron, muttered, 'Yes, Sir.'

'Mrs Armstrong. If you want to continue our chat, pop in any time,' Jim suggested as nonchalantly as he could.

Sue looked at Matthews before answering, 'I will. Maybe later this afternoon. What time are you here till?'

Jim laughed. 'All hours God sends.'

'Oh, you don't have to wait around. I'll aim for about four, if that's okay?'

'Yes. Yes. See you then.'

Matthews stood watching the two adults going through some sort of strange communication.

'Okay, Matthews, shall we go down to my office?'

Without answering, Matthews picked up his bag and followed the deputy.

123

'James, I was wondering if you could tell me more about Mr Shute's visitors. Especially the two boys you named. It's such a serious incident that the police need all the assistance they can get,' Jim explained, hoping to appeal to the boy's sense of doing the right thing. 'Would you mind going over what you saw and anything else you can think of?'

James Matthews squirmed uncomfortably on the chair. 'I dunno really. Can't think of much else. I just used to see Dave and Phil go into his flat quite often. It was unusual 'cos it was so late. Usually after lights out. I thought they'd be getting into trouble with Blacky, their housemaster.'

Mr Cameron waited. Matthews studied his shoes, then gazed around the room.

'Benty used to wear this weird thing. Covered in patterns,' he said suddenly.

'A dressing-gown?'

Matthews thought for a minute. 'No, not really. It had big flowy sleeves. A bit like *Monkey Magic.*'

'*Monkey Magic*?' Mr Cameron wasn't up to date with television programmes popular with teenagers. His children were too young.

'Yeah. You know, the Japanese show with the samurai monkey. He wore the same thing.'

'Ah,' Jim responded, none the wiser. 'How come you saw Mr Shute wearing it?'

'I saw him when the guys were leaving his place. Benty... Sorry, Sir. When Mr Shute was letting them out.'

Jim nodded. 'When you saw Phillip, how did he seem?'

'Um.' The boy pulled at his ear lobe. 'He looked pleased with himself. Bit cocky really.'

'Why do you think he'd be cocky, as you put it?'

Matthews looked at the deputy. 'Phil would have more power because he was 'in' with a teacher and Mr Shute was a teacher that lots of boys liked. He had a big reputation and so those who were close to him would get one too.'

'Do you think Dave felt the same?'

'Doubt it. Dave just did what Phil wanted.'

Jim contemplated the information. Did Phillip enjoy the power gained by associating with a charismatic teacher? But would he, or for that matter, Dave, be willing to have sexual relations with Bentley to belong to his club?

'Did you bump into the boys frequently?' Jim asked carefully. It puzzled him how often Matthews had seen Judd and Sutton. He didn't want to think badly of Matthews, but it did seem odd that the boy was constantly wandering around the boarding house at night.

'I didn't always see them, but I could hear them. My dorm is opposite Mr Shute's flat,' he explained.

'And the bathroom's at the end of the corridor,' Jim reinforced.

'Yeah, it's a pain when you gotta go in the middle of the night,' Matthews said.

'I can well imagine,' Jim said, standing up. 'Thanks, James. You've been very helpful. You may have noticed that the police have been at the

125

school.' Jim held the boy's gaze. 'You realise that the police will want to talk to you and many of the boys whom Mr Shute taught and coached privately and those who lived in his house.' A look of concern flashed across the boy's face.

'James, it is our responsibility to assist the police,' the deputy stated firmly. The boy murmured his agreement and stood. Deep down he knew that Mr Cameron would have to tell the police what he had told him.

THE BOYS ARE INTERVIEWED

In another classroom, or Police HQ, as Stone and O'Shea jokingly referred to it, two students, aged around 17 or 18 stood in the open doorway, uncertain of whether to enter. Both were tall and well-built.

Stone sat at his desk while Sergeant O'Shea walked towards them. He stood, looking from one to the other. 'Morning, gentlemen. Please come in. I'm Sergeant O'Shea and this is Detective Stone.'

The boys stared at the sergeant then looked at the detective, neither one wanting to speak first.

Eventually Phil Sutton wandered over to Stone's desk and stood in front of it. 'I'm Sutton, Sir. Phil, Phillip Sutton.'

Dave Judd, following the lead from his mate, plucked up the courage to tell the police who he was.

'Take a seat, gentlemen,' Stone commanded, and the boys sat down on the two chairs placed in front of the detective's desk.

Judd tugged at the knees of his grey trousers while Sutton looked enquiringly at the detective.

'Will this take long, Sir?' Sutton asked, his arms folded like a statement. 'It's just that we're missing our lunch.'

Stone, who appeared preoccupied with the contents of a manila folder, closed it then looked up.

'Oh dear. We won't keep you long. I'm sure they'll save you something.' He stared intently at Sutton who waited for a few moments before lowering his gaze.

Little prick, thought Stone. Have to put him in his place. Thinks he's God's gift.

Stone, now ignoring Sutton, aimed his first question at Judd. 'You two been friends for long?' he asked curtly. Judd, surprised, mumbled something about being friends since Year 8.

'Right. Must be nice to have such a good mate?' Judd nodded uncertainly.

''Specially, in the boarding house. Must get a bit lonely at times. Away from parents.' Stone paused.

'Bit like *Lord of the Flies.* Who's Piggy? Who's the leader?' Stone turned his head to look at Sutton then back to Judd who was about to speak but shut his mouth quickly.

'I've forgotten the name of the boy who was in charge. Oh well, it was a long time ago. But you have read it, I presume?' the detective asked.

'Yeah. We did it in Year 9,' Sutton answered, staring at Stone, thrown a little by the literary reference. He wouldn't have thought that the police read novels.

'Compulsory reading, I'd say. Teaches you a lot about life and human nature,' Stone said, his eyes lingering on Philip Sutton.

Stone glanced over at Sergeant O'Shea, who had a quizzical expression on his face. 'Not read it, Sergeant?'

'No, Sir. *Go Ask Alice* was about my limit.'

Stone shrugged and turned back to the boys. Sutton was yawning slightly but did not bother to cover his mouth. 'Keeping you up, are we?' Stone asked.

'No, Sir. It's just…,' Sutton paused.

'Just what?'

'I don't know why we're here,' the boy stated sullenly.

'Is that right?' Stone couldn't resist his sarcasm. 'Ah, yes. Better get back to the business at hand.'

Stone made a show of looking again at the folder on the desk and then back to the boys. 'You are probably aware that Mr Shute has died. We are investigating his death and we're hoping that you may be able to help us.'

The two boys straightened their backs. Sutton's arms folded tighter across his chest while Judd appeared riveted by an old photo of the school on the wall behind Stone's head.

The detective opened the manila folder, holding it upright. The boys watched him slowly read, close the folder then place it neatly on the desk, moving his pen to lie parallel to it. He said nothing but looked at Sergeant O'Shea, who coughed gently in reply, his closed hand covering his mouth. The policemen waited. Let the two mummies' boys squirm, they thought.

'I gather the two of you visited Mr Shute in his rooms. After hours,' Detective Stone stated suddenly. The boys jerked involuntarily.

'Who told you that?' Judd asked quickly but peered at his trousers to avoid any further eye contact with the detective.

'We have our sources,' Stone said in his best actor's voice, inwardly laughing at his corny choice of explanation. 'Now boys, we just want to get an idea of your relationship with Mr Shute.' He waited a few beats. 'I gather he helped you with assignments.'

Without waiting for an answer, Stone stood up and wandered over to look out of the window. 'He must have been a great guy to put himself out like that?'

'He was,' Sutton protested, half turning to speak to the detective's back. 'He was the best teacher.'

'And he was your teacher?'

'No. But he knew heaps. He was always willing to help,' Sutton justified.

Stone returned to his seat and sat down. 'So, you would go to his rooms and he'd help you?'

'What's wrong with that?' Judd asked.

'Nothing. Nothing at all.' Stone leaned towards Judd. 'When did you go and how often?'

Judd was about to answer, but Sutton jumped in. 'Not a lot. Sometimes after footy practice or dinner.'

'And he was always helpful?'

'What do you mean? Of course he was helpful. That's why we were there. He helped us with our essays. Checked them,' the student explained.

Stone and O'Shea could hear the desperation in Phillip Sutton's voice. Not quite so cocky now, they thought.

'Did he help other boys?' Stone asked, focusing on Judd.

''Course. Wasn't just us,' Judd replied.

'But he had his favourites?'

Sutton stood up, his chair grating loudly on the hard-wooden floor. 'It wasn't like that.'

'Like what?'

'You know. He was just a good bloke.' Sutton sat down.

'He never tried anything on,' Judd blustered. O'Shea turned towards him.

'Meaning?' he asked.

'Shut up, Dave,' Sutton spat before Judd could answer.

'That'll do, Mr Sutton. Let David answer.' Stone smiled at Judd. 'Carry on. If there's anything you feel you should tell us. It won't go any further.'

Sergeant O'Shea moved his chair backwards with a screech across the floorboards. Both boys flinched. Stone shot a glance at O'Shea who smiled apologetically.

'Anyway. Where were we?' Stone paused. 'David, you were about to say?'

'Nothing, Sir. Nothing. Just that Mr Shute was a good bloke, like Phil says and it's terrible what happened to him.'

131

'So, your visits were purely about homework?' the detective asked, still intent on David.

'Yes, Sir.'

'And he never did anything that you thought was a bit odd?' Stone insinuated, turning quickly to include Sutton.

'Like what?' Sutton asked defensively.

Stone stroked his chin and then picked up his pen and tapped it on the desk. 'Did you know that Mr Shute was a homosexual?' Sutton's mouth clamped shut while Judd's slacked open.

The two students said nothing.

Stone looked from one to the other. 'Did he ever try anything with either of you?'

Sutton's hand went to his face and his fingers found a pimple that had not yet developed a head. He rubbed it then pulled his hand away, suddenly aware of what he was doing. Judd too had begun to pull at the corner of his mouth.

'So, nothing ever happened that made you feel uncomfortable?' the detective stressed again.

'No,' Sutton answered emphatically, staring straight at the policeman. 'He was no poof.'

Stone grimaced. 'Not too keen on gays then, I gather?'

'Fucking hate them,' Judd volunteered, his face revealing surprise at his own audacity. Sutton sat rigidly with his arms folded. The pimple on his chin now red from the attention.

Stone stood up and leaned on the desk. 'Boys, I want you to think carefully. Can you tell me exactly where you were on Saturday night between 6 and midnight?'

'What?' Judd flashed, obviously taken aback by the sudden change of direction in Stone's questioning. 'What do you mean? You know where we were. We were in the boarding house. Ask any of the guys. Ask Mr Black.'

'Your boarding-master?' Stone questioned looking from boy to boy, who grunted that he was. Judd appeared to be on the verge of tears. The implications of the detective's questions were sinking in. 'And he checks that all boys are present and correct?'

Judd nodded vigorously.

'He comes around to the dorm every night to make sure everything's okay.' Sutton explained quickly.

'At what time?' O'Shea interjected.

The boys stared at him in surprise, as if they had forgotten he was in the room. 'About 10,' they replied simultaneously.

'So, no-one would know if you were in the dormitory after 10. I bet some boys take window leave. Isn't that what they call it?' Stone continued knowingly.

Judd protested that they didn't take window leave and he could ask the boarding master.

'I will,' assured the detective.

Sutton's fingers crept back to the festering pimple. 'Ask the guys in our dorm. They'll tell you we were there all night.'

'No doubt. I'm sure you were. You must appreciate that we have to ask everyone where they were that night,' Stone's voice was kindly. The boys' relief at the explanation was palpable.

'Okay gentlemen. Thanks very much for coming. You've been very helpful. Glad we've cleared up the type of help Mr Shute gave you. Just wanted to get our facts straight.' Stone tried not to smile at his pun.

'Sorry to make you feel uncomfortable, but you realise that it's important that we find out who did this terrible thing to Mr Shute.'

He walked from behind the desk, indicating that the boys were free to go. 'If you think of anything else that could help us with our investigation, we'd really appreciate it.'

He put his hand on Judd's shoulder. 'You obviously liked Mr Shute a lot,' the detective said, his voice soothing and non-judgmental.

Judd nodded. 'Most of the boys liked him,' he said then as an afterthought added, 'But some of the teachers didn't.'

'And why was that?' Stone asked, trying not to sound too interested. He could tell that David Judd did not want the police to think badly of him.

'Some teachers were jealous of him.'

'Can you think of anyone in particular?' O'Shea asked, mimicking Stone's tone.

Judd looked at Sutton for permission to continue, but his mate ignored him. 'Most of the lady teachers,' he finally mumbled.

Neither Stone nor O'Shea responded. It wouldn't be hard to work out who did or didn't like Mr Bentley or rather, Mr Ronald Shute.

'Thanks again, boys. Better let you get to lunch. Would hate you to go hungry,' Stone said, unable to resist the dig.

The boys with eyes glued to the floor, left the room.

JIM AND SUE HAVE A CHAT

The school day was drawing to a close and outside in the corridor, an athletic-looking, dark-haired student was reading one of the many student notice boards.

The blazer he wore with its edging and colours denoting status and achievements informed the rest of the school he was in Year 12. The student was memorable, partly because of his athletic physique but also because he was of ethnic background.

There were a few other Greeks at the school, but the majority of students were of Anglo-Saxon background. George was unusual because he was good at rugby union and cricket. Not games normally connected to those of Mediterranean background.

'Afternoon, George' Jim said as he walked closer.

'Hello, Sir.' George's face showed his pleasure at being greeted by the deputy head.

'Great win on Saturday,' Jim complimented. 'Unfortunately, I couldn't get to the game but heard you played well.'

George grinned. 'Thanks, Sir. Yeah, we're getting closer to the final.'

'All the best for the next game.'

'Thank you, Sir.'

Jim turned to walk back to his office but stopped when the sound of footsteps could be heard in the corridor. Sue, seeing them in the distance, slowed but continued towards them.

'Good afternoon, Mr Cameron. George,' she said with a singsong tone and walked into the staffroom, quickly pulling the door shut behind her. Jim was aware of George intently watching Sue's retreat into the staffroom

'Your teacher?' Jim asked.

'Who?'

'Mrs Armstrong.'

'Um. Yeah,' George stammered. 'She's my History teacher.'

'Lucky boy. Mrs Armstrong is a jolly good teacher,' Jim said as George turned back to the fascination of the noticeboard.

'What? Oh yeah. She's pretty good.'

'Anyway, George, keep up the good work with your sport. Hope you're putting as much effort into your studies,' Jim said with a chuckle in his voice. 'It's the HSC this year.'

'Pardon?' George asked distractedly.

'You're sitting the HSC this year,' Jim reiterated.

'Sorry, Sir. Bit tired. Early footy practice. Yeah. This year.'

'Well, good luck.' Jim was keen to put George out of his misery. 'I'll let you get back to it.'

'Thanks, Sir.'

Jim wandered down the corridor but waited before entering his office. He heard the door to the staffroom open again and could see Sue emerge. She headed quickly upstairs to the only ladies' toilets on the next floor. George remained standing by the notice boards but when she had reached halfway, he picked up his school bag and followed.

Good lord. Perhaps there is some truth in the rumours that Shute spread.

Jim opened the door to his office and sat down wearily. This situation was proving very stressful. He didn't particularly like Shute's cronies or the two boys, but he did like Sue. He didn't want to discover something about her which could jeopardise her career or ruin her marriage. He didn't want the gossip to be true and he certainly didn't want an unpleasant man like Bentley to be right after all. Would Sue still come to see him?

Sue arrived a little after four. 'Sorry I'm a bit late,' she panted.

'Are you alright?' Jim asked. 'Can I get you a drink of water? Tea?'

'No. I'm fine, thanks. Just out of breath. Should give up smoking,' she laughed and Jim couldn't help but laugh too.

'Something urgent to do?' he asked.

'Just had to see a student. An assignment that's due. You know George. He needed some help. He spends far too much time playing sport and then gets behind.'

Jim inwardly sighed. Thank God. There was nothing going on. No-one could appear so innocent if there really were an affair. I sound so Noel Coward. In this day and age, does anyone have an *affair* or is it just seen as a liaison or a one-night stand?

Smiling at Sue, he thanked her for coming. 'Much easier to talk here.'

Sue opened her bag, which she'd placed primly on her knees. 'I know I shouldn't, but do you mind if I smoke?'

Jim pulled open a couple of drawers in his desk, found an ashtray at the back of the second one and placed it in front of her.

She lit a cigarette then put the packet and lighter on Jim's desk. 'That's better,' she said as she exhaled and looked up at him. He noticed how blue her eyes were. In direct contrast to his wife's dark brown.

'Mr Cameron, I'm worried that people will think that I had something to do with Bentley's death because I didn't like him and because I was the object of a lot of his gossip,' she blurted out and quickly inhaled again. 'It's as if he's given me a motive.'

'Were other members of staff aware of his gossip about you?' Jim asked weakly. Her objectivity had thrown him.

'Of course they were, Mr Cameron. You know they were. Bentley would say and do anything to be popular. Or successful.' She stopped to flick ash into the ashtray. 'You know what? I answered the phone one day in the staffroom and the caller asked for Doctor Shute. I was flabbergasted. Can you believe it? He'd actually told this person he had a doctorate. If he could lie about his qualifications, he could lie about anything. He's no more a doctor than I am. I don't think he's even got a Masters.'

Jim couldn't help but feel shocked about such a blatant lie. He had seen Bentley's qualifications when he applied for the teaching and boarding master positions and there was no mention of any PhD. Why would he lie? Was his reputation so important that he fabricated a qualification? He was taking a huge risk because such information could easily be investigated. If this had come out when he was still alive, how humiliating that would have been.

He shuddered at the thought and again the reputation of St Cuthbert's occurred to him. If the papers found out that staff lied about their qualifications it would make them look so unprofessional and underhand. Parents would baulk at paying large fees and sending their sons to an institution which practised dishonesty. He'd better warn Robert.

'Can you tell me what he *has* said about you?' Jim asked.

Sue stubbed out her cigarette and immediately lit another. 'I don't normally smoke this much, I promise,' she justified.

'It's a very stressful time at the moment, so no need to make excuses,' he placated.

Sue looked directly at Jim. 'Bentley told his mates, you know, Marlene, Rodney. That lot. And anyone else who'd listen, that I'm having an affair with a student.'

'You intimated that when we spoke the other day. Did he give the boy a name?'

'Yes. Mike. Michael Parker. A student in Year 12.'

Jim laughed. 'Does Michael know that you and he are having a relationship?'

'He does now. Poor boy. I know he's had a bit of a thing for me, but nothing out of the ordinary. He's copping lots of flak from the other students. It's as if Bentley just pulled a name out of the hat and thought he'll do.'

'Have you said anything to Michael about the gossip?' Jim asked.

'No. What can I say? I make a point of never being on my own in a room with any of the boys and I never engage in long conversations with Mike.' She pulled on the cigarette. 'Poor guy. Probably thinks I hate him.' Sue stared at Mr Cameron. 'I didn't, and I don't want to do anything to feed the rumour mill. Especially not Bentley's.'

Jim nodded. Rumour mongering was Bentley's forte. Perhaps he'd been trying to get Sue sacked and then the equilibrium of male dominance or his dominance would have returned.

'Family well?' Jim asked.

Sue frowned in surprise. 'Yes. Why do you ask?'

'Oh, I'm sorry. Hope I'm not being nosey.'

'No. Of course you're not, Mr Cameron,' she reassured him as she stubbed out the cigarette. 'The family's fine. Sometimes it's a bit hard juggling work and home.'

Sue moved forward in her chair and stood up. 'I'd better let you get on.' She put the cigarettes and lighter back in her bag. 'This is a really awful situation, isn't it? Yet, it's hard to take it seriously in a way. It's so surreal,' she said shaking her head.

Jim was not sure what to say. He followed Sue to the door and opened it for her.

'Thanks for talking to me. If you ever want to have a chat, about anything, anything at all.' His words tailed off, aware of his repetition.

Sue touched his arm as she left. 'I won't forget.' And she walked back towards her housemaster's office.

BENTLEY'S BOARDING ASSISTANT

Friday morning always had a more positive air. The end of the teaching week and for Detective Stone and Sergeant O'Shea the feeling was contagious.

Their first interview of the day was with Peter Charteris, Bentley Shute's assistant boarding master. They felt optimistic that he may be able to shed some light on his colleague's activities and proclivities.

Peter Charteris arrived on the dot of nine. His lanky body seemed in contrast to his open and perceptive personality.

'Bentley and I were colleagues, but we weren't mates,' he replied when asked about how well he knew the victim. 'When you work so closely with someone, it's better to keep your distance. Don't want to live in each other's pockets.'

'So you didn't socialise together?'

'No, Detective Stone. It was nothing to do with his being gay. Just felt, well, what I said before.'

Sergeant O'Shea couldn't help but ask, 'Did everyone know he was gay? I would have thought he'd want to keep that quiet.'

'I can see why you'd think that. A boys' school. But times have changed of late so it's not a crime. However, there are some teachers here, especially some of the *straight* men, who are pretty old fashioned in their views and unfortunately, some parents.'

Stone agreed, but still asked, 'Were you aware of boys visiting Mr Shute's apartment in the evening?'

'Yes, I was. He told me that the boys came for extra tuition and I know that happens in other houses, so I wasn't concerned. Why? Do you think a boy or boys could be responsible for Mr Shute's death?'

The two policemen were surprised by the direct question. 'To be honest, we're still investigating every possibility. There are so many students and staff,' Stone justified.

Peter Charteris totally understood. 'So many people to interview. This school has over a thousand boys.'

'Yeah,' Stone sighed. 'We know that Mr Shute was killed on Saturday night between 6pm and midnight. You were on duty that night. Did you see, hear anything, that aroused your suspicions?' Stone asked.

'No. Not at all. I went to dinner with the boarders and then returned to the house. I watched a bit of telly, did my rounds and everything seemed in order. I was in bed by 11.'

'Did you go past Mr Shute's rooms? Hear anything?' Stone questioned.

Charteris thought for a moment. 'Not really, unless you count a radio playing.'

'What time was that?'

'Around 10.30. When I did the last round of the house.' Peter Charteris looked a bit puzzled.

'Actually, I suppose it was a bit odd as I thought he was out for the night. 10.30 is early for Bentley to come back.'

'Did you try his door?' Stone asked.

'No. It was his time off, so I didn't want to intrude.'

'Understandable. And most nights when he wasn't on duty, he went out?'

'Absolutely. Have to admit, he'd look a bit rough most Sundays. Not that there's anything wrong with that, but living so close together, you can't help but notice.'

Detective Stone paused before asking the next question. Charteris was a willing interviewee so how much would he reveal?

'Mr Charteris, can you think of anyone who would hate Mr Shute enough to want to kill him?'

'Mmmm. That's a difficult question. He *was* a popular teacher and had lots of friends on the staff,' he paused, smoothing his hand across his hair. 'I don't like saying this, but he must also have made enemies by his gossip. That's one of the reasons why I didn't want to get too close to him. I don't understand why he did that.'

Neither of the police responded but waited for him to continue.

'I can't think of anyone who would be capable of murder. That sounds so extreme. The staff he gossiped about mostly were the women. Sue

Armstrong, was the main one and then Jenny Bartoli. Lilian Cutler. He was friends with Marlene Bates, so she didn't cop it. The few other women weren't really on his radar. I can't imagine any of them being likely to kill him.'

'Why did he talk so much about Mrs Armstrong?' Stone asked.

'God knows. Perhaps he found her a challenge. And some of his mates probably did too, so they would have supported his chatter. Rodney Addington had his nose out of joint because she was made a housemaster, a position he thought should go to him.' Charteris scratched his head thoughtfully.

'What did he actually say about Mrs Armstrong?' Stone posed.

'Rubbish really. Having an affair with a student. Shagging the headmaster. Unbelievable stuff,' Peter Charteris explained dismissively.

'You don't believe it?'

'God no.'

Stone made a note in his book, then asked, 'Were you aware of Bentley having any relationships with students? Students in the house visiting him at odd hours?'

Charteris reddened slightly, uncomfortable with the question.

'Mmmm. Well. As I said, it's not uncommon for some of the teachers to have the boys over in the evening for study. I knew that Bentley had study groups.'

'Do you know which boys attended?'

'Um. Not really.' He thought for a minute. 'I've seen Robinson, Judd, Sutton, and I think Taylor, but I can't really think of anyone else. Didn't take much notice.'

'Where did you see them?'

'Going into Shute's flat.'

'It didn't strike you as odd?'

'Not really. As I said, some teachers have study groups or music nights.' Charteris pensively fingered his hair again. Sergeant O'Shea began to wonder how long Charteris's hair would last with all this attention.

'On second thoughts, boys like Dave Judd and Phil who aren't in our house used to visit, so that does seem a bit odd. Usually, the boarders are helped by their boarding masters, or teachers straight after school.' The boarding master frowned at this realisation.

Stone fidgeted with his folder. He was reluctant to ask the next question but felt obliged. 'Mr Charteris, sorry to labour the point, but do you think there was anything of a sexual nature going on between Mr Shute and any of the boys?'

The silence in the room made the awkward question more awkward. Charteris pursed his lips before answering, 'I could believe it happening, but honestly I wasn't aware of Bentley being involved with anyone. Student or grown up.'

The use of the adolescent term sounded strange coming from a man in his thirties.

'Surely, in a hot house environment like a boarding house, you would hear rumours. Men and boys are bigger gossips than women.'

O'Shea raised his eyebrows at Stone's words, thinking that can't be right.

Charteris laughed in agreement. 'You're not wrong there. I did hear things but nothing that really involved Bentley. I have a vague idea that he might have had a boyfriend, but I never met him, and Bentley didn't mention him at all. He wasn't one to expose his private life. More interested in other people's activities.'

'Why do you think that was?'

'Maybe power. If you know someone's secrets, you have a hold over them.'

O'Shea and Stone nodded at this observation. Peter Charteris seemed to have a good understanding of human nature.

'Did you and he get on?' Stone asked.

The teacher thought for a minute. 'Yes,' he replied, turning one syllable into two. 'As I said before, we weren't mates but we had a working relationship. When you live so closely together, there's always times when you get on each other's nerves but most of the time we rubbed shoulders okay.'

Stone nodded again. He felt there wasn't much more that Charteris could tell him. He stood up and leant over to shake his hand. 'Thanks, Mr Charteris.

We're grateful for your insights. Just one more thing. Did Mr Shute have many visits from other teachers?'

Charteris had stood to leave but stopped to think. 'Mmmm. Let me see. Rodney Addington, Brian, Ian Walsh, and of course Marlene Bates. Actually, Marlene was the most frequent. She and Bentley seemed pretty close.'

After jotting down the names in his book, Stone repeated his thanks and walked Charteris to the door. 'Anything else you can think of, no matter how insignificant, don't hesitate to let us know. For the sake of the school, the sooner this is sorted out, the better.'

THE FOLLOWING WEEK

Another school week had begun and the bell rang for the end of Monday classes. Boys piled out of rooms and hurried down corridors, eager to catch the bus home or go to sports' practice. Some had mothers waiting for them, blocking streets and causing temporary traffic mayhem with their large expensive cars.

Jim stood at a window on the top floor of the Old Block and watched the flood of students. He could see prefects on duty directing the students on the zebra crossing. Some boys were already on the Oval, casually kicking balls to each other while others headed back to the various boarding houses.

The deputy was about to turn away and go back downstairs to his office when he noticed Sue emerge from the Old Block and walk quickly down to the corner where her car was parked near the Oval.

He admired the way she dressed. Conservatively seductive he would describe it. He wondered how old she was. She had two children, so she must be in her late twenties at least, although women seemed to be having children at a slightly older age than in the past. Her comment about juggling work and home sounded heartfelt. Perhaps she was struggling more than she let on. Her husband seemed a normal sort of bloke, in one of those careers that one word couldn't label.

Sue took out the keys to her car and opened the driver's door. She had started to get into the car when Jim saw George stride up, and appear to pass her something, his hand lingering. It could have been a piece of paper. Sue immediately put it into her handbag, and after placing her bag on the passenger seat, started the car and drove away. George watched the car for a few seconds then walked down the steps to the Oval.

Jim groaned to himself. Oh no. Is something going on after all? But Sue had spoken about George so easily. There was no feeling of any emotion or attachment. He didn't want Sue to be disingenuous. You idiot. You've been taken in by an attractive, young female.

As he walked slowly back to his office with Sue dominating his thoughts, he passed the empty classrooms but in one a senior boy was still seated at a desk reading.

He isn't in a hurry to go home, Jim thought.

The boy looked up and smiled as Jim Cameron slowed in the doorway. It's that boy Michael, the one Bentley said had a crush on Sue. Good timing.

Jim walked into the room and stood next to the boy's desk. 'It's Michael, isn't it?' he asked.

'Yes, Sir. Mr Cameron, Sir,' Michael answered nervously and began to stand.

'Catching up on a bit of reading?' Jim asked noting the text and indicated for Michael to sit down.

'Yes, Sir. Mr Mitchell said we have to finish it by the end of the week.'

'Enjoying it?'

Michael thought for a few seconds. 'It's not something I'd normally read but I like it.'

Mr Cameron understood. 'Yes, having to study literature makes you read works you may never have read and then later, you're jolly glad you did.' He picked up the copy of *Othello* and read the blurb on the back.

'Jealousy is an amazing emotion. Makes people do a lot of things they normally wouldn't do. Don't you think?' Jim asked.

Michael coloured slightly, and Jim quickly placed the book back on the desk. 'How's everything going? HSC this year?'

'Yes. Be glad to get that over with.'

'Happy to be leaving school?'

Michael thought about this question. 'No, not really. I like it here and I really like some of the teachers.'

'Did you have Mr Shute?'

'No. Thank ...,' he stopped. 'Sorry, Sir. Shouldn't comment on the masters.'

'Who's your favourite teacher?'

Michael's face grew redder. 'I couldn't say, Sir. They're all good.'

Good man, thought Mr Cameron. You'll go a long way.

'Anyway, I'll leave you to your studies. Well done.'

With that Jim left the room and Michael sat staring at *Othello* lying on the desk, the main character's black face in torment with the body of his beloved at his feet. The student slowly picked up the book, found the page and continued reading.

Jim walked on. The corridors were now empty. There was the sound of shouts and laughter from the Oval outside the Old Block and the distant sound of cars, but the corridor was a lonely place without the students. He began to walk back to his office, changed his mind and knocked on the door of the classroom used by the police.

'Mr Shute maintained that Sue Armstrong was, is, having an affair with a student. This could give her a reason to do away with him, or for the student to assist her,' Jim informed Alan Stone. 'I'm not saying it's true, but he certainly made her life unpleasant. He also named another student that she was supposedly involved with.'

Jim looked at Alan, his face showing his scepticism at the information, but he felt it was his duty to aid the police with their inquiries.

'Busy woman,' Stone laughed. 'Do you believe the rumours?'

Jim hesitated. Should he tell Alan what he'd observed?

'I really like Sue and would hate to implicate her, but I do think that one of the students mentioned definitely has a crush on her. I'm not sure if it's reciprocal but it might be a good idea to talk to George Stavrou, just to clarify things. Are you going to talk to Sue?'

'We'll interview her and other teachers. Don't worry, Jim. We won't victimise her. You know we have to talk to everyone. What's the name of the other boy who's meant to be having it off with Mrs Armstrong?' Stone asked lightly. Jim flinched at Stone's language, but Kiwis were known for their down to earth personalities.

Despite his reluctance to name Michael, Jim knew he had to. Although it was hard to believe that a student could be a murderer, someone *had* killed Bentley Shute.

'Something else happened that may be of interest,' Jim stated, feeling he was being as big a gossip as Bentley. 'I don't feel comfortable passing on incidents that happen in the staffroom, but you are hardly likely to witness what I can.'

Stone sympathised but reassured the deputy that the more information they had the quicker the murder would be solved. 'Remember, Rarotonga, Jim. It's often the one you least suspect. And something which seems irrelevant may not be.'

'Alan. I know, I know. I just feel, as the boys would put it, like a dobber.' Jim paused for a minute then continued. 'Rodney Addington, a friend of Shute's, had a real go at Sue in the staffroom the other day. He accused her of being happy that Shute was dead. He even grabbed her arm. It was very uncomfortable for everyone in the room.'

'How did she react?' Sergeant O'Shea asked.

'She stood up for herself. But she's very aware that Addington believes the house master's position should have been his. He's a bit old-fashioned in his views about women. Hasn't exactly welcomed an increase in their numbers.'

'Do you think he could try and frame her for the murder?' Alan asked.

'My God. That's a bit Machiavellian. Would someone commit murder because they were annoyed about not getting a job?' Jim looked doubtfully at Alan and the sergeant.

'Stranger things have happened,' Alan said with a grin. 'Anyway, we'll have a chat with Mr Addington and with Mrs Armstrong's young admirer.'

The three sat thoughtfully for a while till Sergeant O'Shea broke the silence. 'Are any of the teachers keen on Mrs Armstrong or the other women?'

Jim felt he could offer no light on the subject and that it would be better to ask Daphne. She was more up to date with the school gossip than he was. Not that she was a gossip, but staff probably talked in front of her while they wouldn't in front of him. The policemen understood his logic.

155

'Sergeant, we might as well strike while the iron is hot, so would you mind asking Mrs Withers to pop in now. If she's not too busy.'

'Yes, Sir,' Sergeant O'Shea answered enthusiastically and quickly left the room. Alan and Jim smiled at each other with raised eyebrows. Not wanting to be present while Daphne was being questioned, Jim returned to his office.

DAPHNE HAS MORE INFORMATION

Sergeant O'Shea held the door open for Daphne who walked quickly up to Alan Stone.

'We meet again. People will start to talk,' she said with a grin. The blue blouse highlighted her eyes nicely. 'Yes.' The two men laughed in unison, both noting how well she looked.

'Sorry to bother you, yet again, Mrs With… Daphne, but Mr Cameron thought you may be able to throw more light on the goings on at the school,' Stone explained, and without waiting for her to reply, asked, 'Are you aware of any of the teachers having crushes on Mrs Armstrong or on any of the other women teachers?'

Daphne frowned. There were always intrigues in a school, the same as in any institution or workplace. 'Do you mean affairs or just fantasies?' she asked.

'Both,' O'Shea replied quickly. Daphne giggled and shook her head a little. Men!

'There are so few women here, you could be 100 kilos and as ugly as sin and still have some of the men and boys fantasising,' she said laughing. Neither of the men joined in as Daphne certainly didn't fit into that category.

Realising that her description undermined women, she put her serious face on before continuing. 'It goes without saying that some of the boys would have crushes on Jenny or Sue and possibly Lilian Cutler. As for the male teachers, I'm not really aware of anyone in particular. If anything, the women, especially the ones I've mentioned, seemed to attract a lot of criticism and jealousy. As I told you before, Sue was always the butt of Mr Shute's gossip.'

Stone waited for her to continue while O'Shea watched Daphne as she studied her nails. Suddenly, she raised her head as an idea struck her. 'Albert. Albert. What was his name? Freeland. That's it. Albert Freeland. I remember Sue telling me that she used to give him a lift to school as they lived near each other and that he developed a huge crush. It became very uncomfortable for her.'

Stone wrote the name in his book then asked, 'What did he do that made her uncomfortable?'

'From what I gather, he told her that he loved her and thought about her all the time. He was married with a couple of kids, but that didn't seem to stop him,' she paused. 'It definitely wasn't reciprocal. Sue was nice to him, but she certainly didn't encourage him.' Daphne stared at the detective. 'Some men misconstrue friendship or being pleasant with flirting.' Stone nodded. 'But why is this relevant to Mr Shute's murder?' Daphne asked.

'It may not be, but we have to look at every angle,' Stone justified. 'What does Mr Freeland teach?'

'He taught French, but he left at the end of last year. Went to a Catholic school in the Western suburbs.'

'Because of his fondness for Mrs Armstrong?'

'I don't know. He was besotted by her, but also, he wasn't a very good teacher. He knew his stuff but didn't have much control over the boys. This sounds snobby, but he wasn't quite the right sort of person for a school like this.'

Sergeant O'Shea smiled his understanding while Stone jotted more notes in his book.

'What sort of man was he?' Stone asked.

Daphne sighed. It was hard to describe Albert. 'He was a nice man. English. A bit different. But I certainly don't think he would be capable of hurting anyone.'

'Was he the butt of Mr Shute's gossip?'

'Not really. Bentley probably didn't see him as a threat. Albert was a bit ineffectual. And Bentley was too busy spreading rumours about Sue with different boys. Stone made another note before repeating his thanks to Daphne. Sergeant O'Shea stood up quickly and escorted the headmaster's assistant to the door.

'You've been very helpful,' O'Shea said while holding the door open for her. She stared at him. He was definitely an attractive man. 'Thank you. More than happy to be of assistance.' And with a slight flutter of her eyelashes, tripped briskly back to her office.

'That'll do,' Stone said with a grin at the sergeant.

'What?' O'Shea whinged as if caught out by his mother.

'You know what,' Stone laughed. 'Get those dirty thoughts out of your head.'

'I only have the purest thoughts when it comes to Mrs W.,' the sergeant protested.

'Yeah. Right,' Stone replied in disbelief but then began to scan the list of names in his book. 'Mrs Armstrong certainly gets mentioned a lot. We'd better have a chat. Soon.'

AN AFFAIR?

Jenny Bartoli popped her head around the door to Sue's office and bounced in.

'Morning Sue. Didn't get a chance to talk to you yesterday. Have a good weekend?'

'Jenny. Hi. God, you gave me a fright,' Sue said breathlessly as her hand went to her chest. 'It was okay. Busy. Can't believe it's already bloody Tuesday.' She looked down at the marking on her desk and moved the papers into tidy piles. 'How was yours? Anything juicy happen?'

Jenny shook her head. 'If only. You coming to the staff meeting?'

'I will be in a sec. Just got to do a bit more marking. Meant to give these essays back last week but been held up.'

'By someone nice I hope,' Jenny said laughing. 'One of your many admirers?'

'Jenny,' Sue whined. 'Stop it. You have your admirers too. Even miserable Marlene has the odd one.'

'Hard to believe. Christ, she's a miserable bitch. Wonder why Benty put up with her. She isn't quite his class.'

'Benty? Classy? Really?' queried Sue. 'I think he had delusions of grandeur but not much else.'

'Yeah,' Jenny sighed. 'Well, I'll leave you to it. Don't be long. You don't want to get into trouble. You'll be put on detention for being late.'

'Yes, Miss,' Sue replied adolescently. 'I won't. Can you shut the door for me, please?' she asked as Jenny left.

Jenny shut the door quietly. Sue waited for a few seconds then reached under the pile of essays and pulled out a folded sheet of paper. She read it quickly, her face flushing. She folded it up but unfolded it again to read a second time. She picked up her bag and stuffed the paper as far down as it would go. The chatter and footsteps of students outside the office could be heard. A quick glimpse at the small mirror on the wall assured her that she looked presentable.

The corridor was now a throng of boys heading for various classrooms but because of the short staff meeting that was held every morning, the pupils felt there was no rush.

One pupil was not caught up in the tide of traffic. George stood peering intently at the notice boards, his head swivelling occasionally to survey the corridor before returning his attention to the tacked on pieces of paper.

Mr Cameron, wearing his gown of authority, walked along the corridor herding the boys off to their classrooms. Boys milled past with a few of the older ones wishing him good morning. He turned to go once the throng had passed but saw that the solitary figure intent on the notice board was George.

'Morning, George,' Mr Cameron called out. When was this boy ever out of the corridor?

George jumped slightly then turned to face the greeter.

'Oh, hello, Mr Cameron.'

'No class to go to?' Jim asked.

George seemed uncertain how to answer. 'Um, yeah. Got History next.'

The deputy smiled at George who, as if to end the conversation, turned his attention back to the notice board. Jim stood, conscious that George was not as eager to chat this time. He went to move away but as he turned, Sue appeared from her office and walked down the corridor in their direction.

She's a bit late for the staff meeting, Jim thought.

'Ah, Mrs Armstrong. How are you?' he asked as she came nearer.

Sue smiled and kept walking as if to accompany him down the corridor. 'Fine thanks. You?'

George swung around. His school bag at his feet.

'Miss, we have you now.'

'I won't be long, George,' she instructed. 'You'd better get to class. The bell will be going soon.'

'Yes, Miss,' he replied and picking up his bag, threw it effortlessly over his shoulder. He sauntered down the corridor towards the stairs to take him to the classroom.

'Everything okay, Sue?' Jim asked.

'Yes, of course,' she answered, distracted. 'I'd better get on.' Sue about-turned and walked back towards the stairs.

She's acting rather oddly. Why didn't she go to the staff meeting? Jim wondered. Was George waiting for her? Did I interrupt something? He began to walk to his office but slowed, turned around and followed in the direction Sue had gone.

Although the second bell hadn't yet rung, the corridor was now empty, and his footsteps echoed slightly. He quietly inched up the stairs but stopped at the top to listen. What on earth am I doing? he muttered to himself. I'm acting like a character in a thriller.

He couldn't see anything of interest, but he could hear muffled voices. Was it George? He was dying to put his head around the corner, but it seemed too risky and he would look a real fool if he were seen.

Another voice could be heard speaking quietly, almost whispering. Was that Sue? He couldn't resist. Jim quickly peeked around the corner of the corridor. Sue and George were standing close to each other; the boy with his hand on her arm. Jim couldn't hear what was being said but the intimacy was shocking. He pulled his head back. *Was* something going on after all?

He waited, not wanting to know but desperate to see if his worst fears were true. There was silence and a door shut. He quickly popped his head around the corner again. Sue was still in the corridor, but

George must have gone into the classroom. Jim waited. Sue waited. A few seconds passed then he heard the door shut again. Her voice could be heard greeting the class. Was she normally so early to class?

Why did this upset him so much? Was he so moralistic or judgmental that he couldn't bear the thought of her possible infidelity? He'd met her husband a couple of times at school functions and found him to be rather reticent. He'd thought then that Sue and her husband seemed an odd match. Perhaps the attention of a young strapping student filled a void that the husband couldn't.

Jim shook his head as if to dislodge the disturbing thoughts and strode back to the security of his office. Soon after, the second bell rang. Teachers poured out of the staffroom and made their way to class.

REVENGE

'You fucking prick, Matto,' Sutton said with his hand around Matthew's throat, the force of his grip pushing the younger boy against the lockers that lined the corridor. 'You dobbed us into the police.'

'I did not,' Matthews gasped. He wished a teacher would walk past. A few boys stared as they made their way to the lockers.

'Then why did the police ask to see us?' Judd stressed and pushed his face into Matthew's.

'I dunno,' Matthews protested, rubbing at his throat now that Sutton had relaxed his hold. 'Aren't they asking lots of people questions?'

Judd stepped back and looked up and down the corridor. He knew they only had a couple of minutes before recess was over. He glared at Matthews. 'If we find out that you've been telling lies to the police, we'll get you. We'll make your life hell. What are you doing hanging around out here?'

'You wouldn't sound so tough if your mate wasn't with you. Ya loser,' Matthews snapped at Judd, ignoring his question and he shoved at the boy's shoulder with the palm of his hand, like an angry baker kneading dough. 'Well anyway, why were you two always going to Benty's place, eh?'

Sutton swiped Matthews' hand away from Judd and positioned himself between the two opponents. 'Just shut up, ya wanker.'

'Make me,' Matto sneered at Sutton. 'You're a couple of poofs. Benty's boys. Everyone knows what he got up to.'

'He never tried anything on with us,' Judd whined angrily, and Sutton agreed although Matthews detected a hint of anxiety in his voice.

'So it doesn't matter if the police ask you questions, then?' Matthews argued. 'Don't you want to help them find his killer? Thought you liked him?'

''Course we did,' Judd answered but was quickly interrupted by Sutton who sneered, 'Not like that, dickhead.'

'Jeez, you two are pathetic. Just worried about looking macho.'

Suddenly, the bell rang for the end of recess and the three boys froze at the sound. Sutton and Judd stepped away from Matthews.

Teachers emerged from the staffroom to mingle with the students heading to class. Matthews picked up his school bag from the floor and quickly walked away. Literally saved by the bell. Sutton grabbed Judd by the arm and marched him down the corridor in the opposite direction.

As Jim Cameron opened the door from his office, Judd and Sutton rushed past. Their faces red and their body language radiating aggression. He quickly glanced up and down the corridor and could see Matthews hurrying in the opposite direction. Had there been an altercation?

Jim shut the door and strode down the corridor to 'Police HQ'. He was pleased to see that both Stone and O'Shea were on their own.

'I could be wrong, but I've a feeling that Mr Sutton and Mr Judd have had a word with Matthews,' Cameron informed the policemen. Both looked at him enquiringly.

'What do you mean?' asked Sergeant O'Shea.

'Just what I said,' the deputy headmaster replied. 'I would imagine that Sutton and Judd didn't take too kindly to being interviewed and I wouldn't be surprised if they accused Matthews of talking to me or to you.'

'But how would they know Matthews spoke to you?' Stone asked.

'Things have a way of getting around, especially in the boarding houses. Matthews may have told a mate and it spread from there.'

Stone and O'Shea's expression showed that he was probably correct.

'I get the feeling that Judd will do anything that Sutton says,' Stone posed.

'Absolutely,' Jim said. 'He's a follower. A pretty weak boy. I seem to remember he had a few social issues so being friends with Sutton gave him kudos.'

Stone nodded at the description. Boys like Judd could be manipulated into doing things which stronger boys suggested but were unwilling to do themselves. But was Judd, or Sutton for that matter, capable of murdering a teacher? Had Shute made advances to one or both of them and they'd reacted violently in defence of their masculinity? Was Shute waiting for them in his bed and they'd attacked him?

'We'd better keep an eye on them and Matthews. Make sure no-one does anything stupid,' Jim suggested. 'The stigma of being gay doesn't go down well in a boys' school. Some can get away with it, as long as they're not too blatant. Bit like affairs amongst the upper classes in the past, as long as one was discreet.'

O'Shea raised his eyebrows at the analogy. Where did these buggers come up with such ideas?

'Maybe all schools should be co-ed,' the sergeant suggested. 'Then no-one would get tempted.'

Jim and Alan Stone glanced at each other and shook their heads at the naïve suggestion. O'Shea had obviously not fully appreciated the genetic responsibility of nature over nurture.

'Yes. Well. Enough of your theories,' Stone answered, unable to keep the sarcasm out of his voice. 'Perhaps Shute's being gay has nothing to do with his death. Could he have known something that was threatening, or did he make someone angry? It's obvious from what people are saying, that although he had his followers, he wasn't liked by everyone.'

'Very true,' Jim Cameron agreed. Hell had no fury like Bentley scorned. The gossip mill would start, and the non-believers would find themselves excluded and ostracised. Jim's unpleasant memories were interrupted by a question from Detective Stone.

'Do you think we're barking up the wrong tree when we're assuming that the murder was caused by someone who was fed up with his gossip or maybe it was someone with a sexual grudge?'

Jim stood up and paced to the back of the room then returned to his seat. He needed time to think.

'In any school, sexual matters are always of interest,' Jim explained. 'Schools are a hormonal minefield.' He coughed slightly, unsure of what to say next.

'How do you mean?' asked the detective, although fully aware of what the deputy was referring to.

'Well. It's an age when many of the students are discovering who and what they are. What their leanings are. If you get my drift?'

Stone said that he did.

'So, you're saying that some of the boys are queer?' O'Shea asked.

Again, the two men looked at him. O'Shea's insensitivity was threatening the collaboration. The sergeant was a good man but he held common prejudices that did not sit well with the investigation.

Detective Stone appreciated Jim's loyalty to the school and so far, he was being helpful with their enquiries, but he didn't want to push the deputy too far, despite their connection.

'Sergeant, would you mind asking Daphne if we could have some tea? Jim, do you fancy a cuppa?' Stone requested.

O'Shea stood up from his desk, sensing he'd overstepped the mark but not quite sure why, and left the room.

'Sorry about that, Jim,' Stone said, shaking his head. 'Ray is a great guy, and a good policeman, but sometimes he's a bit, um, abrasive in his views. He's young. Anyway, where were we? The fact of the matter is, do you think Bentley was having relations with any boys?'

'Obviously, I don't really know, but now we're wondering about Sutton and Judd. Whether there was any homosexual activity, I'm not sure.' It was such an awkward topic. 'Alan, I think you must appreciate that homosexual activity goes on everywhere, but in such an environment as a school, it's hidden. It's like the old saying, what you don't know doesn't hurt you. Many of the boys may investigate their sexuality, but as long as it's under the covers, so to speak, it's ignored,' he said carefully, but Stone couldn't help but grin at the innuendo.

'So, it is possible that Mr Shute may have had, um, intimacy with the occasional boy?' Stone stressed.

'Put it this way, I know it's happened in the past. Maybe not Bentley, but other masters.'

171

Stone ran his hands through his hair. 'Did the head know about this? If he did, how could he let it continue?'

Jim thought for a moment. He knew that his answer would not satisfy the detective and only make the head appear weak. 'You have to understand that an institution like this has its own set of rules and code of behaviour. Like I said before, a bit like marriages in the Victorian era. As long as one was discreet, affairs were acceptable. The stability of the family and its position were all-important. The same with the school. Discretion, valour etcetera,' Jim tried to explain.

The 1960s and '70s had changed the morality of the Western world. The music, the hippy movement, the use of drugs, the advent of the pill. Women's Liberation, the protests against the Vietnam War, had promoted an era of different thinking and not accepting the status quo.

'The times they are a' changing,' he quoted self-consciously, then added, 'Alan, you know how things are more... How can I put it? More liberal of late.' Jim came to an abrupt halt. He knew that his explanation was the opposite of acceptable. The school could be viewed as allowing behaviour which was morally corrupt, especially when it involved a teacher and a student, despite homosexuality having been legalised quite recently.

Stone tapped a cigarette out of a packet he had on the desk and looked quizzically at Jim who said,

'Go ahead. At times like this, I wish I still smoked. Don't know why I gave up. Actually, I will have one. It's been awhile.' Jim reached over to the packet that Stone held out in front of him and took a cigarette. Stone lit it for him, surprised by Jim's decision. He must be stressed.

The two men sat in uncomfortable silence. Cameron's loyalty to the school was being tested and Stone's understanding, equally so. He lit his own cigarette and took a long drag. 'What about the AIDS issue? How could the headmaster overlook that?'

Jim didn't know how to reply. This new epidemic was something which couldn't be explained. It didn't happen in a school, or did it? Could Judd and Sutton have the fear that they had become infected and therefore struck out at Bentley? Was that a motive to commit murder?

'Jim, we've got to get the bottom of this and the sooner we do, the better,' Stone emphasised. 'And there's a murderer out there.'

'I know. I know,' Jim said coughing.

'This murder may be just the first of others,' Stone suggested.

The deputy took another drag, hoping he wouldn't choke again. This premise had never occurred to him. 'Is that possible? A serial killer in our midst. Sounds like a television show.'

'It does but we have to be prepared for any eventualities.'

Jim thought for a few seconds. 'Do you think it could have been the two boys?' he asked as he thankfully stubbed out his cigarette.

173

'It's a possibility but somehow I don't think so. If Mr Shute had tried something sexual with them they'd've been more likely to slag him off to other boys and have nothing more to do with him. They seemed to admire him, if anything.'

Jim listened before suggesting, 'You know, we're focusing on the school. Could it have been someone from outside? A jilted boyfriend?'

'Maybe. Are you aware of his having visitors, friends from outside the school?'

'Not really. But then I wasn't part of his circle and he certainly wouldn't have exposed himself like that to me.'

Stone grinned at Cameron's inadvertent pun. 'No, mate, don't suppose he would've.'

A slight tap on the door was followed by Daphne's face appearing around the door with Sergeant O'Shea standing closely behind her. Stone beckoned for them to enter and they came into the room carrying mugs of tea and coffee. Daphne was about to leave after depositing the cups on the desk when Stone, in what seemed an afterthought, asked if she could stay.

'Of course. How can I help?' Daphne asked as she sat down on the chair next to Mr Cameron, her knees close together, her hands placed on them as if posing for a school photograph.

O'Shea leant against the classroom wall, surreptitiously looking at her, his eyes lingering over her legs. He noticed the shiny texture of her stockings.

'Daphne, sorry to keep interrogating you, but it seems that whoever got into Mr Shute's flat used a key or the door was left unlocked. Is there any way that someone from inside or outside the school could get into his flat?' Stone asked.

Daphne shook her head. 'Not really, not unless they got a key from someone who works here.' She stopped and thought for a minute. 'Actually, that wouldn't be hard as there are sets of master keys for the different areas and all boarding masters have keys to each house. Or, they could just ask me. But whoever attacked Bentley is hardly going to ask me, surely?'

The three men nodded. It didn't seem likely that the murderer would want to draw attention in such a way.

'Where are the keys kept?' Stone continued.
'They're in the cabinet behind my desk,' Daphne answered.

'Would you mind going and getting them?'
'Not at all.'
Daphne hurried off to her office.

'All present and correct?' Stone asked once she had returned.

She stood at his desk, rolling them through her hand. 'This is the one for Mr Shute's house. It would open all the doors, his place, the dorms. The rest of the keys are for the other boarding houses.'

'So, unless you showed which key was which, the person would have no idea which key did what,'

Stone surmised. 'Did many people know you had the keys?'

'Yes, but not everyone. Most teachers wouldn't know. Only those like the boarding masters, Bill, the HODs and some admin staff.'

'HODs?' Stone queried doubtfully.

'Heads of Departments,' Daphne explained.

'Ah, right. Is the cabinet locked?'

'No. Not normally. If there's an emergency it's important to have access to the keys.'

'Perhaps Mr Shute gave a copy to a friend,' Stone wondered, changing tack. 'Did he have a friend, Daphne? I don't mean his colleagues at work. Someone from outside?'

'I'm not sure. He seemed to socialise mainly with the staff and the odd parent. Mind you, I'm not here at the weekend unless it's a special event so I wouldn't really know what visitors he had.'

Daphne stared at Jim, then turned to Detective Stone. 'This may sound odd, but I don't think he was a very sexual person. He may have had a boyfriend, for all I know, but he seemed to get his kicks from being nasty and stirring up trouble. He seemed to suppress himself. Sorry, I'm not explaining myself very well.'

The three men muttered unanimously that she *was* making sense.

'Thanks, Mrs... Sorry. *Daphne*. That was a great help,' Stone said, as Daphne left the room.

DOTH THE LADY PROTEST TOO MUCH?

The school was quiet. The boarders had returned to the boarding houses and the dayboys to their respective homes. Jim and Daphne had departed for the day leaving Stone and O'Shea alone to sum up the day's revelations.

Both smoked despondently, gazing out of the window at the playing fields below.

Stone turned to the sergeant. 'We definitely need to interview Mrs Armstrong tomorrow. She is an obvious candidate as Shute took a real dislike to and he seemed to make her position at the school very uncomfortable.'

'But would she be capable of inflicting such a blow to his neck like that?' O'Shea asked doubtfully. 'Surely, she wouldn't have the strength.'

'Yeah, it does seem highly unlikely, but she does have a motive. Shute made her life a misery. Perhaps she got someone to do it for her.'

O'Shea seemed sceptical. 'Isn't that a bit farfetched? It's not *The Godfather.* Having someone bumped off. Unless she's got a very wealthy husband, how on earth could she convince someone to do her dirty work?'

Stone wandered back to his desk and flicked open the manila folder as if it may contain the answer and suggested, 'Maybe it's got nothing to do with money. Maybe she and another member of staff decided to do it together. A person with a bit more strength. Mind you, we haven't met her yet. She could be a body builder.'

Both men laughed at the thought.

'Perhaps it was her and Daphne and a few other women on the staff who didn't like him. Strength in numbers,' O'Shea proffered doubtfully, although his doubts didn't stop his imagining a group of women frolicking together wearing very little clothing. He could picture Daphne in a skimpy superwoman outfit.

Stone nodded. 'Maybe. Stranger things have happened. Anyway, let's get Mrs Armstrong in first thing. Also, the fingerprint guys have been over his room with a fine-tooth comb, so we'll have to start matching up the prints with staff and boys.'

'Bloody hell. It's going to be a long job. So many people have been into his rooms. Unlikely any of the boys would have a police record, or staff for that matter.'

'It's got to be done,' Stone stressed. 'We'll talk to Sue Armstrong tomorrow, asap. And after the fingerprint guys have done their job, there might be some prints that can't be accounted for and that may lead to other possibilities.

'Yes, boss,' O'Shea replied.

The following morning Sue Armstrong sat facing Detective Stone, his jacket draped over the back of the chair while Sergeant O'Shea appeared busy with papers at his desk.

'Thanks for coming, Mrs Armstrong. Sorry to take up your free period,' Stone said politely, wanting to put her at ease. 'I know how busy you teachers are.'

Sue smiled uncertainly, unsure of his tone. 'Not a problem. It's Sue, please.'

'Yes. Sue,' Stone repeated and fiddled with his tie as if it were causing him some irritation. 'Jolly hot in here.'

Sue didn't answer but waited for the detective to take the lead. Stone peered around the room.

'Classrooms never change, do they?' he asked rhetorically.

Sue laughed slightly. She noticed the ashtray on the desk. 'Do you mind if I smoke?'

'Not at all. I'll join you.' They both lit up as O'Shea looked on wondering when Stone was going to get down to business. Sue was a lot younger than he'd imagined and prettier as well. The couple of women teachers who'd passed them in the corridors had not been head turners.

'Anyway, Sue, we won't keep you long. Just going to ask you a few questions.'

'I gathered that. I presume it's about Bentley's death.'

179

'It is,' Stone concurred then hesitated before asking, 'We've heard that you were the victim of Mr Shute's... how can I put it? Gossip?'

'That's right. He did talk about me a lot,' Sue answered quickly. 'But of course, I wasn't the only one.' She thought for a moment. 'Bentley was a bit put out when the three of us started on the staff together.'

'Why was that?' O'Shea couldn't help but ask.

Sue turned towards him. 'He didn't seem to like women very much so when we arrived that put his nose out of joint.'

'Weren't there other women on the staff?' O'Shea asked again.

'There were a few, but we were a bit more of a threat.' Sue slowed, not sure how to explain that the women already on the staff were either older or not particularly attractive. 'Put it this way, the three of us got a lot of attention from the men on the staff. And from the boys. Bentley didn't like sharing the limelight.'

'What did he do that indicated to you that your presence was a threat?' Stone asked.

Sue smiled at the detective. 'You've probably heard that I'm meant to be having an affair with a student or students. That was one of the rumours Bentley started. Then there was the gossip that I must have slept with the headmaster to gain the role of housemaster. Bentley was very inventive when it came to me.'

'Would you mind telling me the names of the boys Mr Shute said you were having relationships with?' Stone asked cautiously.

Sue looked sharply at the detective. 'Surely you don't think that a student could be involved in his death?'

The detective fiddled with his pen before replying, 'Mrs Armstrong. Sue. We have to think of all possibilities. It's a process of elimination.'

'Of course it is,' she agreed emphatically. 'This whole situation just seems so unreal.' She shifted in her seat and reached for another cigarette. Stone reached across to light it for her, waiting for her to tell him the names of the students. Sue sucked deeply on her cigarette. Stone noted that the filter was white unlike his typical brown one. An unusual brand.

'Well, apparently, I'm having a thing with George Stavrou. Oh, and I've heard via the grapevine that Mike, Michael Parker and I are an item. And what about Mr Pritchard? Don't know how I have the time to do my job and take care of my family,' Sue said sarcastically.

Stone smiled. 'Quite. Sounds exhausting.' He placed his elbows on the desk and rubbed his chin with both hands. 'What about the other two women teachers who started when you did?' Stone asked.

'What did Bentley say about them?' He could see that Sue was relieved to have the subject changed.

'Similar sorts of things but not quite as bad. He knew that the Head of Commerce was very threatened by Mrs Cutler, so Bentley fed him with stories about how she wasn't a good teacher. And stuff the boys said about her. That sort of thing.'

Stone nodded and sat quietly for a moment. 'So, the stories about your having an affair with a student are not true?'

'Of course, they're not,' Sue stated indignantly. 'Why on earth would I risk my job by doing something like that? And I'm perfectly happily married.'

Stone didn't answer. Shakespeare's words, 'Me thinks the lady doth protest too much' sprang to mind. The quiet in the room was broken by the occasional sounds of students passing in the corridor, a low murmuring of conversations.

'How did you know he had spread such gossip?' Stone asked, straightening the manila folder on his desk.

Sue laughed despondently. 'Probably the same way you've heard about it. There are a number of teachers who are more than happy to spread rumours.' She looked directly at the detective. 'As a man I doubt if you know what it's like to work in an environment where you are the minority. A traditional school like this has only recently started employing more women teachers and some men don't like it. Not just Bentley. And, how can I put it?'

She forcefully stubbed out her cigarette before continuing, 'The male chauvinist element lapped up the gossip and it was obvious when they were talking about me. The silence when I walked into the staffroom, the surreptitious looks, the smirks.'

'It appears that you had every right not to like Mr Shute. And some other members of staff,' Stone stated, his eyes searching Sue's face.

'You're right. I didn't like him, but I certainly didn't want this to have happened. It's awful,' Sue protested.

'You'd have been at home with the family on the night Bentley died?' Stone posed his question as a statement to which Sue nodded, a blush flooding her face.

'Yes. Yes, I was. My husband can vouch for me. Think my kids are a bit too young to be reliable witnesses,' Sue answered wearily.

'Am I actually a suspect? Do you really think I'd kill someone because they gossiped about me?' She stared intently at the detective then at the sergeant.

'Schools are hotbeds of gossip. There would be no one left alive if everyone got that upset.'

The two men smiled. 'True. True,' they agreed.

Stone stood up, the grating noise of his chair scraping along the floor echoed around the room.

'Thank you, Mrs Armstrong. Sorry to have to ask you such questions.' Then he added quickly, 'Must be hard working full time and taking care of young children. And a home?'

Sue frowned at his change of questioning. 'It can be. But I manage,' she defended.

'I'm sure you do,' he responded sympathetically. 'But it can't be easy with both of you working.' He could see that Sue's composure was waning. 'And working in this, how can I say, rather old-fashioned institution, wouldn't help?'

'It doesn't, but...,'

'But what?'

Mrs Armstrong thought for a moment before replying, 'Detective Stone, I like working. I'm not cut out to be a stay at home mother. I'm not blaming those who do like it, but I don't. It is hard juggling everything, but it's worth it.'

'The money, I suppose?' Sergeant O'Shea threw in.

'No. Not just the money. It's more than that,' Sue stated, her tone indicating that the sergeant was a dinosaur in his attitudes. He sounded like so many of the men on the staff. How very 1950s.

'There's such a thing as job satisfaction. I'm sure you must feel that too, Sergeant?' Sue asked, not caring if she sounded sarcastic.

O'Shea looked suitably admonished and nodded his head as if to agree but continued his questioning,

'Must be nice teaching boys, Mrs Armstrong? I used to like being taught by women teachers. A nice change after some of the men.'

'I wouldn't know. I am a female after all.'

Both men laughed and exchanged a quick glance. 'Anyway, thanks again. We'll just have to confirm with Mr Armstrong about that night. We're asking everyone, so please don't feel that we've got it in for you,' Stone justified, concerned as he saw her frown.

Sue bent down to pick up her bag from the floor, rummaged through it, and pulled out a crumpled tissue from the jumble of contents. A piece of paper, dislodged by her search, fell out landing at Stone's feet and he quickly reached down to retrieve it. Sue too grabbed for the paper, their heads colliding.

Embarrassment permeated the room; the two rubbing their foreheads while O'Shea couldn't help grinning at their discomfort.

Stone placed his hand on her arm. 'You okay?'

'Yes. Yes. Sorry,' Sue replied, reaching out to take the piece of paper which Stone still had in his hand.

'Important?'

'Oh, just something I need for a class,' Sue said as Stone handed it to her, and she stuffed it back into her bag.

Stone walked with Sue to the door and opened it for her. 'Thanks again, Mrs Armstrong.' Sue did not reply and left the room.

The detective closed the door and waited for a few seconds till he thought Sue was out of earshot. O'Shea stood expectantly.

'What was that all about?' he asked.

'Definitely something she didn't want us to see.'

'But did you?' O'Shea asked.

'Put it this way, it didn't look like it was written by a teacher.'

'Yeah. She really didn't want you to read it.' O'Shea hitched at his trousers. 'And she didn't seem too keen on the idea of us talking to her husband either. Her manner was quite defensive.'

'It was. But then who would want to be a suspect in a murder case?' Stone rationalised.

'Not sure that's what she's worried about,' O'Shea stated.

'God knows,' Stone answered. 'This school is bloody odd.'

REVENGE BACKFIRES

The arc lights over the Oval were switched off. The streetlamps gave some visibility but the walk back from the Oval to the boarding houses was virtually in darkness. Most boys clung together in groups as they trudged back to their dorms after rugby practice.

James Matthews lingered on the field, stuffing his rugby boots and an old beach towel into his bag. He wasn't in a hurry. The routine of school activities had become disjointed since Mr Shute's death and the regimen was not adhered to with the same deliberation. The school was distracted.

The boy made his way to Churchill House; the route so familiar he didn't need any lighting. As he approached the heavy doors to the entrance of the house, he heard behind him the crunch of footsteps on the concrete path. It was the limping sound of rugby boots on a hard surface.

'We've come to get you, Matto,' a voice whispered threateningly.

Matto stopped. Turned. A punch knocked him to the ground. Football boots kicked randomly. Matthews grabbed at a leg and pulled. A body fell. 'Fuck!'

Matthews scrambled to his feet. He could see there were two boys, both in rugby kit and wearing the school tracksuit top with the hoods pulled down over their eyes. A scene from *Rocky* flashed across the screen in his head. The boy who had fallen was pulled roughly to his feet by the other and side by side they faced Matthews. The light from the doorway silhouetted them but Matthews knew instinctively who they were. Why did they even bother to try and hide their faces?

As the boys inched forward, their fists clenched and held up like old fashioned bare-knuckle boxers, James stood waiting, his arms folded.

David Judd pushed his face at James. 'We've been questioned by the police because of you. Arsehole.'

'We don't like shits like you who get us into trouble,' Phil Sutton reinforced, lowering his voice, and stressing each word to add to the menace. He lifted his fist again and whacked James across the ear.

Now Judd, aping his mate, continued the attack.

Matthews wind-milled his arms in the hope of deflecting some of the punches, but it was difficult fending off two attackers. A push from Judd felled him onto the path. Matthews wrapped his arms around his head and decided to wait until they had run out of puff or became bored.

A foot was raised and about to strike when a deep male voice yelled, 'What the hell do you boys think you're doing? Stop that fighting at once.'

The foot was stayed. The three boys were paralysed by the words. It was the School Sergeant.

Bill MacGregor stormed out of the boarding house and yanked Matthews to his feet. He grabbed the other two by their hoods and roughly pulled the clothing back to reveal their faces.

'Mr Sutton and Mr Judd. Well. Well. Tell me. Who started this little fracas?' The sergeant's nose was a centimetre from Sutton's. Sutton could smell whisky and traces of stew.

The boys remained silent. The sarge turned to Matthews. 'Can you enlighten me, Mr Matthews? Or has the cat got your tongue too?'

Matthews remained silent.

'Right. If that's the case, the three of you had better get to your dorms right this minute and then report to me before breakfast tomorrow morning. Have a good think about what you want to tell me. The cane hasn't had a good work out for a while so maybe that will jog your memory about who and what started this. Matthews, get inside right now.'

Judd and Sutton, with arms hanging by their sides and sullen expressions, were told to wait. They watched their victim pick up his bag and tread carefully towards the front door and make his way slowly up the stairs to the dormitory.

'Now, I'll see you two to your place of residence. Don't even think about returning to finish off whatever was started,' MacGregor warned. 'I'll have your guts for garters if you do anything out of line.'

The boys pulled their hoods back over their heads and with shoulders hunched, followed Mr MacGregor back to their dorm. MacGregor was not in the mood to make conversation. Just as well he'd been doing his rounds. Ever since Shute had been murdered, he'd made a point of patrolling the school grounds after lights out. You never knew if the murderer was going to strike again.

The following morning the three boys stood silently in a row in the deputy headmaster's office. Mr MacGregor, a few paces away, also stood quietly but with a cane clutched tightly under his arm.

Mr Cameron paced in front of the boys as if they were on army parade. He stopped suddenly in front of Phil Sutton. 'Mr Sutton. Could you please explain to me how James here, received these injuries?'

Quickly, rounding on David Judd, he asked the same question. Neither answered.

'Perhaps, Mr Matthews, you can enlighten me as to why your face is covered in bruises?'

'I fell over, Sir,' Matthews explained. His face blank.

'Pardon?' The sarcasm in Jim Cameron's voice was very obvious.

'I fell. Footy practice.' This time he attempted to eye the deputy head.

'All right. If this is the way you want to play it, I'm going to hand you over to Mr MacGregor. He's got all day. You'll have plenty of time to think about what actually happened.'

Mr Cameron pointed his index finger at each boy in turn stating loudly, 'I will not tolerate violence of any sort in this school. You are gentlemen. Not louts. Now go. Wait in the corridor till you're called for.'

The boys picked up their school bags and left the room with Matthews at the rear. Outside the deputy's office a row of chairs was positioned against the wall. Many a nervous student had sat waiting to be called into the office for an 'interview'.

The three sat as far away from each other as they could. Students stared curiously at them as they passed on their way to class.

The time dragged, the bell rang, teachers and boys moved between classrooms. The boys slouched further back into their seats as they wondered what was going to happen.

Mr MacGregor finally emerged from Jim's office. 'Sutton. You come with me. You two, wait here.' Sutton stood up, relieved that something was happening. Anything to beat the boredom. He followed the sergeant down the corridor to his less impressive office.

Judd and Matthews slumped further, their legs stuck out, ankles crossed, both pretending the other wasn't there. Time dripped by. Seeing other boys going to class made them envious. Just sitting was torture. Finally, David Judd could take the silence no longer.

'What are you gonna say to Mr Cameron?' he mumbled, without looking at James.

Matthews sat up in his chair, flexing his shoulders. 'What I've said already.'

Judd glanced at him. 'Why?'

'Why what?'

'Why aren't you gonna dob us in?'

'What's the point? What's happened's happened.'

'Fuck, Matto. You're sounding weird,' Judd said, scratching at the pimples covering his cheeks.

The silence returned although Judd couldn't help but admire Matthews. He certainly wasn't a wuss or a dobber.

Unable to resist, he whispered, 'Did you like Benty? You were in his house.'

'He was okay. Did *you* like him?' Matthews continued, deflecting the question back to Judd. A conversation was better than sitting all day doing nothing.

'Yeah, I did,' Judd answered, distractedly scratching at a whitehead on his chin. 'Some of the boys didn't know how to take him, but.'

'Well, he could be a bit moody. You never wanted to get on the wrong side of him,' Matthews admitted. Judd's revelation had come as a bit of a surprise.

'I'll say. Maybe that's 'cos he's…. You know,' Judd's analysis petered out.

Matthews didn't reply but the rise of his eyebrows and the downturn of his mouth showed that he knew what David Judd was implying. Now that Matthews had bought into the conversation, Judd relaxed and shuffled his chair closer to James.

'He never tried anything with us, but I heard from other boys that he wanted… you know,' Judd blustered, his cheeks reddening. 'I'd have punched his lights out if he'd come near me. So would Phil. He can't stand all that fag rubbish.'

'Nah, suppose not. But why'd you go to his room all the time?'

Judd grimaced. What was Matthews insinuating? He felt he had to explain. He didn't want anyone thinking that he was a poof. 'Dunno really. Phil liked to go. Hear all the goss.' Aware that his explanation sounded rather lame, he still wanted Matthews to understand. 'Makes you feel a bit powerful knowing the teachers, especially one like Benty. Be part of the in-crowd.'

Matthews's lips tightened into a thin line. Jeez, these guys sound so bloody insecure. Neither spoke, one not sure how to reply to such information, the other aware that he'd given away too much.

The sudden reappearance of Mr Cameron came as a relief to both of them. 'James. David.' The two stared at him expectantly, then quickly stood up.

'Bring your bags and come with me. Mr Pritchard has asked me to keep an eye on you. We don't want any more of the events of last night. We'll go back to my office and continue our chat.'

Silently, the boys followed Mr Cameron back into his office and sat down as directed.

'What's going on between you chaps?' he asked benignly. The boys peered at the floor.

'David. I was extremely disappointed to hear that you and Phillip took it into your own hands to attack James. Do you think that was the right thing to do?'

Judd, embarrassed, shook his head. He knew that Mr Cameron was a fair man. 'We were just pissed off with him 'cos what he told the police got us into trouble.'

Cameron smiled at him sympathetically, ignoring the swear word. Now wasn't the time to haul him over the coals for using bad language. 'I can understand that you wouldn't like being interviewed by the police. No one does. But that doesn't excuse what you and Phillip did. You have to remember that there has been this very unfortunate incident concerning Mr Shute and so many of the staff and boys have been asked questions. It was wrong to take your anger out on James.'

'Suppose so,' Dave agreed reluctantly, then as if a burden had been lifted, blurted out. 'We wouldn't have hurt Mr Shute. We just went to his rooms sometimes. We weren't the only ones.'

'No-one thinks you were, David. Nor Phillip. It's a very stressful time for everyone. And for you as well, James.'

Both boys looked relieved. Mr Cameron was very understanding.

'Can either of you think of anyone who may have wanted to hurt Mr Shute?' Cameron's tone hinted at confidentiality. Appealing to their ego, especially Judd's, may result in useful information.

James was about to reply when Judd jumped in. 'Not really. Everyone keeps asking that. The only people who didn't like him were some of the women teachers. But they wouldn't do anything like that. Women don't murder people.'

Cameron didn't bother to refute this opinion. 'What were you going to say, James?'

James struggled to voice his thoughts. 'The same as Dave, I suppose. Mr Shute didn't like some of the women teachers, but women don't do that sort of thing.'

'Women can be pretty tough, you know. But, you're probably right.' Cameron realised that life would teach them about female strength after they'd been in a few relationships.

'What about any of the other students who visited Mr Shute?' Mr Cameron asked, addressing his question to the room. Neither boy spoke. Neither wanted to implicate anyone and Cameron decided that asking such questions would be futile. There was no point in putting them offside by insisting that they dob in mates and they were unlikely to tell him anything in front of each other.

Mr Cameron pushed his chair back and stood up, asking the boys to do the same. 'I want the two of you to shake hands like gentlemen and put this nasty incident behind you. We have to respect each other and not take out our frustrations by using violence. That never solved anything.'

He walked around his desk to stand between the boys. They slowly raised their right arms and as if pulled by magnets their hands met. A quick shake, a

195

moment of eye contact and the awkwardness was over. Jim patted each boy on the shoulder. 'Well done, lads. Now off you go and remember, fighting is not the answer.' The boys murmured their agreement.

A VISITOR TO THE SCHOOL

Graham Russell parked his car near the school and sat watching. He twiddled the radio knob until he found a station he liked and was pleased to hear *The Pet Shop Boys'* latest release being played.

It was Wednesday morning and he'd waited since Saturday for an explanation why Bentley had not arrived at the pub for their date.

Apart from a solitary car driving along the road, which divided the school grounds, there wasn't much to see as the pupils were in class and the staff equally occupied. The sun glinted on the trees lining the street and a quiet haze hung over the buildings. It was the dichotomy of a school environment, noisy and active one minute, silent the next.

Russell took out his Olympus camera from the battered brown satchel on the passenger seat and after checking to see if anyone was observing his actions, clicked a couple of quick photos of the buildings on either side of the road. He put his camera on top of the satchel, opened a cigarette packet, snicked out a cigarette, lit it and continued watching.

Two men suddenly appeared at the top of the steps, which exited from a building on the right side of the road, and they made their way to a car near the entrance. One of the men was in police uniform while the other wore a dark suit, shirt and tie. Graham again picked up his camera and surreptitiously snapped them about to get into the car, a regulation police Holden. He made a note of the time on the small pad he'd taken out of his shirt pocket. These two must be the ones sent to the school to investigate the accident that had occurred recently on an excursion. Bentley had talked about it, but as a journalist, Graham wanted to learn of the legal aspects.

His informant at the police station had given him very rudimentary information about the drowning. Perhaps he needed to take Stan out for another drink to find out more. Usually, the desk clerk at Waverley was fairly forthcoming with news about possible stories but this time, he'd only given a few hints. Why the reticence? What had happened at a boys' private school to cause such secrecy about the event?

The current leftist political climate was ideal for a story feeding prejudice against privileged private schools and the silver tails. With Bob Hawke as Prime Minister, many segments of society were fighting against old conservative right-wing attitudes.

Articles arguing against the private school system resonated with some members of society especially as a number of the State schools in lower socio-economic areas were doing badly in the Higher

School Certificate rankings and the readers wanted to know why.

Russell easily ignored his personal hypocrisy of having gone to a private school as the desire for a front-page story certainly wasn't going to interfere with an emotive exposé or be affected by personal experience.

It was so easy to manipulate the reading public. Journalists could nourish the prejudice against what was considered privilege. Few readers would have thought about the negative effects on academic results by the decline in discipline in public schools. Or how governmental interference in the structure and running of schools impacted badly on academic outcomes.

The reporter was fully aware of how the lack of respect for teachers, their low pay compared to other professions and the interference by parents who thought they were authorities on education because they'd been to school, aided the negative perceptions of the education system. If parents could afford the fees and even if they had to struggle to pay them, preferred to send their offspring to a private school where discipline was still enforced and where teachers were not so beaten down by bureaucracy.

Flicking his butt into the street, Graham Russell immediately lit another. He was willing to wait. Why had Bentley not turned up? It wasn't like him to be unreliable, especially with what they had planned for later in the evening. Of course, the boarding house had its issues but to go this long without hearing from him was most unusual.

His memory slid back to how the two of them had met over a year ago in a gay bar on Oxford Street. It was a regular haunt for men who felt safe away from the prying eyes of the straight community, the gay bashers and for Bentley, sufficiently removed from the possibility of bumping into any boarders who had taken 'window leave'.

Although prejudice against the gay community had eased somewhat since the '70s, the advent of AIDS had reinvigorated the intolerance, especially from the religious right-wing crowd. The Fred Nile followers would love any opportunity to point the finger. Their preoccupation with the sexual activities of others swung from it being an endless source of fascination to disgust. The plague of gayness had to be stopped. Only God knew when it would end.

Graham finished his cigarette and again flicked the butt into the street. How long would he wait? Perhaps he should go in and ask for Bentley? See what the reaction would be.

Retrieving his satchel from the passenger seat, he replaced the camera into the bag and locked the car.

He strode quickly to the building from where the two policemen had emerged, walked down the steps, and pushed open the heavy double doors. He peered along the corridor and saw the sign for the headmaster's office. There should be an assistant somewhere nearby. It was better to deal with underlings rather than the top dogs. An unsuspecting personal assistant may let something slip.

He made his way down the corridor as if he had an appointment, catching glimpses of students sitting in classrooms and soon came to an office with a sign indicating that Mrs Withers was the Headmaster's secretary.

Graham tapped on the partially open door and walked in without waiting for an answer. Mrs Withers was sitting at her desk engrossed in something on the computer. She looked up, surprised to see a face she didn't recognise but then quickly composed herself.

'Can I help you?' Daphne asked, taking in the tall, rather long-haired youngish man carrying a satchel and dressed in what only could be described as shabby chic. He didn't have the appearance of a teacher nor a policeman. His outfit of jeans, shirt, leather jacket and the ubiquitous R.M. Williams didn't place him as a parent either.

Graham smiled confidently at Daphne. 'I hope you can. I'm here to see Bentley, Bentley Shute. Popped in on the off chance that he's free at the moment.'

Daphne's smile stopped and put her hand up to her hair. 'Mr Shute?'

'Yes, Mr Shute,' the journalist repeated. 'I've known Bentley for some time,' he added, using the Christian name to reassure Mrs Withers that he was indeed a friend of Bentley's and wasn't making a random call. He could see that she was flustered.

'Oh. Um. Well, Bentley, Mr Shute isn't here. At the moment,' Daphne stammered, uncertain of what to divulge. 'Are you a friend of his?' she asked, blushing at her question.

'You could say that,' Graham responded. 'Look, if it's a problem, I'll give him a ring later. I don't want to put you out.'

'No. No. You're not putting me out. Sorry, I must seem rude. It's just that...' Daphne stopped again. 'I'll let him know that you came.'

Daphne scrambled to pick up a pad and pen. 'If you give me your name, I'll tell him you wanted to see him. Can I tell him the reason for your visit?'

'No. Nothing urgent. Just tell him that Graham Russell came.'

'I certainly will, Mr Russell. Do you have a phone number?' Daphne asked, reverting to her secretarial mode.

'He knows it, Mrs Withers. Thanks for your help,' Graham said as he backed out of the room.

Daphne made a note on the pad in front of her. There was something about Graham Russell that didn't seem quite right. Was he really a friend of Bentley's or was he snooping? Daphne didn't know much about journalists but for some reason she felt that he may be one. His style of dress, his manner, especially after what had happened.

Or perhaps he was a 'friend'. He didn't appear to know that anything was amiss. Was he fishing for information? Should she tell the police about Mr

Russell's visit or tell the boss? Her hand dithered over the phone then picked it up and spoke to the headmaster.

Robert Pritchard stood at Daphne's desk; his agitated state concerned her. The memorial for the dead teacher had not yet been decided. The nature of his death made the organisation of such an event difficult, more from the psychological aspect than the practicality of the arrangement. And now there was this visit from a supposed 'friend'.

'Robert, don't worry. We can sort this out. We'll just have to check the school calendar and work out a date,' Daphne said, her words sounding more confident than she felt. It was going to be an uncomfortable function.

'I know. I know. But also who's this chap nosing around, asking for Shute?' Pritchard asked tugging at his tie. 'Was he really his friend? Why did he turn up now?'

'I don't know. Maybe it's just a coincidence. Bentley must have known people outside of the school.'

'I suppose so. But it's odd that whoever he is, comes here so soon after Bentley's,' he paused, 'death'. There was no other way of saying it and the two were aware that the news of the teacher's death could have spread outside of the perimeters of the school.

'What was he like?' Pritchard asked tentatively, not sure how to word the question. To imply the visitor could be gay was full of judgement.

Daphne ran her fingers through her hair. What was that man like? Was he gay? Did it have any relevance if he were? This whole fixation on whether someone was gay was so annoying.

'Well, he wasn't a parent or the police, Robert,' Daphne replied, trying to keep the irritation out of her voice. 'He may have been gay, but we can't assume that, just because Bentley was. We really didn't know much about his life outside of the school. Perhaps he had a whole other life. Straight friends as well as gay.'

Robert, sensing her annoyance, thought it wiser to change the subject.

'Yes. Yes. Sorry. This bloke turning up is a worry, but there's also the other stuff. I feel that I'm not in control of the situation. And this bloody memorial service. Sorry to swear, but God, Daphne, it's all driving me mad.'

'I know. I know. It's very stressful,' Daphne said soothingly and walked around the desk to put her hand on the headmaster's arm. 'It'll be alright.'

He placed his hand on top of hers in gratitude and squeezed it. 'I don't know what I'd do without you.'

'Well, Robert. Don't worry. I'm not going anywhere,' Daphne reassured him as he let go of her hand. 'Do you want me to let the police know that this Russell chap came?'

Pritchard looked wearily up at the ceiling as if for an answer. 'Yes. Yes. You'd better tell them. We can't be seen not helping the police.'

WILL HE OR WON'T HE?

Sergeant O'Shea stood over Daphne's desk, the photograph of her children disconcerting in its message that she was a married woman. He felt a shiver of jealousy at the thought, although logically he knew he had no right to feel possessive of her. He thought he'd detected a connection between them, giving him the freedom to imagine a relationship.

He pictured the two of them sitting knee to knee at a bar, her sheer stockings rubbing against his leg, the exciting thought of suspenders twanging undone when they undressed in his bedroom. Did women still wear suspender belts? O'Shea hoped so.

A wave of desolation came over him at the realisation that this may never happen. His face sagged, and a slightly queasy feeling churned his stomach.

'Are you alright, Sergeant?' Daphne asked, enjoying saying his title.

'Shit! What?' the sergeant answered, shocked by the surprising arrival of the woman in his imagination. 'Oh, sorry to swear. You just gave me a fright.'

'Do all policemen scare so easily?' Daphne asked, smiling at him and as she walked towards her desk, leant out as if to steady him.

Sergeant O'Shea could feel his temperature rising, a mixture of embarrassment and arousal as she was so near to him.

He coughed and fiddled with his police hat, turning it around in his hands like a steering wheel.

'I was just admiring your kids. They look like you,' he paused, 'especially your daughter. She's very pretty.'

Daphne slowly turned to face him unable to hide her pleasure at the compliment. She hesitated, not sure what to say, but aware that this could be a moment which defined the future. 'Thank you. You're very kind. Do you have any children, Ray?'

'No. Not married. Not even in a relationship,' he answered carefully.

The air seemed heavy with the importance of his reply. Daphne picked up the photograph and ran her hand across the glass. 'The best part of my marriage. At least something good came out of it.'

She let the words sink in. O'Shea swallowed. Was she telling him this for a reason? Standing there in a police uniform made him feel vulnerable. It wasn't the most flattering outfit. The light blue shirt was too wishy-washy. He'd feel much more comfortable in jeans while standing next to Daphne in a pub. Fuck, he'd kill for a cigarette right now.

O'Shea faltered. Should he ask her out? But what if she was still married? But she seemed to imply it was over. He said nothing.

Daphne's face clouded over. Had she been rejected? Had she misread his interest? She'd been wrong before.

Hoping he hadn't seen her disappointment, she walked to her desk and while fidgeting with some papers, told him crisply, 'A man came asking for Mr Shute this morning. He may be of interest to your inquiry.'

The sergeant, despite his usual insensitivity, had noticed that her tone had cooled. You bloody idiot. Why didn't you say something?

'Oh, Daphne...' He put his hand out uncertainly then withdrew it. Daphne looked down at his hand and then at him. Her face softened. He *was* a young man after all.

Despite his uniform, which she thought fitted him very well, the blue highlighting his eyes, harking back to his Irish ancestry, he seemed gauche and insecure. He had the uniform to give him confidence and the authority that went with it, but he probably hadn't had much experience. The odd one-night stand perhaps, and maybe that was limited because some women could be put off by his profession. It was like going out with a psychiatrist who might be analysing your every action or word. But in this case, any guilty move. Would he arrest his bed partner if she rolled a joint before having sex or would he become self-righteous at the possibility of being over .05 after a few drinks?

'What is it, Sergeant?' she asked.

'It's just. Um. I wondered…' he dithered.

'Perhaps we could discuss this case over a drink one night,' Daphne suggested, putting him out of his misery.

'That would be great,' Ray O'Shea gushed adolescently. 'Tell me when.'

Ray pulled himself up like a sentry on guard, his manner becoming more official as he realised how eager his words sounded.

Daphne nodded, smiling, relishing his embarrassment but pleased with the result. 'I'll let you know.'

She picked up her pad with a secretarial flourish then said, 'I'd better give you information about Bentley's visitor.'

'What? Oh, yeah. Can you describe him for me? Did he give you his name?' Ray asked enthusiastically and sat down. He felt safer in his role as a policeman.

Daphne told him about their conversation and how she had the feeling that Graham Russell was a journalist.

Ray O'Shea listened attentively, impressed by her observations. 'Did he give you an address or a phone number?' Daphne said no, explaining that she'd asked for it, but the man told her Bentley already had it.

Ray got up from his chair and thanked Daphne for her help. It was much appreciated. It was her pleasure she told him as he left the room.

Out in the corridor, his shoulders dropped as the tension rolled off him. He'd finally done it. Or rather she had done it. Either way, he could now ask her out properly. It was against protocol but who cared? She couldn't possibly be involved in Bentley's murder, so he wasn't really doing the wrong thing, was he?

Ray wandered jauntily back to their HQ to find Detective Stone sitting at his desk, studying the information in his notebook.

'Mrs Withers said a man came to visit Shute. This morning, in fact. She wonders if he might be useful to the investigation,' O'Shea stated, unable to keep the smugness out of his voice.

Stone raised his eyebrows and looked quizzically at O'Shea. 'You're sounding very formal all of a sudden. Nothing to do with the attention of a certain headmaster's assistant?'

O'Shea laughed. 'I don't know what you mean?'

'You'd better be careful, mate. There's more to Mrs Withers than meets the eye. I'd hate to see you done like a dinner.'

'No worries. She's cool. I can handle myself,' Ray asserted.

'Ah, the ignorance of youth,' said Stone sagely.

'Bloody hell, mate. You're sounding like an old fart.'

'You may sneer, young man, but there's a lot of truth in those old sayings. Why do you think they've lasted so long?' posed Stone.

Without waiting for a reply, he continued. 'What's this about a man asking for Mr Shute?'

Sergeant O'Shea, attempting to continue sounding professional, replied, 'Daphne said a man came to her office asking to see Shute. She'd never seen him before, but she thought he may have been a journalist. Although he did say he was a friend of Shute's.'

Stone smirked at his colleague's territorial use of her Christian name. 'And does this man have a name?'

'Yes. Graham Russell.'

The detective jotted the name down. 'Right. We'll need to talk to him and we also need to talk to James Matthews again. His altercation with the two boys may have nothing to do with anything, but it won't hurt to learn more about what goes on in the boarding houses.'

With a sly grin, he instructed the sergeant to ask Mrs Withers if she could locate Matthews and bring him to HQ. Sergeant O'Shea willingly agreed to do so and quickly left the room.

WHO WAS THAT MAN?

Daphne knocked on the door to Police HQ, opened it and followed by Matthews, walked up to the two policemen. Both men nodded at the boy who had the air of someone rather tired of being in the limelight but could not return to what life had been before.

'Hello, James,' Detective Stone greeted him in an attempt to put the student at ease and motioned for him to sit down while thanking Daphne for her assistance. Matthews slowly sat and placed his feet squarely on the floor, reminiscent of a victim in front of a firing squad in World War One. All he needed was the blindfold.

'Been getting a hard time from Judd and Sutton, I gather,' Stone stated in an understanding tone, while noting the bruises on the boy's face. Matthews didn't reply but pulled at his socks as if to make sure they were totally even. 'It's okay, James, you did the right thing telling us about the boys' visits to Mr Shute,' Stone reassured him.

The formal setting was reminiscent of a teacher, pupil situation. 'I'm not asking you about the boys, but I wondered if you have ever seen anyone else visit Mr Shute on a regular basis? Someone not from the school? A man? Or men? Even a woman?' Stone leant forward, splaying his fingers on the desk as if he were going to trace around them like an Aboriginal hand painting on a cave wall. 'Tell us anything you can think of. It doesn't matter if it sounds weird.'

Matthews twisted his bottom on the chair as if to find a more comfortable spot on the hard wood. He rubbed his chin with the back of his hand. 'Can't really think of anyone else that I haven't told you about already.'

Stone waited, his fingers dragging slowly along the desk. 'I really appreciate the information you've given us but if there's someone, anyone you can remember who went to visit Mr Shute. Someone you normally wouldn't see.'

He knew it was difficult for boys like Matthews to dob in mates, but he'd also gathered that this boy seemed keen to do the right thing.

Matthews fidgeted as if movement would jog his memory. Did he really want to help the police? Dave and Phil had already bashed him and maybe they'd do it again. Who cared if Benty was dead? He'd been a bit of an arsehole and his mates on the staff were losers. Not like Mrs Armstrong and other teachers. They didn't bully or make you look stupid. They weren't on a power trip.

Finally, James Matthews answered, 'There was a man who came to watch the game a few Saturdays ago, and he seemed to know Mr Shute. He wasn't a teacher.' The boy kept thinking. 'He didn't look like a parent. Didn't seem old enough for a kid at high school.'

'Can you describe him?' the detective asked, not wanting to sound too eager.

'Dunno really. He was a bit of a cool dude. Jeans. Leather jacket. He had a camera. Big flash thing.'

'How did you know he was with Mr Shute?' Stone asked.

'They were standing together watching the game. It looked like they knew each other.'

'Was anyone else with them?'

'No,' Matthews stated emphatically then thought again. 'Actually, Miss Bates joined them and then this guy moved off. Benty looked a bit annoyed that she'd interrupted them.'

'You're very observant, James,' Stone flattered. 'Why did you take such an interest in Mr Shute?'

Matthews frowned as if he were being reprimanded. 'I didn't. It was just that Mr Shute used to make us stand near him to support our team. Not much happens at school so you can't help notice anything different.'

Stone, realising he may have put Matthews offside, was keen to reassure him that his observations were greatly valued. Matthews, placated, nodded.

'James, I want you to hear Mrs Withers' description of a man who came looking for Mr Shute this morning. It may be the same man.'

Matthews' face showed his curiosity at hearing about a possible connection to the crime.

'Mrs Withers, would you mind describing the man so that we can all get a picture of his appearance?' Stone asked.

Daphne sat down on one of the chairs which were grouped around Stone's desk, firmly crossed her legs, and began her description. 'He was about mid-30s. Reasonably tall. Fairish hair. He seemed quite hip, if you know what I mean. Jeans. Boots.'

'Did he have a beard, moustache?' Stone queried.

Daphne's brow furrowed. 'No. I don't think so, but he did have quite long hair. He was well-spoken, as if he'd been to a private school.' Aware of how this sounded, added, 'I don't mean that only private school students speak well.'

'I know what you mean,' Stone quickly reassured her. 'Did he have an appointment with Mr Shute?'

'No. He said he'd popped in on the off chance. But he did seem to expect Mr Shute to be here.'

Detective Stone turned to Matthews asking, 'Does this sound like the man you saw watching the game with Mr Shute?'

'Yeah. Yeah. It does,' he confirmed eagerly.

'Was that the only time you ever saw him with Mr Shute?' Sergeant O'Shea interjected. Matthews took a moment before answering, 'I think I've seen him before, but not very often.'

Stone focussed his attention again on Daphne and was about to ask her whether she had any indication that he and Mr Shute were friends but instead stood up, giving Matthews the impression that he could go.

He led the boy to the door, thanking him for his help and shut the door decisively once Matthews had left the room. Daphne and O'Shea surreptitiously smiled at each other and waited patiently, both appreciating why Stone had seen fit to make the teenager leave the room.

'Thought it better if he left. Didn't want to ask if you thought this man was a homosexual in front of a young boy.' Daphne and O'Shea nodded, understanding the detective's sensitivity about the possible answer.

Daphne pondered for a few seconds. 'I didn't pick up the fact that he may have been gay but there was something that made me slightly suspicious about him. I couldn't tell if he really was a friend or as I said, maybe he's a journalist. Something about his style of clothing and the way he asked about Bentley. It made me wonder if he did know him, but after what's happened, I'm probably being over suspicious.'

'Understandable,' reassured Sergeant O'Shea in a protective way, causing Stone to look slightly askance at the sergeant before asking if she'd noticed anything else.

'Actually, he had a satchel with him, a big arty thing. Brown. Made of leather, I think. Quite worn and it had something bulky inside it.' She ran her hand under her chin. 'I honestly can't think of anything else,' Daphne said with finality to the two men.

O'Shea sensing Daphne's imminent departure, stood up and slid quickly over to the door, which he opened with a flourish. Daphne, queenly in her exit, murmured her thanks.

Once the door was shut behind her, O'Shea returned to his desk and perched himself on it, placing his feet on the chair. 'Do you think any of this is relevant to his death?' he asked Stone, his demeanour mirroring the electric impact that Daphne had on him.

'Who knows, but we have a name and a description. It sounded as if Shute mainly socialised with the staff but maybe he had another life that no-one knew about. I get the impression that even among his mates at the school, his homosexuality didn't go down too well, so I'd assume that he kept his private life to himself.'

'Not surprised,' O'Shea responded but didn't continue after seeing annoyance pass across his boss's face.

'Jesus Christ, Sergeant, you've got to get over your paranoia or prejudice or what-ever you call it. You can't be so judgmental in our position,' the detective reprimanded. 'Don't think you're going to win any favours with Daphne with your antiquated attitude.'

'Sorry, Sir. You're right,' O'Shea apologised with a sufficient look of contrition and heaved himself off the desk and went back to his chair which he made a great show of shuffling it and himself under the desk.

AFTERNOON TEA

Like old mates, Jim Cameron sat with Daphne in the deserted staffroom. The bell had rung an hour ago to signal the end of the school day. The two sipped at their tea, comfortable in each other's company and judging by the close proximity of their bodies were chatting intimately.

'So, his name was Russell? Bentley's friend?' Jim reiterated.

'Yes. Graham Russell. I gave the police all the information I could. I wondered if he was a journalist. The coincidence of Bentley's death and his coming to the school. Do you think he could be?' Daphne asked anxiously.

'Who knows, but I'll give Des Campbell a call. If Russell is a journalist, then he should know. It does seem coincidental but maybe he is just a friend.'

'Who's Des Campbell?' Daphne asked.

'A mate of mine. He's the editor of a local Sydney paper.'

'Could you ring him now? I'm dying to know,' Daphne pleaded.

'Just for you,' Jim agreed, then prised himself out of the comfy chair and walked towards the phone booth at the back of the staffroom.

Daphne watched him pull out a small tattered address book from an inside pocket of his jacket, flick through the pages before dialing a number. She could see Jim's face change from one of greeting to concern, and the nodding of his head signalled his thanks and goodbyes.

He opened the phone booth glass door and returned to sit next to Daphne.

'Well, you're right. He *is* a journalist,' Jim informed her. 'But he doesn't work for Des' paper. He works for the opposition. Des *has* wondered if Graham Russell is gay, but in that industry, it's not really an issue. The media is full of all types.'

'Did he say what he's like?' Daphne asked eagerly.

'Not really. Just that he's a respected 'journo',' Jim said waggling his fingers around the word, 'and has a good nose for a story.'

'Oh God,' Daphne groaned. 'It'll be in all the papers before we can say Jack Robinson.'

'Or Graham Russell,' Jim countered. Daphne tittered slightly.

'Maybe I could ask Des to contact the editor of *The Daily Herald* and ask him to find out on the Q T, if they know anything more about Russell.'

Daphne agreed. This whole drama was becoming more like an Agatha Christie novel every day.

'What about Shute's memorial service? Has that been organised?' Jim asked, changing the subject.

Daphne explained that she and the headmaster had decided on the dates and that there were going to be two services. The second one followed by drinks and nibbles for a select group.

Jim dreaded the thought of standing around with a glass of warm chardonnay or beer, desperately trying to think of something to say. Some of the staff were experts at doing the room, partly because of the mothers who came. The predominance of male teachers, a number of whom were single, made a social evening with a large group of eager mothers highly desirable.

By the time their sons attended St Cuthbert's, many of the women had been married for years and some of the marriages had grown a little stale. Chatting to a young male teacher in a kilt or an army uniform, depending on the occasion, was titillating. Mind you, the tension in the car going home afterwards was often chilly.

He remembered a cocktail party at the beginning of one year to welcome new staff. When the new female teachers entered the function together, some of the fathers, pathetic in their eagerness, rushed to get them drinks and those who had left their run a little late, circled, waiting to step in the moment one of the attendees vacated the group.

Over the years, Jim had seen the slow disintegration of some marriages. Couples turned up to school gatherings to put on a show of togetherness for the sake of their sons, but after a couple of drinks it was clear that they preferred to socialise separately, their body language hinting at emotional isolation. They were merely keeping up

221

appearances as the only real bond they had was the son, or sons, at the school.

Also, they wanted, for a short while, to enjoy the sense of community and belonging that the school provided. For a few hours, they could pretend that everything was normal; the rugby grand-final, the cadet camp, the HSC, the coming excursion to New Zealand. These topics shielded them from the reality at home and the worse-case scenario of how to tell their son that he would soon be a product of yet another divorce.

'Do you ever remember Bentley taking anyone with him to the school dos?' Daphne asked, sensing that Jim's attention had wandered.

'Pardon?'

'Bentley. Did he ever have a guest with him at the school social occasions?' she repeated.

Jim thought for a minute. 'I don't remember. Do you?' he asked smoothing down his tie.

'No. He seemed too preoccupied with fawning over the wealthy and well-connected parents. And, of course, entertaining his entourage of followers,' Daphne said with a rise of her well-defined eyebrows.

Jim Cameron didn't bother to respond, knowing full well what she meant. The two sat silently. Nothing seemed to be making sense. They both wanted the situation to be resolved but it wasn't because either of them had any sense of loss for their colleague, it was because everything seemed so unbelievable.

When Daphne returned to her office the phone was ringing. The number that lit up on the handset showed it wasn't the headmaster's extension. She picked up the receiver. 'St Cuthbert's. Daphne Withers speaking.'

As she listened her face brightened but she hesitated before speaking. 'A drink tonight? Ooooh. That would be nice. No need to pick me up. I'll meet you there. I know the pub. 7ish. Which bar? Lovely. Okay.'

She replaced the receiver, smiling self-consciously. He'd finally had the courage to ask her. Was it the right thing to do? Oh, bugger it. A bit of fun wouldn't go astray in this time of stress. Daphne rummaged through her handbag and pulled out her compact. Her face reflected the pleasure she felt. She still had it.

THE DATE

Sergeant O'Shea, dressed in jeans, check shirt and a jacket, waited nervously in the bar nearest to the entrance of the pub.

It was busy despite being mid-week. He'd bought a midi as he didn't want to look as if he had already been drinking copiously before she arrived. He lit a cigarette quickly and sucked deeply. Did Mrs Withers smoke? He hoped she did. A post coital cigarette was a real pleasure and he imagined lying next to her after a session of unbridled sex, the two of them puffing indulgently in the sweaty sheets.

He was about to light another when he spotted Daphne walking through the entrance. His stomach lurched at the sight of her. She was wearing a light blue, close fitting ribbed knitted top and a tight short black skirt with sheer stockings and stilettos. Her blonde hair flicked out slightly at the shoulders.

She had retained the fashion of the 1960s without making it seem incongruous in the current era of bold colours and shoulder pads. Her age flicked across his mind. It was obvious that she was older than him, she had two kids, but she was so hot. He'd wondered many times about the age difference but even he knew better than to ask a woman her age. Weight and age were two forbidden topics according to his mother.

Ray stood up quickly, fumbling to put down his drink without knocking it over and signalled to her, his other hand automatically checking that his fly was done up. He stopped, embarrassed, hoping to God that she hadn't seen him do that, and went to shake her hand when she reached his table.

For fuck's sake, he thought, she's not a bloke. Daphne, sensing his discomfort, shook his hand and then stood on tiptoes to give him a kiss on the cheek. Their heads collided.

'Oh shit, I'm so sorry,' the sergeant groaned. This was a disaster. He shouldn't have asked her out. She was way out of his league.

'It's fine. How about you get me a drink? I'll have a glass of bubbly, please,' she instructed and sat down at the small table. Daphne watched him wend his way through the drinkers to the bar.

Poor man, she thought. Don't think he's done this before. Or at least, not with someone older than twenty.

Ray returned carrying the drinks and gingerly placed the champagne in front of Daphne. He was going to buy champagne for himself as well but then thought that maybe it would make him look a bit feminine. Champagne was a girly drink. Only poofters drank it. For God's sake stop thinking like that. Stone had already told him off for having such prejudices. Maybe Daphne liked queers. Gays.

Whatever the politically correct term was now. Women seemed to these days. Better be careful how to talk about Shute. If he came up in conversation.

He grabbed the cigarette he'd been about to light before Daphne arrived and lit it urgently then realised that he had not offered her one. Things were getting worse. Where were his manners?

'Would you like one?' he asked, fumbling with the packet, and holding it open to her.

Daphne pulled one out of the packet and waited for him to light it for her. Ray flicked the unwilling lighter a couple of times and finally, she was able to draw on her cigarette. They looked at each other and laughed. The sergeant felt his inadequacy drain away and he leant back in his chair.

The conversation veered around inconsequential subjects, neither of them wanting to be the first to bring up the murder.

O'Shea was conscious that technically he shouldn't discuss it and Daphne not wanting to appear nosey.

Another round of drinks was bought and then another. The noise in the bar was getting louder as more drinkers arrived and with the alcohol kicking in, it lubricated the chat up lines and responses. Women were flicking their hair at admirers and laughing appreciatively at the comments potential suitors were making.

Daphne and Ray nudged closer to each other in an effort to hear what the other was saying. Daphne, conscious of Ray's buying all the drinks, offered to buy the next one on her way back from 'powdering her nose'.

She found the Ladies and noted that for such a large pub there was the usual lack of female facilities. Older pubs often had few toilets for women, harking back to the days when a hotel was a male domain.

There was the usual queue and the girls chattered about their desperation to go and the typical shortage of loos. Finally, an empty cubicle became available much to Daphne's relief. The strength of her pelvic floor certainly wasn't what it was since the birth of her two children. She'd always meant to do the exercises but somehow hadn't got around to it.

The moment of quiet made her think about what was happening. Did she really fancy this man or was she flattered because he was younger? Was it worth wasting her time on someone with whom there may be no future? But then, shouldn't she just enjoy the moment? She found Ray a lot more attractive than men of her age or older. As men aged, they seemed to become beige in manner and appearance.

Daphne made her way back to the table with the drinks. Ray's relief clearly visible. 'Wondered if you'd gone home,' he said.

'Why would I do that?' Daphne asked with a smile on her face. 'I have a uni student who lives at my place and she babysits when I need her. They're not quite old enough to be left alone yet.' She stopped talking, worried that she sounded too much like a mother. '*And* I am enjoying myself.'

Ray reached out and took her hand. 'So am I,' he said squeezing it and leant in to kiss her quickly on the cheek.

'Shall we finish these and go?' Mrs Withers suggested, leaving her hand in his but seeing his confusion and disappointment, added, 'Your place?'

The post coital cigarettes were the bliss of the anticipated ending to what O'Shea believed was the best sex he'd ever had. There was nothing like an older woman who knew what she was doing and what she wanted. Daphne didn't have the hang-ups of younger women who fretted about their body or if performing certain acts was wrong.

The words from Rod Stewart's *Maggie May* looped through his head. He hoped for the 'morning sun to really show her age' as that certainly didn't bother him and how wonderful it would be if she stayed the whole night. He was already imagining their next meeting even though it was only a matter of minutes since their session had climaxed.

While Ray went back to the kitchen to pour them another drink, a beer for him, a red wine for her, Daphne lay back thinking about Bentley. Had he had a relationship that had gone wrong or was his malicious gossip the reason for someone to kill him? What about Sue Armstrong? She was married, and, she had a position of responsibility at the school so

Bentley's constant rumour-mongering about her and the student gave Sue a motive to want rid of him. But she came across as a nice woman and the student had always behaved well. It seemed highly unlikely for them to take such drastic action. Yet, in TV shows it was often the least suspected who were the murderers. Or was it a double bluff where the obvious was so obvious it was disregarded? And what about Graham Russell or a boy at school who had an unrequited crush, or a colleague who was anti-gay? The possibilities seemed endless.

Her thoughts were interrupted by Ray's return and she took the wine held out to her. Daphne, smiling her thanks, pulled the bed covers back so that he could slide in next to her.

WHERE IS BENTLEY?

While Daphne and Ray sipped their drinks, languishing in the afterglow, Graham Russell walked glumly down Oxford Street, peering in the windows of various bars. He could see groups of men drinking and laughing. Music drifted out into the street; Gloria Gaynor or Helen Reddy pleading the rights of women.

Finally, he entered a dark doorway and walked up the stairs into a smallish, intimate room with views over Oxford Street and Taylor Square, the clientele predominantly male. He could make out a couple of men at a high table entwined, their moustaches blending together. A tender picture. He ordered a drink from the barmaid, Jess, whose tattoos could be seen on slender white arms, her tea towel tucked into the back of her tight black jeans.

There was a vacant seat at the end of a long table and he eased himself onto it, while glancing quickly around the bar. He didn't really expect to see anyone he knew but there was always a chance of meeting a familiar face in the tight gay community. Gays stuck together not just to mingle and pick up, but for safety. Despite a more liberal attitude prevailing, tourists from less open-minded suburbs still came hoping to bash a queer.

He couldn't help but stare at the two men passionately kissing. They were sitting in the same seats where he and Bentley had sat after their eyes had met across the pulsating testosterone ridden room. Graham lowered his eyes after sensing the two men had noticed his interest. He didn't want to be asked to join them. He'd never been one for group sex. Why hadn't Bentley got back to him? Something wasn't right. He didn't fully believe that woman's explanation and she'd seemed thrown by his appearance. Winter, Withers, or whatever her name was, certainly wouldn't win prizes for lying.

His journalist's intuition told him that something was fishy. Bentley had always met him when they arranged a date. Even if he'd had a school function, he'd come as soon as he could after it had finished.

Surely his judgement of Bentley wasn't wrong. He was positive that they were both committed to their relationship. But he'd been wrong before. How well could you know a person? The world was full of people who were shocked and dismayed by the realisation that their partner had been deceiving them.

Bentley had been an entertaining although complex partner. His stories of the school and its occupants constantly amused them both. He loved the way Bentley could manipulate the attitudes of his colleagues and some of the boys. It reminded him of how as a journalist he could force his opinions onto readers and twist their thinking. He chuckled

231

inwardly. So much for an unbiased and objective press. His paper was one that could influence the outcome of an election. A bit of dirt about a politician, fact or fiction, stuck and a political party which once held the majority was kicked out. He loved the power of his reporting and his paper had no qualms about printing misrepresentations of the 'truth'. His stint working for *The Sun* in London had taught him well.

Graham downed the dregs of his drink and walked back to the barmaid. She knew both him and Bentley as she'd worked here for at least a year, a long time for bar staff. Perhaps she'd seen Bentley. He ordered another Heineken and leant against the bar waiting till she gave him his change.

'Just wondered if Bentley's been in lately?' he asked, trying to sound noncommittal. Jess was friendly but protective of her customers and he didn't want to put her offside by sounding like a policeman or a possessive boyfriend.

Jess thought for a minute. 'No, not recently. Not since the last time you were both in here. When was that? About three weeks ago?'

Graham nodded, impressed by her memory. They'd been here on a Saturday night to celebrate their anniversary of one year together and their good mood was heightened by the E's they'd taken earlier. The whole bar seemed to find their mutual enjoyment contagious and the evening had been one of sexual frisson and anticipation on everyone's part. Bentley's humour, albeit extremely bitchy, ensured they were the centre of attention.

Later, the two wove their way arm in arm back to his unit in Surry Hills, but once inside and away from the exhilarating atmosphere of the pub, Bentley's ebullient mood had drained away. Bentley, lucid because of the drugs and yet drunk, recounted his concern about the death of the student on the recent excursion. His suppressed memories of the tragedy were unleashed, and he lurched determinedly through the events of that day.

Graham tried to veer the conversation away from the subject, but Bentley had gone on and on and on. Although he was not held responsible for the accident, he was angry with one of the other teachers who'd been on the school trip. Some guy called Addington. Apparently, they still socialized when there was the buffer of other teachers in attendance, but their relationship had cooled somewhat.

Bentley's reaction to the boy's death shocked Graham. Obviously, the death was extremely upsetting but it was unusual for him to be obsessive about past events and what others thought about him. Normally, Bentley couldn't care less about public opinion and he positively thrived on the power of his gossip. It was hard to equate the emotive response to the boy's death with his usual dismissive and careless attitude to others' feelings.

Graham did not particularly admire F. Scott Fitzgerald as a writer, but his use of the word careless was appropriate in relation to Bentley.

Perhaps Bentley had been in love with the student, or at least in lust. Not surprising, as teenage boys were in their prime.

The suggestion that he write an article about school responsibility and the dangerous position students were placed in on excursions, did not appeal to Bentley. It wasn't just because of his loyalty to the school but as a teacher he genuinely believed that students needed to be put out of their comfort zones, especially those from protective families with parents who mollycoddled their sons.

Attending the occasional school sporting events with Bentley had been fun. Like naughty schoolboys, they relished the secrecy and naughtiness of the pretence that they were merely friends from university days. However, Benty considered it was too risky for him to accompany him to more formal social functions. Even if some of the staff had their suspicions that he was gay, it wasn't advisable to push the relationship under their noses.

Although Graham had bowed to Bentley's wishes about not writing the article, he was still storing the idea in his head and soon he was going to write it. However, he couldn't think about that now. He had to find Bentley and learn the truth.

THE MORNING AFTER

The next morning, Daphne was busy putting her makeup on in the bathroom of her own home. She carefully applied eye shadow, eyeliner and blush. Ray would no doubt be at the school today and she wanted to look her best. Despite Ray's constant asking, she hadn't wanted to stay the whole night, as there was nothing worse than waking up in the morning with smudged makeup and messy hair. That could come later. It was too soon to be sharing bathroom intimacies. She had no desire to hear Ray doing a wee or God forbid, a fart.

Meanwhile, Sue chivied the kids into their seats, buckled them in, threw small, colourful backpacks filled with lunches and changes of clothes on to the front seat but before starting the car peered at the rear vision mirror and put on lipstick. She'd apply mascara once she'd got to school if she had a spare minute.

George packed his rugby kit, threw his books in his bag, yelled to his mother who was busy in the kitchen before she went to work in the family milk bar, that he'd be late home as he had practice after school and rushed out the door, slamming it shut behind him.

Ray O'Shea and Detective Stone, using their portable shavers, sat in an unmarked police car parked near the school, with paper cups of coffee positioned precariously on their knees, while two Bacon and Egg MacMuffins, still in the wrappers, were waiting to be eaten.

Michael Parker slowly packed his school bag and after eating a bowl of cornflakes, kissed his mother goodbye. He walked around to the shed behind the house, wheeled out his bike and rode off to school.

The boarders, including Matthews, Judd, and Sutton, showered, tormented each other with wet flicks from towels, put on school uniforms then meandered across the Oval to the boarders' dining room where they ate the usual breakfast of cereal, toast and vegemite. Some grabbed the fruit from a large box placed near the door as they returned to the boarding house to pick up the books needed for the day.

Graham Russell didn't bother to shave. George Michael had made it fashionable to have a three-day growth. He pulled on his jeans, navy blue shirt and boots and walked across the road to his regular coffee shop. He ordered a latte to have with a croissant, shared opinions with the barista about the political events of the last few days, returned home to pick up his car and headed off to work.

Gary, Brian, Marlene, Ian, and Rodney completed their ablutions, and each with a degree of reluctance to face each other, dressed and prepared themselves for another school day. All were wary of the atmosphere of incrimination at the school. The once easy conversations were now short and careful. A murderer could be amongst them and none of them wanted to inadvertently associate themselves with whomever that was. The Friday drinks at the local yacht club down the road were currently postponed.

Whether on foot, bike or by car, the road up to the school, past the walled houses with long private driveways, was full of students, parents, and teachers, all ruled by the bell.

Jim parked his car, unaware that Stone and O'Shea were sitting nearby watching the arrivals, and he made his way up the street towards his office in the school Old Block.

Stone held his cigarette to his lips, took a drag, and as the smoke curled out of his mouth, asked Sergeant O'Shea what he felt about Mr Cameron.

O'Shea's eyes followed the man as he walked briskly along the footpath. 'Why ask me? You know him better than I do. You must have a good idea what he's like.'

'Yes, but it was a long time ago and I want a different perspective. I don't want my judgement clouded by past events.'

'Fair enough.' The sergeant thought for a minute before he said, 'Seems a decent bloke. Fought in Vietnam from what I've heard. He seems to be doing all he can to help us. Not like the headmaster. Bit hard to fathom. Surprised he's the head. Cameron seems a better choice.'

237

Stone nodded. 'I agree. Maybe it's because Jim has an Asian wife. Aussies can be pretty racist.'

O'Shea didn't comment. Bloody Kiwis making judgements.

Jim entered the school by the steps down from the street and he soon disappeared through the double doors. More four-wheel drives stopped in the road, discharging their passengers.

As boarders, Judd and Sutton had no mothers to drop them off and they made their way one behind the other, down from the boarding house that was on a rise behind the school. They walked slowly across the grass to the footpath which led to the school entrance.

O'Shea nudged Stone and they watched the two boys. Sutton, a few steps ahead of Judd, appeared to be ignoring his mate but as they neared the entrance he slowed, allowing Judd to catch up. Sutton said something urgently, their heads almost touching. Judd stepped back and waited till Sutton had gone inside the building, then resumed his entry to the school.

'They don't seem very happy,' O'Shea observed.

'They certainly don't,' Stone replied. 'I don't like either of them. Two little boys who are up their own arses. 'Specially that Sutton.'

Neither of the policemen had noticed Mrs Withers pulling up in her car and parking on the opposite side of the street in the staff car park. She got out of the car after a quick peek in the rear-view mirror then retrieved her handbag from the passenger seat.

Stone's head swivelled to see more of the arrivals and grinned when he spotted Daphne walking quickly towards the main entrance.

'Oi oi. Look who's just arrived. She's a bit late. Isn't she usually the first one to arrive? Get the school up and running.'

O'Shea quickly turned his head to see Daphne, his colour rising but he didn't speak.

'Wonder if she had a big night. Slept in perhaps?' Stone stressed slyly.

'Wouldn't know,' O'Shea muttered.

Stone was about to speak but changed his mind. What O'Shea did in his own time wasn't his business but shagging a possible suspect was a bit dicey. It might jeopardise the investigation but then who was he to get in the way of romance? And anyway, perhaps he'd imagined O'Shea's attraction to Daphne. Would Daphne really want to date someone like Ray, someone limited in his philosophy of life, someone with a bit of a chip on his shoulder about those from other backgrounds, especially the more educated and wealthier?

'Well, this won't buy the baby a new bonnet,' Stone said as he snuffed out his cigarette in the car's ashtray.

239

O'Shea faced him with a puzzled expression. 'What the hell does that mean?' he asked.

'My father used to say it. Means we'd better get cracking,' Stone explained patiently.

O'Shea shook his head in disbelief. 'Mate, you come out with the oddest things.'

The two men got out of the car and joined the throng entering the school.

MARLENE

The Geography teacher sat stiffly on the chair in front of the detective's desk, her arms still folded. A flicker of disapproval crossed Sergeant O'Shea's face. What did this woman have that was worth protecting? Her tits didn't compare to Daphne's. What was it about Miss Bates that was so unattractive? She had reasonably pleasant features, hazel eyes and wavy brown hair but her expression was one of suspicion and her manner, defensive. O'Shea noticed that she seemed to find it hard to meet Detective Stone's eyes.

'I gather that you were a good friend of Mr Shute's?' Stone asked in a friendly tone.

Marlene shrugged her shoulders a little, the shoulder pads of her green jacket rising in unison and answered that she was.

'Did you know he was a homosexual?' the detective continued.

'Of course, I did. So, what?'

The detective stared at her. 'Well, it seems that some of his colleagues didn't.'

Marlene stared back. 'They might have known. But it was something we never talked about.' Her face took on a possessive look. 'It didn't matter to me. I understood Benty.'

'Maybe it didn't matter to you, but do you think it would to some of the men? Being at a boys' school, he probably didn't want the staff to know. Or the boys.' Stone waited for a few seconds. 'Do you think some of the teachers would have been worried if they'd known that he was gay?'

Marlene frowned at Stone and tightened the grip across her chest. 'No. It didn't matter. And anyway, if it did, it was because they were more worried about themselves. Their reputation.'

'What do you mean?' both men asked at the same time, causing Stone to flick a warning glance at the sergeant.

'Nothing,' Marlene snapped.

Stone and O'Shea waited. Her annoyance was obvious. They couldn't decipher whether she was angry with her male colleagues or for opening up to them. She clamped her mouth shut and hoicked at her breasts with her crossed arms.

'Miss Bates, we know this is difficult for you and that Mr Shute was a good friend, but we do need to find out who killed him. Can you think of anyone who could have hated him enough to do that?'

Stone leaned forward in his chair to stress his words. Marlene's eyes flicked around the room then her facial muscles softened slightly and the grip on her chest loosened.

'He was a good friend, especially as it wasn't easy for me in the beginning. Being one of the few women teachers. He was very supportive.'

'I gather he wasn't always as supportive of some of the other female members of staff,' Stone suggested carefully.

'Yeah, well, they made it hard for themselves.'

'How?'

Marlene stared dismissively at the detective and swivelled her head to include Sergeant O'Shea.

'Some of them like the attention of the boys and the staff. It's pathetic.' Her arms again protected her breasts, her jealousy masked as disapproval. Her lips tightened into a thin line. 'Some women are just on an ego trip.'

Silence settled over the room with both men aware that Marlene saw herself at a disadvantage against the other more attractive women teachers. Her emphasis on what she stated as weakness only highlighted her own. Stone straightened the manila folder on his desk and placed it parallel to the square glass ashtray.

He waited before raising his eyes and asked again, 'Miss Bates. Can you think of anyone who wanted to hurt Mr Shute? Was there anyone who hated him enough to kill him?'

Marlene vigorously shook her head. Her eyes had become bloodshot. Stone wondered if she were about to cry. She shook her head again as if to dislodge the thought that anyone could hate Bentley.

'I don't think so. I can't imagine any of the women having the strength to kill him. Poison maybe or with a gun, but...,' she tittered.

Her sudden change from possible tears to laughing, made Stone wonder about the stability of her mental state.

'What about the men?' Sergeant O'Shea asked quickly.

Marlene ran her fingers through her hair, pulling at a strand. 'I suppose some would be strong enough. But Bentley was so admired. I can't imagine any of the men wanting to hurt him.'

'The boys?'

'They loved him too. He was a great teacher. Entertaining. Knew his subject. Got good results,' she explained parrot-fashion. This was a recurring description of the dead teacher.

Stone subtly raised his eyebrows to O'Shea then added, 'Miss Bates, you certainly admired him.'

He gazed at the blackboard then turned back to face the Geography teacher. 'It may have been a crime of passion. It looks as if someone could have been in love with him.' He stopped, waiting for the suggestion to sink in. 'Were you, Miss Bates?'

Marlene's face pinched itself together and she glared at the detective. 'Of course, I wasn't. That's ridiculous.'

Sergeant O'Shea coughed slightly, the atmosphere in the room had cooled again. Detective Stone waited for Miss Bates' indignation to fade. 'I certainly didn't mean to upset you, Miss Bates. You must realise that we have to ask questions.'

She blinked quickly and again squeezed her bosom like a vice. Stone could see from the pursing of her mouth that she had something to say but he didn't want to push. Usually, most of those being questioned would volunteer information as the presence of the police commanded authority and obedience but Miss Bates didn't seem intimidated.

Aping the teacher, Stone sat back in his chair with his arms folded. O'Shea, watching, was reminded of his school days when two kids stared each other out till one blinked. Marlene loosened her grip, her jacket front springing back after being squashed for so long.

'No-one I know would want to hurt Bentley, although I wouldn't put it past Sue's, Mrs Armstrong's, student friend.' The sarcastic stress Miss Bates had placed on the word 'Mrs' was not lost on Stone or O'Shea.

'And who is that friend?' Stone asked, hoping not to sound equally sarcastic.

'George. George Stavrou. The Greek boy. In Year 12,' Marlene said, unable to keep the gloat out of her voice.

The two policemen gave each other a quick glance. This was not the student who'd been named previously. 'Does Mrs Armstrong have more than one admirer?' Detective Stone asked casually.

'We all have our admirers but not all of us do anything about it. Some of us don't need the ego boost,' Marlene stated smugly. 'She already has a husband, so I don't know why she has to be so greedy.'

'Are you married, Miss Bates? It's hard to tell these days by your title. What with Women's Liberation. And kids always seem to call women teachers, Miss. Not sure what to call people anymore,' Stone placated, hoping he hadn't put her completely offside.

'No. No, I'm not. I've got better things to do,' she replied tartly.

Not surprised. Miserable bitch, thought Ray O'Shea. She's not in the same league as Daphne, or Sue Armstrong for that matter.

'So, is it common practice for the teachers to have relationships with students?' Stone continued.

Marlene shrugged. 'Not really, but Sue is definitely going out with George. Has been for a while. Whole school knows.'

'Do they? Or was this relationship something that Mr Shute suggested?'

'Why would he do that if it wasn't true?' she asked the detective with disbelief in her voice.

'Well, I've gathered that Mr Shute, how can I put it, enjoyed a good gossip. Did he often talk about other teachers? Spread rumours? Say things which could have caused offence?'

Marlene waggled her head. 'No, no. Not really. Just the usual staffroom talk. It was sometimes about Sue and George. He made the odd comment about the other women teachers, but he really didn't like Sue.'

'Why? What could have given him cause for such dislike?' Stone asked. Marlene's acceptance of Shute's opinions and gossip was staggering.

'I suppose Bentley could see that she was trying to win favour. Sue turns up to the school demanding attention. She went out of her way to make the boys like her,' she paused then continued self-righteously. 'And a lot of the men. She's married. It's not the swinging '60s anymore. It's the 1980s. She should know better.'

The two men couldn't help but glance at each other, her vitriol so obvious.

'Mrs Armstrong created a lot of jealousy then?' O'Shea asked quietly. 'And you're sure she's having a relationship with a student. This George Stavrou.'

The teacher gave him a withering stare. 'Of course she is.'

'Because Bentley said so,' Sergeant O'Shea stated. Her gullibility was embarrassing.

Stone broke in. 'Has anyone ever seen them together?'

'No. But why would Bentley make it up? They must meet in secret. They'd hardly be going out in public. Far too risky,' Marlene justified knowingly. 'And he was always hanging around outside the staffroom.'

The policemen raised their eyebrows at her logic. She seemed determined to believe everything Shute had said.

'Do you think that Mrs Armstrong and her 'boyfriend' had reason to kill Mr Shute?' Stone asked, more to see what her reaction would be than to hear anything reliable.

'It's possible. Wouldn't put anything past her or her boyfriend,' Marlene responded.

'That's a very strong reaction, Miss Bates,' Stone said.

O'Shea frowned. The woman sounded mad.

'Well, stranger things have happened,' Marlene said. She glared at the detective as if to question him.

'You've obviously given this a lot of thought, Miss Bates. We value your observations greatly, but we'd better let you get back to work.' Stone felt he could get no further with his questioning. He made to stand up but changed his mind and sat down again.

'Just one more question, Miss Bates. Where were you on the night Mr Shute was murdered?'

Marlene's face paled. Her aggressive demeanour shrivelled and Stone wondered if she were about to cry.

'I don't mean to upset you, but we have to ask everyone where they were that night,' Stone consoled. He found her sudden change puzzling. She'd seemed so confident before and now so vulnerable. They waited for her answer.

Marlene pulled a tissue out of her sleeve and rubbed her nose vigorously. Was she playing for time?

'I was...,' she stopped speaking to blow her nose. 'I was at home after going to watch the game. The

Firsts played at 3.15,' she explained as if they had no idea about how the private schools and their games were timed.

'And can anyone vouch for that?' Stone asked.

Marlene wiped her nose and pushed the tissue back up her sleeve. 'I live by myself, but my neighbour saw me drive back. You can ask her. I got home about 6.'

'Can you tell me her name and address? That would be helpful. As I said, we're asking everyone where they were. Nothing to worry about,' Stone reassured.

The teacher gave the neighbour's name and an address in Maroubra. O'Shea quickly wrote down the details.

This time Stone did stand up. He thanked the teacher and led Marlene to the door, shutting it carefully once she'd left the room.

'Bloody hell. That was hard going,' Stone sighed. 'She's obviously no fan of Mrs Armstrong's and she seemed to believe every word that came out of Shute's mouth. However, we do need to have a chat to this George boy,' he said as he walked back to his desk. 'And, and it's a big 'and', why has Shute named more than one boy supposedly 'going out' with Mrs Armstrong?' He grimaced at his use of the adolescent term.

'It looks like our mate was really trying to paint her as a bit of a tart,' O'Shea said as he gazed around the classroom. Its lack of colour was stultifying. Thank God there was at least a window which let in natural light and had a bit of a view. 'Did he like stirring the pot? Didn't care about the consequences of his gossip. Or did he tell a different story just to give himself a kick? A pathological liar?'

'I've no idea, but it does seem odd that he said there were two boys. It would make the story harder to believe. One is feasible, but surely, only someone who got their jollies thinking about such a thing would accept she'd be having it off with two boys.'

Stone leant back in his chair, peering at the ceiling. It was bad enough dealing with a murder, but the school seemed full of strange personalities whose honesty and reliability were in doubt. Apart from Jim was anyone telling the truth.

O'Shea wandered over to the chair vacated by the teacher and sat down. 'I'm not convinced by Miss Bates' story,' he said, stressing the Miss. 'Is she that gullible to believe everything Shute told her? I wonder if Shute was actually the one who was gullible. Maybe someone started the rumour about Mrs Armstrong and George knowing that Bentley would lap it up and continue spreading it.

'Mrs Armstrong has a guilty secret, which is now exposed and so it would seem she had every reason to want Bentley silenced. Perhaps whoever killed Bentley wanted to establish her motive beforehand. Sue had a reason to hate Shute because he'd gossiped about their affair, therefore she and George killed him. The killer would know that this is the assumption. Her 'guilt' has already been established.'

'But what about the other boy? Surely, it didn't include him as well. It all seems so far-fetched,' Stone said in disbelief.

'I get the impression that Bentley, with that fucking stupid name, would say anything to get attention. Pull any boy's name out of the hat to cause a stir. It's like he had to know everything about everyone, even if it wasn't actually true,' O'Shea stated, his disapproval of the dead man all too clear.

Stone listened intently, his head nodding more vigorously as O'Shea continued his explanation.

When the sergeant slowed, Stone jumped in.

'Could Sue have done something to someone who wants revenge? Our Miss Bates said Sue is very popular with the men and the boys. So, did someone have a huge crush on Sue, but she rejected him? Hell, hath no fury like a man, in this case, scorned.'

O'Shea smirked at his boss's choice of expression.

'Love can make people do stupid things.'

'You're not wrong,' Stone agreed, looking O'Shea straight in the eye.

MR ADDINGTON

After a phone call to the main staffroom, Daphne left a message for Rodney Addington and within a few minutes there was a firm knock on the door to her office and without waiting to be asked, the teacher hurried in.

'You wanted to see me, Mrs Withers?'

'Oh. Hello, Rodney. No. Not me. The police. They're in Room 36. Their little office while they're investigating. They asked to see those who were closest to Bentley. And other people of course,' she added after seeing the concern on Addington's face.

'Right. Right. Of course,' Rodney muttered. 'Room 36?'

Daphne repeated the number and Rodney strode out of the room. He walked down the empty corridor till he came to Room 36 and rapped sharply on the door.

Sergeant O'Shea opened the door slowly, almost as if he were going to suddenly swing it back and shout peek a boo. He resisted the urge and signalled for Rodney Addington to come into the room.

'I gather you've asked to see me,' Addington demanded rather than questioned as O'Shea stepped aside to make room for the teacher to enter. Addington marched briskly up to Detective Stone's desk and stood as if at attention.

'Good morning, Detective,' Addington barked, assuming that the man in the suit was the superior, while both Stone and O'Shea wondered if he were going to salute. Stone nearly told him to stand at ease but thought better of it, instead indicating for him to sit down.

'How can I be of assistance?' Addington asked after positioning himself carefully onto the chair. He undid the bottom button of his jacket and smoothed his tie.

'Thank you for coming,' Stone answered firmly, deflecting Addington's attempt at taking control.

'We're talking to those closest to Mr Shute. We're hoping someone can shed some light on who could have killed him and why.'

'Dreadful business. Good man, Bentley. God knows why anyone would want to hurt him,' Addington puzzled, plucking at his bristly moustache with thumb and forefinger.

'Yes. It's certainly a mystery. Bit of a whodunnit,' suggested Stone.

Addington wasn't sure whether to laugh or not so decided against it while Stone felt he'd better get to the matter at hand. 'You were good mates with Mr Shute,' Stone stated rather than questioned.

Rodney Addington shifted a little in his seat and answered that they had been friends although he was not as close to him as some others.

'Oh? I'd gathered that you and he were good friends,' Stone stressed again, noticing that Addington's face had reddened slightly.

'Well, yes,' he replied, his hand returning to his moustache. 'We were, but not so much of late.'

'Why was that?'

The discomfort the teacher felt was clear but the police were the police and one should follow the rule of law. Addington coughed; his hand fisted to block any spray. 'After the excursion things were a bit strained between us.'

'The accident with the student?' O'Shea chipped in.

Addington turned his head quickly to stare at the sergeant. 'Yes, the accident.'

'Why did that affect your relationship?' Stone continued. 'It was an accident after all.'

'Of course it was, but Bentley took it badly and as we were the two masters in charge, we couldn't help but feel re...' his explanation tailed off, then he started again. 'It made us a little uncomfortable with each other. There was nothing we could have done. It was a freak accident but seeing each other reminded us about what had happened.'

'Understandable,' Stone comforted. 'The boy drowned.'

'Yes. Terrible. Terrible,' Addington confirmed.

'Did you feel that you were responsible, even though it wasn't your fault?' the detective asked.

'No. No,' Addington replied, his face grim.

'Mr Shute?' Stone continued.

Addington tugged at his tie. 'No. No. But…'

'But?'

'I can't really say.' Addington pulled his shoulders back indicating that he couldn't continue.

Stone thought it wise to change the subject and asked if Mr Addington was aware if Mr Shute had any enemies, to which he replied that he couldn't really think of any.

'Not even those who bore the brunt of his gossip?' Stone asked.

'Well, she deserved it,' Addington almost snarled, unsettled by the change in questioning. His manner defensive.

'Who? Deserved what?' Stone jumped in.

'The gossip. Mrs Armstrong,' Rodney Addington answered as he fiddled with his tie. 'How can I put this nicely? She's a bit of a slut, if you'll excuse the term, so it's not surprising people gossip.'

'That's a bit harsh,' O'Shea cut in.

'Well, you must have heard the talk. Going out with Mike. What's his name? Boy in the Sixth Form. Year 12,' he corrected himself.

'Mike? But what about…?' O'Shea stopped himself after seeing Stone's warning look.

'Mr Addington. Do you think that some members of the staff were jealous of the fact that Mrs Armstrong was made a housemaster even though she hadn't been at the school very long?' Stone asked.

'Damn silly idea making a woman a housemaster. Doesn't have the right control. You have to have the respect of the boys. The boys only like her because they...she's...,' he paused, his expression challenging any sympathy Stone and O'Shea may have had for Sue. 'You know.'

'Know what?' both men asked.

Addington shook his head and closed his mouth firmly. Stone stood up and walked towards the window.

'Do you believe the position of housemaster should have been yours, Mr Addington?' he asked staring at the view.

Addington craned his neck to look at the detective. 'Well, no, but...,' and closed his mouth again.

Stone decided to change tack and as he walked back to his chair asked quietly, 'You knew that Mr Shute was a homosexual, didn't you?'

Addington laughed bitterly. 'That old chestnut. Some people used to say so but it's because they were jealous of him. Straight as a die.'

'But what if he had been? Would that have changed your relationship?' Stone asked.

'Of course not. I'm not prejudiced against queers,' Addington answered, turning his head from one man to the other as if expecting agreement in his use of the term but the blank expressions on their faces indicated that he hadn't won any favours with either of them.

'Mr Addington, good to see you have no prejudice against homosexuals. Attitudes *are* changing. People are becoming more accepting and tolerant,' the detective stated firmly as the teacher shifted uncomfortably on his chair not sure whether there was a reprimand in the words. 'However,' Stone continued, 'can you think of anyone on the staff who did have intolerant and outdated views about gay men?'

Addington shook his head again and fidgeted with the cuffs of his jacket. Was the detective being sarcastic? His conceit in his prejudices made him forget that his views were no longer as widespread as they had been.

The advent of the Sydney Mardi Gras in the last decade had begun a revolution in thinking but Addington and his type had been left behind. He'd had a sneaking suspicion that Bentley didn't bat for the same team but as long as he kept it to himself then he and the others in Bentley's circle could ignore the truth.

'When did you last see Mr Shute?' Stone asked, watching Addington closely to see his response to the implied accusation.

'At the staff meeting after school. On Friday,' he stopped speaking. 'Steady on. You're not assuming I had anything to do with this?'

'Just checking when Mr Shute was last seen by you and other members of staff,' Stone replied smoothly. 'How long was the staff meeting?'

'The usual. Finished about 5 then a few of us went down to our regular for a couple of drinks. Normal practice,' Addington answered.

'Was Mr Shute with you?' Sergeant O'Shea butted in.

Addington glared at him with disapproval. He could tolerate questions from a detective but not from a sergeant. 'No. As a matter of fact he wasn't. On duty.'

O'Shea, sensing Addington's superior attitude, persevered with his questioning, 'Duty doing what?'

'In the boarding house. Overseeing prep,' Addington answered, his tone implying that anyone who'd been to a private school would know full well the procedure.

'Ah. Is that how it works?' O'Shea responded trying to keep his sarcasm to a minimum.

'So, if Mr Shute didn't go for a drink with you after the meeting, who did?' Stone enquired.

'Me. Gary, Miss Bates, Ian.' Addington thought for a few seconds. 'And Brian. Oh, and Don popped in for a quick one. Didn't stay long.'

'So not everyone goes? Just a select few?' Stone observed.

'Yes. Well. There are some people,' Addington paused. The policemen waited for him to explain.

'Some members of staff you don't want to have a drink with. You know how it is. Can't always get on with everybody.'

'No. Of course not,' Stone agreed politely. 'So, you didn't ask Mrs Armstrong, or Ms Bartoli, or Mrs Cutler to join you?'

'Oh no. They only come when it's a full staff function.'

'The staff sounds quite divided,' Sergeant O'Shea pointed out. Mr Addington shrugged.

'How do those who are not included in the Friday drinks feel about being left out?' Stone asked.

'No idea.'

'And it was Mr Shute who decided who went to the drinks?'

Addington shifted slightly in his seat. 'No. It was just accepted that only certain staff members would be included.'

The detective scribbled on the sheet of paper in his manila folder. Addington watched carefully.

'The women have families and other commitments,' he blustered.

'But Miss Bates was included,' Stone countered.

'Well, she's not...,' Addington began.

'Not what?' the two policemen asked together. In another situation they would have laughed, but not now.

'Look here. I don't want to be critical of Marlene.'

'But?'

Addington moved his bottom again. 'She's a good woman, but I would prefer to go for drinks with just the men. The conversation changes when there's women around.'

Stone nodded in encouragement. Addington sensing agreement, continued, 'Marlene has a few

259

issues. Not married and no-one on the horizon. She can be a bit of a… how can I put it? A bit painful. Seems obsessed with Bentley. All a bit odd. Makes it uncomfortable. I can't be doing with romantic nonsense and Bentley had no time for that either.'

'Nothing to do with his being a homosexual?' Stone asked.

'Look. He wasn't. I wish people would stop going on about it.'

'I'm sorry to go on about it, as you put it, but Mr Shute was a homosexual,' the detective stressed hoping that his assertion was one hundred percent true. 'Was it the boy's death that caused a rift between you or that you didn't like his sexuality?'

The teacher's lips tightened. 'I really can't help you any more with your investigation. There's nothing to add. I'd better get on. Work to do.'

The three sat in silence. Stone realised that he wasn't going to get much more out of Rodney Addington. This man obviously had an issue with the idea that Bentley was a homosexual. It wasn't clear whether Addington believed it or refused to. Was the student's death on the excursion the real reason why the two of them felt uncomfortable in each other's company?

'Mr Addington,' Stone began, 'just one more question. Can you tell us where you were on Saturday night? The night Mr Shute was murdered.'

Colour drained from the teacher's face. He sat staring in disbelief at the detective. 'Murdered.

Murdered,' he repeated. 'What a terrible word. Dreadful.' Addington lent his head back with his eyes closed then with a sigh opened them and said, 'I just can't believe it. At a school like this.'

The room was quiet again as Stone and O'Shea waited to see if the teacher had anything more to say. 'Saturday?' Stone reminded him.

Addington lowered his gaze and rolled his shoulders in an attempt to compose himself. 'Yes. Of course. Saturday.'

'Yes, Saturday,' Stone repeated.

'I didn't go to the game. Normally do but didn't feel up to it. My wife can vouch for me. We stayed in. Wish I had gone. Maybe things would be different.'

The policemen looked at each other acknowledging that the interview was over. Stone stood up while O'Shea walked towards the door. Addington, following Stone's lead, stood up swiftly, smoothing the front of his jacket and straightened his back before leaving the room.

'Bloody hell,' sighed O'Shea once the door was shut. 'Even I'm shocked by the prejudice. Talk about old school.'

Sue Armstrong, at home after work, stood at the kitchen divide. The bubbly in the bottle was at a low ebb and the ashtray needed emptying. She lit another cigarette before dialling a number. She sipped at her drink and took a drag on the thin white cigarette while looking at the kitchen door to make sure it was closed.

'Hello. Hello,' Sue spoke, her hand cupped around the mouthpiece. 'How are you?' Her face brightened at the response to her question. 'This whole situation at school is awful,' she stated, tugging at her hair, pushing it behind her ears while she listened, 'I know. I know. We'll have to wait till things are sorted out.' Sue nodded her head in agreement at the response. 'It'll all be over soon.'

The grating noise of a key in the lock could be heard and with a hasty farewell, Sue hurriedly replaced the receiver and composed her face as the kitchen door opened.

NO PROGRESS

Stone sat at his desk in the police station reading the notes he'd made on the Shute investigation. It was quiet as most of the administration staff had left for the day. He read the facts and hypotheses about the case. He knew that the likelihood of there being any fingerprints on the Samurai sword was slim but as the murderer had so blatantly left the weapon at the scene of the crime, he wondered if this could be another tease. But as he'd predicted, there had been no fingerprints.

Shute's flat had been thoroughly dusted and the laborious task of taking the staff's prints had been underway for some time. The headmaster had called for any boy who'd visited Mr Shute's flat to come forward and this had resulted in a large number being checked. Perhaps the excitement of taking part in what seemed like an episode from *Magnum P.I.* encouraged the high number of fingerprint volunteers.

The flat had been searched from doorknob to bedstead, carpet to ceiling, but the sword was the only item that the police found that had any bearing on the case. Owing to Bentley's fastidious nature and the school cleaner, who owed him a favour, the number of fingerprints left behind by any visitor was minimal. The doorknob on the outside of the door was the most productive but the attempt to match them was proving a long process.

Stone wearily closed the folder, turned off the light in his office and left the building.

Jim stood in the kitchen of his home, sipping a glass of red wine while he related the latest developments in the investigation to Anh. The children had gone to bed. This was the calmest moment of the day.

After taking a large swig, as if to give him courage to say what was on his mind, Jim said, 'What worries me is that Sue did have a motive to kill Bentley.'

Anh put down her drink on the kitchen island and looked closely at her husband. 'You're not being influenced by what you've heard about her, are you?'

Jim stared into his drink. 'I hope not. But she was the one most victimised by Bentley. And if the gossip is true, George is a strong young man who could easily have had the strength to kill someone. If he's besotted by Sue, then perhaps he was willing to attack Bentley for her.'

Anh topped up Jim's drink and her own. 'Maybe it's not anyone at the school.'

He drank again before speaking, 'That reminds me. Did I tell you that a man came asking for Shute?'

'No. Who?'

'A man called Graham Russell and I rang Des and asked him if he's a journalist. Apparently, he is, but he also said he's a mate of Shute's. A bit coincidental that he turns up just after the murder.'

'His boyfriend?'

'Possibly. But I've never seen him.'

'Jim,' Anh said doubtfully. 'Do you really think anyone who's gay would take their partner to a school function? At a school like St Cuthbert's? They've only just accepted me, so can you imagine them accepting a gay partner?'

'No. No. You're right,' Jim said, putting his arm around his wife. 'But I accept you. You're the best thing that ever happened. Sounds like a song,' he said laughing.

'Silly man,' Anh responded, running her hand gently up and down his arm.

'In some ways I am being silly,' Jim responded, staring at his wife. 'I hate the thought that it could be Sue. Others like Addington and the rest of Shute's cronies, I don't really care about, but I do like her. It wouldn't really bother me if any of them lost their job, but if Sue did, I'd be jolly upset. Surely, she'd realise the danger to her career and her family.'

'I'm sure she would,' Anh comforted and with a sly grin asked how much he liked Sue. 'Not too much, I hope,' Anh said.

'Nooo. It's just awful the way she's been picked on. And it's one of those situations that is very difficult to control. Most teachers gossip a bit, so it's hard to single out one person and tell them to stop.'

265

Anh sipped her wine before making another suggestion. 'Well, what about the men on the staff who don't like gays?' she asked. She could see Jim weighing up what she'd said, then added, 'And what about the parents of the boy who drowned on the excursion. They must be very upset with Bentley and Rodney.'

'Good point. The Sinclairs lost their only son. Imagine how we would feel if anything happened to our boys? But would they be upset enough to commit murder?'

'Grief can make people do things never thought possible,' Anh stated, peering into her glass. 'It would be unbearable. To lose the most precious possession.'

All Jim could do was nod grimly. He knew what Anh had been through during the war, the loss of family members to the Viet Cong, the suffering and the devastation.

YES OR NO?

The following school day began as normal. Roll call, two classes, morning break, two classes, lunchtime.

Jim wandered onto the staffroom balcony after the bell had rung for lunch and leant his elbows on the railing, gazing across the Oval to the sea beyond. He could see cars parked in the street that curled around the school grounds and the large houses that profited well from the view. Boys, some running, some ambling, made their way onto the Oval or to the dining hall to eat their lunch.

A splash of colour amongst the khaki uniforms drew Jim's attention. It was Sue Armstrong. What was she doing? Where was she going? She walked quickly along the edge of the Oval and strode up the grass path to the street full of parked cars. She climbed into an older model Toyota and drove away.

He was about to return to the staffroom when George could be spotted coming from the back of the classroom block, heading down the same street.

The boy looked at a few of the cars, then unlocked the door of one, a somewhat dishevelled Ford Falcon, got in and drove off.

'Gi's a lend of your car, mate,' George had asked his friend Nick, one of the small band of 'wogs' at the school.

'No dramas,' Nick replied, pulling a set of keys out of his trouser pocket, and giving George a knowing smile, threw him the keys.

Jim glumly watched George drive off in the same direction as Mrs Armstrong. There were about 40 minutes of lunchtime left. He went inside to make a cup of tea then returned to his position on the balcony, holding the mug, slowly sipping. His eyes on the road. The time dragged but he felt he had to wait and watch. If they returned within minutes of each other it indicated a possible rendezvous away from the school. The risk they were taking staggered him.

It would be worse for Sue if they were ever caught. Sue was the teacher and her job and reputation were at stake. Such behaviour could even lead to prosecution. Also, society tended to have a way of condemning women for illicit sexual behaviour while men, or in this case, a very young man, were admired for their prowess and success at attracting and seducing the opposite sex.

A number of teachers joined Jim on the balcony, eager to chat, but his short answers to their questions soon made them leave him alone. Usually polite, Jim found it hard to make small talk as his mind raced with the thought of what he might be witness to. He wanted to be alone when Sue returned. And George.

The 40 minutes dragged by. His tea had cooled, and Jim had little interest in the activities of the boys on the Oval. His attention was constantly drawn to the cars driving around the perimeter of the school.

The bell to indicate that lunch was nearly over was about to ring when Jim saw the car that George had borrowed, race back to its original parking spot. George could be seen dashing to the school, just in time for the second bell.

Sue's cutting it a bit fine, Jim thought as he kept watch. George is back, so surely she can't be far behind?

The staff began to head to classrooms and the Oval was now empty of students. Jim wavered. Should he wait to see if Sue returned at all? Maybe she had a free period after lunch? Daphne would know. She had all the individual timetables.

Jim walked through the staffroom and straight to Daphne's office. 'Daphne, would you mind checking Sue's timetable for me? Does she have a class now?'

Daphne pulled open a filing cabinet and rifled through the alphabetical list of staff members. Sue was near to the top. 'Here she is,' she said, pulling out the timetable with a flourish.

'She has a free period now. Doesn't start teaching till Period 6.' Daphne looked quizzically at Jim.

'What's the matter?' she asked, tilting her head.

'Nothing. Just want to check something with her,' Jim explained, hoping that he sounded convincing.

'Fair enough,' Daphne replied. 'She'll probably be in the staffroom now or in her office.'

'Thanks, Daphne. I'll go and see if I can find her.'

Jim wandered slowly back to the staffroom. He doubted if she would be there. After a lunchtime dalliance, facing the teachers seemed highly

269

unlikely. He pushed open the door and walked in.

The room was virtually empty as lunchtime had finished at least five or more minutes ago. There was no sign of Sue, so the next option was her office.

Like the staffroom, the corridor was deserted as well. Jim walked past the familiar relics of the wars, the sporting achievements and school memorabilia.

Sue's office was at the end near the door to the quadrangle. As he neared the closed door, he could hear whimpering. Bloody hell, she can't be busy with her young man in her office? Jim's stomach lurched. To knock or not to knock?

The deputy raised his hand to knock on the door, but it was suddenly flung open. A frazzled Sue appeared holding the hand of a young boy. Tears could be seen drizzling down the child's face.

'He's not well. Had to pick him up from childcare. Now he's dying to go to the toilet,' Sue said sounding stressed as she led him down the corridor to the Ladies' toilets. 'And, I'm going to have to take him into class with me,' she shouted over her shoulder.

Jim ran after Sue and bent down to talk to her son, 'Hello Tom. Are you feeling poorly?'

The little boy pulled a miserable face.

'Sue, I'll mind him for you. I'm sure Daphne and I can cope for 40 minutes,' Jim offered. Sue's thanks were heartfelt as she took the little boy up the stairs.

Jim stood and watched. The flood of relief he felt was dizzying. She'd been to pick up her son from childcare. There was nothing untoward going on. Thank God for that. But where had George been?

THE POLICE PAY A VISIT

Graham Russell had just flipped the cap off a bottle of beer when the doorbell rang.

'What the fuck?' he muttered, taking a quick slug of his beer before answering the door.

He didn't appreciate unannounced guests, except of course if it were Bentley, but that seemed highly unlikely now. It'd been a few days since he'd visited the school and there still had been no word from him. Maybe he'd been dumped but somehow he didn't really believe it. His gut told him that there was another explanation.

'Yes?' he asked suspiciously when he opened the door to find two men standing like Seventh Day Adventists waiting to convert any takers.

Detective Stone held up his police identification as he introduced himself and Sergeant O'Shea.

Graham gave the I.D. a cursory glance and indicated for them to enter.

'Mr Russell? Graham Russell?'

Graham replied that he certainly was.

'Sorry for the intrusion at this hour, but we'd like to ask you a few questions,' the detective explained firmly, noting that Russell didn't seem particularly fazed by their presence. Was he used to the police coming around or as a journalist, was he used to dealing with the police?

Graham led Stone and O'Shea into the lounge which was littered with books and newspapers. A computer on a large wooden table was active, showing the home page of St Cuthbert's.

'Doing a bit of research, Mr Russell?' Sergeant O'Shea asked as he peered at the screen.

The journalist nodded. 'Bit of background for a story,' he offered.

'Why is that?' Stone asked.

'The public always loves a story about the silver tails, especially when there's a bit of a scandal. Makes them feel good,' Russell answered dismissively. 'Word travels fast.'

'Oh?'

'I went to St Cuthbert's the other day. The headmaster's secretary was a bit shocked to see me. Perhaps she thought I was sizing up the joint.' Russell laughed.

'It's not a crime to visit a school, Mr Russell. We've come about another matter entirely,' Stone explained.

'Do you mind if we sit down?' Stone asked and sat before being given permission. O'Shea followed suit.

'A beer?' Russell offered as he picked up his stubby and had a swig.

'Love one, but unfortunately on duty.'

O'Shea looked longingly at Russell's beer. Bloody Boss. A stickler for the rules.

273

'Anyway, Mr Russell, you'll be wanting to know why we *are* here,' Stone continued. 'Mrs Withers, the headmaster's secretary told us that you went to St Cuthbert's asking for Mr Shute. We need to talk to his associates. Anyone who's seen him recently or been in contact.'

Russell listened, his face showing no surprise at their knowledge that he'd visited the school.

O'Shea's eyes wandered around the room. It wasn't very tidy for a gay man. Maybe it was because he was a journalist. It certainly wasn't like Bentley's flat.

'You're a journalist,' O'Shea stated more than questioned.

'Sure am. Is that a crime?' Russell asked with a hint of sarcasm.

'Not at all, Mr Russell. We're more interested in your relationship with Mr Shute,' Stone said carefully.

Russell's eyebrows raised at Stone's use of the word relationship. How much did they know about him and Bentley? He supposed that it was inevitable that someone would have put two and two together if they'd been spotted at a school game. Or on Oxford Street.

'When did you last see Mr Shute?' Stone questioned.

Russell seemed thrown by the question or perhaps it was the detective's reference to a relationship.

'Before I answer, can you tell me why you want to know? Has something happened to him?' Russell asked, trying to keep the desperation out of his voice.

Stone thought for a second, Didn't Russell know that Shute was dead? But then, why would he? It wasn't in the papers yet and when he went to the school, he wasn't told that anything about what had happened.

'I don't know how close you were to Mr Shute, but I'm sorry to inform you that Mr Shute is dead.'

Russell stared at the detective; his jaw dropped. It was what he'd half expected, or at least some kind of accident. God knows why he'd had such a premonition. There was no obvious reason why Bentley had ignored him. No fight. No argument.

'Did you know he was a queer?' O'Shea asked. 'A homosexual,' he corrected himself.

'Yes. I did,' Russell answered the sergeant with a disparaging grimace. Fucking police and their fucking antiquated attitudes. 'So what?'

'Sorry, Mr Russell. My colleague doesn't always choose his words wisely,' the detective reprimanded. Russell's resigned expression showed that he'd heard the prejudice before. 'I'm sorry to be the one to give you the bad news,' Detective Stone commiserated as he ran his hand slowly down his tie.

Graham Russell's fingers gripped the beer bottle tighter as he watched the detective smooth his tie. Bentley was dead. Was it worth trying to explain to these two men that he had indeed been in a proper relationship with Bentley? The sergeant seemed to have the sensitivity of a toilet seat.

'What do you mean by close?' the journalist asked Stone, his eyes narrowing.

Stone's face flushed a little. 'More than friends?'

Graham could see the detective's discomfort, but he wasn't going to help him. 'You mean, were we two queers having sex?'

'That's exactly what I mean,' Stone said. This interview wasn't going as planned. 'We don't want to take up too much of your time,' he placated. 'The thing is that Mr Shute was murdered sometime over the weekend before you came to the school and we have to talk to everyone who knew him.' Stone couldn't help being blunt. There was something about this man that stopped him from being tactful.

'Murdered? My God. Fuck.' Graham gulped at this beer.

'I know it must be a shock, but we do need to know how well you knew Mr Shute? Were you in a relationship?' Stone asked directly. Did Mr Russell presume he was as prejudiced against gays as O'Shea? He felt annoyed to be tarred with the same brush.

Graham went into the kitchen and took another beer from the fridge.

He's taking his time, O'Shea thought. Planning his answer? But as Graham returned to his seat the policemen could see that his face had crumpled. He flicked angrily at the beer bottle lid with the opener.

'He was my partner. My boyfriend,' he stated, staring intently at each man. 'If you can bear the term.'

Neither answered. Such honesty was unsettling.

'Maybe, we will have that beer,' the detective said, aware that the journalist had exposed a fact that many would not have had the courage to do so.

Graham got up again to return to the kitchen. His face was recomposed as he handed the beers to the men.

Stone, his beer placed on his knee, leant forward to ask another question, 'So how long had you and Mr Shute been friends?'

'About a year,' Graham answered after a quick sip of his drink. 'Obviously, we didn't live together although we discussed it. Maybe go and live somewhere more tolerant. God knows where. But there must be somewhere less uptight than Australia.

'We were meant to meet on Saturday night, but Bentley didn't show up. That's why I went to the school. It was odd as he's usually very reliable and I wondered why.'

'Of course. So, you were meant to meet. Where was that? Did you go there and wait for him?'

'Yes. I waited for a couple of hours. It was the bar above the Oxford Hotel. You can ask the barmaid. She knows both of us.'

'And after that?'

'I went home.'

'And you never saw him again?' Stone continued.

'No.'

'Can anyone confirm that you were at home that night?'

'No.'

'So, you waited for a few days and then went to the school? Weren't you worried?'

'Yes. But I assumed that something had come up at the school. I presume you know he was a boarding master, so anything could have happened.'

'Why didn't you ring him?' O'Shea interjected.

Graham stared at the sergeant. He wasn't some teenage girl with a crush. Stone too was puzzled.

'Didn't you think something could have been wrong?'

'Not really. Of course I was disappointed he didn't turn up but because of Bentley's position that sometimes happened. Also, he didn't want me to ring his flat too often in case someone else was there.'

Stone nodded and waited for Mr Russell to continue. The journalist picked up his beer and tipped the neck into his mouth. A few drops trickled down his chin. The policemen watched the beer drip onto his shirt. Graham wiped at them distractedly. The detective uncrossed his legs, thinking about his next question.

'Mr Russell, can you think of anyone who would want to hurt Mr Shute? Did he have any enemies?

Graham laughed sadly at the question. It was like a line from a B grade movie. 'From what I gathered he had lots of friends on the staff. Seemed pretty popular,' he answered dismissively. If this was the quality of the detective's questioning, God knows how they'd find the murderer. Did they expect him to immediately confess that he'd 'dunnit'?

'What about people from outside the school? Old lovers?' Stone asked. 'People from his past?'

The journalist laughed again. 'He had no contact with anyone from that ghastly small town where he grew up. Didn't even see much of his parents. They weren't really his type. You know how narrow-minded country folk can be. Being gay isn't considered normal in those sorts of areas.' He ran his hand through his hair. 'It's hard enough even in a city like Sydney.'

'I thought the prejudice wasn't as bad these days?' Sergeant O'Shea asked, surprised by the comment about Sydney.

Graham rolled his eyes sarcastically. 'Yeah, right. It's not easy even in my profession. They connect gays with paedophilia. As if I'd want to molest little children.'

Neither policeman said anything. Graham took an angry swig of his beer.

Daphne's words came back to the sergeant about her disgust at the way homosexual men were viewed. He was beginning to see her point.

'We really are sorry for your loss,' the detective sympathised.

Graham shook his head then taking a deep breath, said emphatically, 'You'll probably find this hard to accept, but I loved Bentley and he loved me.

I can't think of anyone who'd want to hurt him. And, I hadn't seen him since the weekend before he died.'

The policemen couldn't help but feel sorry for the man. Despite his defensive manner, it was clear that he cared deeply for Bentley Shute. They stood up in unison, neither wanting to add more to the man's grief.

'Well, Mr Russell. Thank you for your time. If you do think of anything that could help us with our enquiries, we'd really appreciate it. Anyone Bentley may have mentioned. Any arguments he had, no matter how insignificant they may seem,' Stone said hoping that his tone would ease Russell's fears that they were anti-gay.

After seeing the police to the door and an awkward shaking of hands, Graham grabbed another beer from the fridge and sat sipping, tears oozing down his cheeks. Bentley really was gone.

ANOTHER STUDENT IS INTERVIEWED

By Friday, Stone and O'Shea were beginning to feel like they belonged to the school. Their use of the classroom, the interviewing of students and staff, the ringing of bells, the rules and regulations had become familiar and normal. They now understood the hierarchy of the school and some of its unwritten codes of behaviour. They realised that it was Daphne who really ran the school and she had organised for them to interview George Stavrou and Michael Parker at lunchtime.

They didn't want to take the boys out of class and draw attention from the other students, although neither student seemed surprised at the request to be interviewed as a number of their mates had been already.

Mike proved to have been of little help other than to say he'd gathered via the gossip that his name had been connected to Mrs Armstrong but despite his admiration for her as a teacher, he'd had no interaction with her other than as her student. And although lots of boys had crushes on teachers, Mike believed it was just a form of showing off. He'd had no contact with Mr Shute. Never had him as a teacher and had never been to his flat.

George was next. He sat nonchalantly in the classroom next door, seemingly unconcerned, with arms loosely crossed, his thick black hair gelled back. His ethnicity was his talisman in such an Anglo environment.

Ray O'Shea, watching him through the small window in the door, felt his hackles rise at the overtly confident attitude of the student. Stone, detecting his antagonism, had a quiet word to the sergeant before they called him in. He didn't want to put George offside before they'd talked to him.

They could see that George was strong and athletic. He would have been quite capable of striking Bentley Shute with the sword but the question was, of course, why would he do that? If he were having an affair with Sue Armstrong, he had a motive. That's if Shute's constant insinuations he was Sue's lover were correct. But what about Michael Parker? Was he as innocent as he seemed? He too would have had the strength to wield the sword. However, it was difficult to imagine that Mrs Armstrong would be spreading herself so widely. Also, Michael didn't seem to have the courage to act so unconventionally. Most teenagers were too worried about their reputation to be different from the crowd.

Sergeant O'Shea brought George in from the neighbouring classroom, but Stone let him sit for a while. Perhaps the silence might corrode his arrogance. He had the confidence of a young man who had always got his own way. An indulgent mother perhaps. Weren't Greek mothers renown for spoiling their sons?

Although the detective had no reason to leave the room, he stood and indicated that O'Shea was to join him. The two left and waited outside for what they hoped was enough time to disconcert George. Leaving the interviewee alone was a technique frequently used as isolation put the wind up most people.

Both men returned to the room after what they thought was a suitable amount of time and walked purposefully back to the desk. They sat facing the student, their faces serious while looking above him at the wall beyond. George now sat with his hands under his bottom as if to warm them. His childish action contrasted with his previous nonchalance.

'Right, George. You don't mind if I call you George, do you?' Detective Stone asked in a man to man tone.

'Uh. No,' George muttered, obviously surprised by the question. Then added 'Sir'. His manners ingrained by his training at the school.

'Good. Then let's get on with our chat. There's nothing to worry about. We're talking to lots of students and staff.'

George nodded but remained silent.

'Now George, we want to ask you about Mr Shute. Was he your teacher?' Stone asked.

'No. Well, not now. I had him in Year 9 but not now.'

'You're in Year 12,' Stone confirmed. 'And you liked him?'

'He was okay.'

'Who's your favourite teacher?' Sergeant O'Shea asked quickly.

George shrugged. 'Don't have one.'

'That's unusual. I thought most students had favourite teachers,' O'Shea stated as he stared hard at George. You really think you're the boy, matey.

The boy raised his shoulders again, denying the sergeant's assertion.

'We've heard that you're a pretty good sportsman,' Stone said. 'Rugby. Cricket. Tennis.'

George couldn't hide his pride at the compliment and although he shrugged as only adolescent boys can, he smiled a little. Sport was his area of expertise. It gave him kudos despite being a 'wog'.

The detective looked at him closely. Was his confidence an act? Perhaps George was used to being bullied. Being of Greek background in such an Anglo environment, maybe he'd learned to put up a brazen front. Although, judging by the size of him, bullying seemed pretty unlikely.

'George. We gather that there is a lot of gossip and some of it includes you,' Stone explained.

'We don't necessarily believe it, but there are insinuations that some boys are having relationships with teachers. Are you aware of this?'

'Yeah. I've heard about it. Doesn't mean it's true.'

'So how do you feel that your name is connected to Mrs Armstrong?' Sergeant O'Shea asked.

'What?' George asked frowning. His cheeks coloured slightly.

'Well, word has it that you and Mrs Armstrong are an item,' Stone said. 'We're not saying it's true, but a number of people have said that you're in a relationship with your teacher.'

'That's bull shit. She's my teacher. She wouldn't go out with me,' George responded angrily. 'They're talking crap.'

'So, there's no truth in the rumour that you and Mrs Armstrong, how can I put it? Are more than teacher and student?' Stone persisted.

'No there's not. Why would she go out with me?' George questioned as his hand ran through his hair.

'Okay, George. Fair enough. But you must realise that Mr Shute has been murdered and we're trying to find out who did it.'

George's body stilled. 'Do you think I had something to do with it?' he asked defensively. It was dawning on him why he was being questioned.

'Why do you think that?' O'Shea asked.

'I dunno. But you're asking me questions. Is it because I'm a wog?'

'Of course it's not. It's because Mr Shute is dead, and we have to ask questions,' Stone justified, trying to keep the irritation out of his voice. This boy certainly had a chip on his shoulder.

'Suppose so,' George agreed sullenly.

'What were your feelings about Mr Shute? I know you haven't had him as a teacher for a few years. But do you have any thoughts about who might have had a grudge against him?'

'A grudge? What does that mean? Someone who wanted to kill him. How the hell would I know?'

'Come on, George. Don't play games. You must have known that Mr Shute spread negative gossip about Mrs Armstrong and that your name was included,' the detective said. Was George acting dumb?

Sergeant O'Shea stood up and leant towards George, his hands splayed on the edge of the desk.

'We know you two were having an affair and we know that Mr Shute said some pretty nasty things about you both. Can't you see why we think that you and Mrs Armstrong had a good reason not to like Mr Shute?'

'Yeah. He was a big gossip. But Sue, Mrs Armstrong, would never do anything like that. She'd never hurt anybody.'

Stone nodded before continuing, 'So, you're saying there is nothing going on between you and your teacher?'

''Course not. She's just been really good to me. She knows that it's not easy for me as I'm one of the few ethnics here,' George explained, unable to keep a tinge of self-pity out of his voice.

'You're a big strong boy. You could easily have attacked Mr Shute. What did you use to kill him?' O'Shea asked aggressively.

'What the fuck?' the student asked wildly. 'I didn't kill him. Why the hell would I do that?'

'Mrs Armstrong is an attractive young woman. You obviously have a high regard for her. And you sound incredibly grateful for her assistance,' the detective insisted, as he watched the boy wriggle in his seat.

'Yeah. But I wouldn't kill anyone. That's crazy. Benty, Mr Shute was a bit of an arsehole but I fucken wouldn't do that to him,' George argued, no longer concerned about his use of bad language.

'Can you think of anyone who would?' Stone asked. He was beginning to feel that this interview was leading nowhere. George, although he was defensive, wasn't giving much away. An 18-year old would normally be intimidated by the police.

'Nah. Not really. Some guys loved him, and others didn't.'

'Love is a strong word to use. Is that how you feel about Mrs Armstrong?' Stone shot back at George.

'For fuck's sake. I'm not in love with her. She's older than me. She's married. Has kids. She's not Greek.'

'It looks like you've thought a lot about her. Why does it matter that she's not Greek?' Stone asked.

'Because she wouldn't be accep...' George stopped.

'Wouldn't what?'

'Nothing,' the boy almost groaned, his bravado fading. 'I just know that I would never do anything like what happened to Mr Shute and neither would Sue,' he pleaded, his dark eyes staring at the floor.

287

'Where were you the night Mr Shute was killed?'

George thought for a few seconds. His face flooded with relief. 'I was at a Greek do. Ask my parents. Ask my brothers. They'll tell you.'

The policemen glanced at each other. The boy's anguish at being questioned was obvious but whether it was to do with his affection for his teacher, his ethnicity or his guilt, they were not sure.

THE PLANS

Preparations were underway for the memorial services for the dead teacher. Although the students and some of the staff did not fully know what was being planned, there was an air of excitement as if something dramatic was about to happen. The teachers talked urgently among themselves about who might be invited and what type of service it would be considering that Bentley had not died of natural causes.

Bentley's body was still in the morgue waiting to be taken back to his hometown for a funeral service but that was to be a private family affair. However, the memorial service at St Cuthbert's was to be held on the next Saturday, following the Friday service which would involve the whole school.

The cause of death was well established, a blow or blows to the back of the neck by one of his own samurai swords. His body had been tested for drugs and a small trace of the drug ecstasy had been found but it wasn't of sufficient quantity to cause death and had been imbibed at least a week before his murder. Tranquilisers were also evident but there was no sign of poison or dangerous chemicals, so the final cause of death was from a blow by a sharp sword-like instrument. The Coroner had agreed to the release of the body and Bentley's parents would be able to farewell him.

Mr Pritchard would attend the funeral service in Bentley's hometown, as the representative of the school. It was not something he was looking forward to. Nor was he looking forward to the two events at the school. The thought of facing parents and friends who might have questions about who killed Bentley, which he could not yet answer, was very stressful and uncomfortable. He was unable to give the answers, and nor could the police at this stage. However, he would have to face that whether he liked it or not.

He was more preoccupied with the memorial and at least he had the support of Daphne and thankfully, Jim, who, according to Rudyard Kipling, kept his head when all around were losing theirs. The memorial would have to be a tasteful and solemn affair, a PR event for the school.

The three of them had spent hours finalising the guest list. As well as the memorial service itself, there was to be a social function after it. This could not be seen as disrespectful or frivolous but should still be a celebration of Bentley's life and the contribution he had made to the school.

Invitations to the Saturday memorial had gone out to the School Board, prominent Old Boys and those who supported the school and its community. All the staff and students were expected to attend the service in the school assembly hall on the Friday prior to Saturday's service but only a select group from the school were included on the guest list for the second function; Heads of Departments, Boarding Masters, School Prefects, staff with positions of responsibility and those members of staff who were known to be Bentley's closest friends.

Sergeant O'Shea and Detective Stone were to be invited to Saturday's service. Their presence could cast a shadow over the 'celebration' but on the other hand, Bentley had been murdered and for them to attend might help the investigation.

Daphne was careful not to push too hard for the policemen's invitation. Her 'fling' with the sergeant was a clandestine affair. They had met again at the weekend and to her surprise her affection was deepening.

At first, Daphne had felt flattered by Ray's interest, especially as he was younger than her, but now she was starting to see a different side to him. He'd shown that he was a thoughtful and kind man who had the courage to go against convention while Ray admired Daphne's age and experience.

Jim Cameron knew that the school had to make a fuss of Bentley Shute and his role at the school, but the thought of listening to glowing eulogies praising a man who had caused such emotional disruption was not something he was eager to hear. He felt guilty harbouring such thoughts about a person who had died but the hypocrisy of the situation could not be ignored. He also couldn't ignore the fact that Shute had been killed in such a brutal manner and this seemed indicative of the murderer's intent to make a statement about his or her attitude to the victim. Again, Jim wondered what Shute had done to cause his own death. At the moment, the school was seeing the teacher as the victim, which indeed he was, but was his death an act of revenge?

The headmaster had similar misgivings. He had never felt comfortable with Bentley. Robert Pritchard had been aware of Bentley's attempts to ingratiate himself into the upper echelons of the school, but these attempts had failed with him. Bentley couldn't be trusted. He saw gossip as power and Robert didn't want to be closely associated with a man who used knowledge as a weapon. If he'd had his way, he would have got rid of the teacher but Bentley's popularity with boys, staff and parents would have caused a stink, one which he couldn't justify. To speak with sincerity at the memorial service was going to test his acting ability.

He was grateful to Daphne for contacting Bentley's parents, and arranging their flights and accommodation at a hotel in Double Bay. The school would pick up the tab. It was the least they could do. Mr and Mrs Shute were due to arrive on Thursday, yet it was strange that no-one else seemed to be coming from his hometown. Perhaps, the funeral back home would see a big turnout for a favourite or not so favourite son.

At first, Detective Stone had been surprised by Mr Pritchard's insistence that both he and Sergeant

O'Shea were welcome to attend the memorial service on Saturday. He assumed that the headmaster asked them as a formality, but thinking about it, he saw this as an opportunity to observe members of staff and the other invitees. Emotions would be running high and if a few drinks were consumed at the do afterwards, there was every chance that someone could let slip a revealing comment.

Attending a memorial service for a dead queer, was not something that would normally have appealed to Ray O'Shea, but he was rethinking his attitudes after conversations with Daphne. She'd opened his eyes to his prejudices. Daphne would give him a bollocking if she heard him use the term 'queer'. To him, it was just a word, but now he had to be careful, although it was difficult breaking the life-long habit of using derogatory expressions.

But if he were really honest, he was titillated by the thought of being in such close proximity to her at the service. He pictured Daphne in black, kneeling submissively at a chapel pew, acting demurely and sweetly, while knowing that his eyes would be undressing her. The two of them would have to pretend they hardly knew each other, but even the excitement of a shared sly glance, the brush of a sleeve, was arousing.

Sue Armstrong, as a housemaster, knew she'd be invited and part of her felt reluctant to attend, as she, like Jim Cameron, saw her presence as hypocritical. The death of anyone was awful, but as the service was for Bentley, she didn't feel any sense of loss or grief. Rather relief. Yet, despite it being hard to admit, part of her wanted to go to the service out of curiosity. As well as members of staff, and those connected to the school, who else would attend? She was also curious to see what Bentley's parents were like. She imagined that they could be quite flash or were they too, a pretence as Bentley had been?

The boys had mixed feelings about the loss of Mr Shute and in Matthew's case, the death of his boarding master. Sutton and Judd had admired him, as occasionally being included in Benty's inner circle had its rewards, but there was also the gay element.

Other students were envious of their connection to the charismatic teacher but at the same time, the two boys knew that the teacher's reputation as being a poof made their elevated status questionable. Matthews was more pragmatic in his opinion. Although he had admired Mr Shute as a teacher and for being an avid supporter of the school, he'd seen the other side of the man. In the boarding house, Benty had shown favouritism, but for those who weren't his favourites, his sarcasm and mockery could leave a boy feeling dispirited and isolated. However, like many of those who suffered abuse, a victim would still want the teacher to like him.

Marlene pummelled her pillow with clenched fists, frustrated tears coursing down her cheeks, her nose reddening and swelling with emotion. The thought of the memorial service was unbearable. It meant that Bentley was dead. She couldn't bring him back. Deep down she knew that a relationship with Bentley was unrealistic but somehow the thought of his companionship had offered solace.

Was she going to be alone forever? How was she ever going to meet anyone at this school? Maybe she should go somewhere else or change careers. Teaching could be such a soul-destroying occupation. Plus, the male teachers at St Cuthbert's weren't real men. Well, the ones who were, had been taken. It wasn't fair that teachers like Sue had admirers when they already had a partner.

Addington couldn't suppress the feeling of relief that washed over him when he thought about the pending memorial service. It signified that soon Bentley would be out of his life forever. Their relationship had never been the same since the boy's death and Bentley's presence was a constant reminder of their involvement in what had happened. Rodney had had his suspicions that Bentley batted for the other team but as long as it wasn't made public, he could live with that. But now the murder investigation associated him with a man whose sexual behaviour was seen by many as perverted. Logically, he knew that Bentley's farewell would not end the association, but to him, it symbolised that life was moving forward.

Bentley's other cronies were also eager to put Bentley's death behind them. Ian reflected on the impact the man had had on him and looking back saw that it hadn't been the healthiest friendship. It had been too easy to get caught up in the gossip and he felt ashamed of his enjoyment in seeing the unpleasant positions in which Bentley had placed some of his colleagues. If he continued to teach at this school, perhaps he should distance himself from the other teachers who had been a part of Bentley's circle.

With his death, Brian, Gary, Marlene, and the others had started to look pathetic. Losers, if he were being completely honest. People with no life. He didn't want to be connected with them now that Bentley wasn't here to add kudos to the group. After the memorial services and the function were over, he'd distance himself from them. Maybe, he should start looking for another position, in a different school.

THE SCHOOL ASSEMBLES

Friday, the day of the service for the whole school had arrived. The previous night, Mr Pritchard and his wife, Chrissie, had welcomed Bentley Shute's parents at their hotel. They solicitously dealt with the parents' grief and shock. Pritchard guiltily acknowledged his surprise at their ordinariness.

They were Mr and Mrs Average; bland, non-threatening, and their ocker accent grated on the ear. Bentley had sounded so different. Almost upper crust English. The headmaster wondered if Bentley had been embarrassed by his humble origins, or whether his parents were embarrassed by him. They were from the country but could not be considered landed gentry by any means.

After the taxi had dropped them at the school, Mr Pritchard shepherded Mr and Mrs Shute into his office, while Daphne organised a reassuring cup of tea and some hearty sandwiches brought over from the boarders' dining room. Jim was on hand to alleviate the stress and to act as a buffer to possible emotional demands.

The school had been thoroughly spruced up and boys were instructed to be at their smartest. Every tie knotted correctly, every shirt tucked in, every sock pulled up to the correct height with shoes blackened and shiny.

Mr and Mrs Shute sat awkwardly on the large Chesterfield armchairs, unpolished hands holding teacups. They were used to drinking tea of course, but to be doing so in this incomprehensible situation had never been envisaged. Mrs Shute looked from Pritchard to Cameron to Daphne, her eyes red from crying. She blinked at each person as if asking in code why her son had been killed. Murder was something that happened in the pictures, not in real life. Jim sat wanting in some way to comfort her but did not know what to say. He wondered if she knew her son was a homosexual. He doubted that being gay in a country area would be readily accepted, and men of Mr Shute's generation probably found it hard to deal with.

This thought had crossed Daphne's mind as well. When she'd lived in a small town in the west of New South Wales before moving to Sydney, she'd become good friends with Craig who'd struggled with being gay. He'd lived in denial for a long time but finally came out in his last year of high school.

When Craig told his parents the truth about his sexuality, his father's reaction had not been positive or supportive. He wanted his son to play league and be one of the boys as he had been in his younger days. Craig, for the sake of his father, flirted with heterosexuality while at school and Daphne had played along with the charade, partnering him to the end of year school dance. But it didn't work. Craig was gay and that was that. He knew he was disappointing his father, but he had to be fair to himself. Needless to say, Craig left town as soon as he'd completed Year 12 and went to the anonymity of Sydney. Daphne wondered if that was how Bentley had lived and why he'd created a new persona.

'Would you like another cup of tea, Mrs Shute? Mr Shute?' Daphne asked, breaking the anguished silence. Both declined and sat with heads cocked to one side as if waiting for an explanation. Mrs Shute's blouse from Millers added to the pathos of their predicament. The Ken Done splashes of colour on synthetic fabric did nothing for her ruddy complexion.

'Let me run through today's procedures,' Mr Pritchard stated eagerly, uncomfortable with the parents and the silence that couldn't be filled with small talk. 'We want to give Bentley a great send-off.'

Mr and Mrs Shute glanced quickly at each other. 'Why do you keep saying Bentley?' they asked. Pritchard gulped, his colour rising.

'Bentley. Your son,' he explained. Oh my God. The parents hadn't questioned their son's name before. Had they been too upset to ask the previous night? Were they so overwhelmed with the unfamiliar situation that they didn't want to query the headmaster? Embarrassment enveloped the room like a blanket. Jim and Daphne raised eyebrows at each other in puzzlement.

'His name's not Bentley. It's Ronald,' Mrs Shute snuffled. 'Did he call himself Bentley? That's a funny name. Why would he do that?' She stared intently at Daphne as if another woman would have the answer to the mystery of her son's name.'

'We've always known him as Bentley, Mrs Shute. The name certainly suited him,' Daphne said soothingly as Mrs Shute blew loudly into a tissue while shaking her head.

'Do you mind if we continue to refer to him as Bentley, Mrs Shute? That's how the whole school knew him,' Mr Pritchard asked, hoping that he didn't sound rude.

The parents nodded at each other glumly in agreement. Their looks of resignation indicated that they may have been in this type of uncomfortable predicament before. Why on earth hadn't Ron told us that he'd changed his name? But then, why would he? Mrs Shute thought.

Mr Shute pulled his shoulders back. He would like to hear the order of events. The details would give him something to focus on other than the death of his queer son. Where the hell did he get that stupid name from? Sounds like a bloody car. He did that at high school once. Called himself some poofter name. Luckily, that got knocked out of him.

He was devastated by Ron's, or rather, Bentley's death but he couldn't fight the niggling thought that life might be a little easier without his challenging son. He scratched his head, pushing the judgmental thoughts aside and waited to hear what the headmaster had to say.

'All the boys and staff are going to the auditorium for the service today at 1pm. We'd better get a wriggle on as it'll start fairly soon,' Pritchard informed them, glancing at his watch. 'We've cancelled classes from lunchtime today. I'll deliver a eulogy after the head boy has spoken. The chaplain will lead the prayers. Of course, there will be hymns. We know which ones were,' Pritchard paused self-consciously, 'ah, Ben… your son's favourites. We talked to his friends and colleagues. They were very helpful.'

The Shutes nodded, pleased to hear that their son seemed well liked. Mrs Shute, still clutching her cup and saucer, leaned forward to hear more from the headmaster.

'Afterwards the boys will go home, and you can have time to yourselves at the hotel,' Pritchard continued, gazing questioningly at both of them, hoping that they would be happy with the arrangement. The thought of having to spend another evening entertaining Bentley's parents was ghastly. What on earth would they talk about? Where could he take them? He imagined that their idea of a night out would be at the local Leagues club.

Mr Pritchard hoped he hadn't sounded too eager for them to have a night to themselves, but he found their passivity challenging. They were so obviously out of their comfort zone and sat like children waiting to be told what to do. Again they nodded, glad they did not have to make a decision.

Relieved by their acquiescence, the head continued with the details. 'Tomorrow is the main memorial service. It's at 4pm. The boarders from Bentley's house will attend the service in the Chapel as well as the prefects and Year 12. There'll also be the boys in Bentley's army cadet unit. And selected staff,'

Pritchard paused to let them absorb the information then began again. 'The school board, certain old boys and members of the school community will also attend and once the service is over, we'll all retire to the boarders' dining room where refreshments will be served. Obviously, the boys won't be going to that as there's alcohol involved. Oh. And some parents will be coming.'

He looked from Bentley's mother to the father. 'I hope this, suits you both. Are you sure you don't want to invite anyone?'

Mr and Mrs Shute shook their heads. No, there was no one they wanted to ask, thank you very much. Mr Shute shifted in his seat. He'd had enough. Listening to all this bullshit about prefects and cadet units. No wonder Ron had never wanted them to visit him at the school.

Jim's mouth twitched as he listened to the parents' reply to the headmaster's questions. Like Mr Pritchard, Jim wondered whether they were so embarrassed by their son that they didn't want anyone they knew to attend. This seemed very sad. Perhaps they didn't have many friends, but what about relatives, old school mates? It all seemed a bit strange.

Memories of past school functions when families and friends were included, made Jim realise that he'd never seen Bentley with any family members. Even fussy Rodney Addington had brought his wife and father-in-law along to the ANZAC Day parade on the oval. Or, had it been the other way around, and it was Bentley who didn't want his colleagues to meet his parents? Was it their ordinariness? They weren't even quaint country folk, just a middle of the road couple from the sticks.

What was it that Sue Armstrong had said about Bentley having called himself a doctor, a lawyer or some such? What the hell was he thinking? Did your parents matter that much? Wasn't Australia meant to be one of the most egalitarian countries in the world? Well, anyway, they didn't seem to have seen much of each other.

Jim's mental meanderings stopped when Mr Pritchard stood up and walked over to remove his academic gown from its hanger on the back of the door. He slipped it on over his suit and turned towards Mrs Shute. She looked around for somewhere to put her cup and saucer and then began to heave herself out of the leather chair.

Seeing her difficulty, Pritchard reached out and put his hand under her elbow, supporting her rise. Mr Shute quickly followed and the group, as if one, moved towards the door. Daphne came up the rear, straightening her black skirt and pulling the door shut behind them.

THE ASSEMBLY

The disparate group made their way down the corridor to the double doors which opened onto the outside walkway which led to the auditorium. By now the boys were seated, and the staff, dressed in full academic regalia, were in position on the stage. The whole school was hushed.

Suddenly the whining of bagpipes could be heard as Mr Pritchard, Mr Cameron, Mrs Withers and Mr and Mrs Shute solemnly made their way to the assembly hall. The shrill strains of *The Soldier's Return* cut the air, blocking out any distant noise of traffic. Mrs Shute's face flushed with emotion and she pulled another tissue out of her sleeve. Mr Shute walked stiffly, seemingly unmoved by the haunting sound of the Scottish classic.

Daphne, following behind in step with Jim Cameron, watched the parents closely and had to check herself not to judge Bentley's father and mother harshly. She could feel their discomfort. They seemed so out of place in this environment. Their unsophisticated appearance contrasted sharply with the obvious affluence of the school and its sense of tradition and privilege.

The school rose to its feet as Mr Pritchard led Bentley's parents onto the stage from a side entrance and ushered the Shutes to their seats at the right of the lectern. Daphne and Jim quickly stepped around the perimeter of the teachers' seats and stood in the back row waiting to sit once Mr Pritchard and the guests had sat down.

Following directions from the chaplain, the boys, and teachers, including Daphne and Jim, stood to recite *The Lord's Prayer*. Once the staff and boys had settled after the prayer, the headmaster stayed standing to welcome Bentley's parents, solemnly conveying the school's sympathy for their tragic loss.

The boys shuffled their feet slightly in discomfort at hearing words of a sentimental nature, while some peered with curiosity at Benty's parents. It was funny to think a teacher had parents.

Jim sensing that Robert would not feel comfortable speaking about Bentley in such a manner, felt relief when the Head Prefect was introduced. Alistair McLeod, a redheaded boy, made an eloquent and at times, funny eulogy reminding the school of Mr Shute's passion for his subject, his wit and how effective he had been as a teacher. The familiar hymn, *Praise, my Soul, the King of Heaven*, followed, sung with gusto; the high pitch of the Year 7 boys contrasting with the low rumblings of the older boys.

Mr Pritchard waited till the final note had faded, picked up his sheaf of papers and slowly returned to the lectern. Acknowledging Mr and Mrs Shute, the staff, then with a bow of his head, began his eulogy. Although public speaking was part and parcel of a principal's position, Mr Pritchard struggled to find the sincerity he needed to convince the audience of his grief at the loss of such a fine member of the school community. He knew that some of those listening to him would wonder if he'd disliked Bentley because he'd been a homosexual. It would be hard to convince them that it was nothing to do with his sexuality, but rather his personality. Pritchard finished with the well-used phrases that Mr Shute would be sadly missed, the school would not be the same without him, nor would he be forgotten.

The Shutes, unaware of Mr Pritchard's inner conflict, stared at the floor, willing the time to pass. Their sitting in isolation on the stage added to the pathos of the situation.

Sue, between Bruce and Jenny, towards the back of the stage, nudged her foot against her friend's, at the words that Bentley would be sadly missed. Jenny returned the pressure. Stifled coughs and the blowing of noses could be heard. Rodney Addington, Marlene, Gary, Brian, and Ian, sat side by side across a row of seats. Together but separate, Bentley's friends faced straight ahead, ignoring the sea of faces gazing up at them from the assembly floor.

Near the back of the auditorium George sat with his Greek mates. Their posture cocky, legs widespread, arms folded. Their manner indicated that they saw themselves as a group apart from this very traditional assembly.

Jim peered at the mass of students and managed to single him out. He was watching to see where the student's attention lay. George didn't appear to be interested in any of the teachers or anyone on the stage. If anything, he was busier picking at a thread on his tie or leaning down to fiddle with shoelaces.

What on earth had he expected George to be doing? Mouthing 'I love you' to Sue on the stage? He was being ridiculous. Other boys were focusing on Sue though and Jim could see them appraising her and Jenny while making sniggering comments to their neighbours. Jim spotted Michael, sitting a couple of rows behind George, and noted that his eyes kept coming back to Sue's face. Did that mean anything? Nearly every older boy in the auditorium had their eyes fixed on the women teachers and not just on their faces. Even Matthews had seemed more interested in the female teachers than listening to what Mr Pritchard or the Head Prefect had to say.

Further down the tiered rows, Phillip Sutton, despite being surrounded by other boys, radiated a sense of isolation. His face scrunched into a sneer as his eyes ran up and down Mrs Shute. What the hell was she wearing? And why wasn't Benty's father wearing a suit? They looked like a couple of westies. David Judd made no such observation. He was too aware of Phil sitting away from him on the other side of the hall. Why had Phil told him to sit somewhere else? It pissed him off when Phil got all bossy and acted like a dickhead. He'd been really weird since Benty died.

To everyone's relief the service came to an end and Mr and Mrs Shute shuffled their way awkwardly off the stage chaperoned by the headmaster. The boys, unable to hide their delight at the early mark from school, noisily made their exit out of the auditorium and once they'd collected their bags from the heaps piled along the corridors, quickly left the school grounds or made their way back to the various boarding houses.

Bruce leaned back against the balcony railing as he reached out and lit the cigarettes that Sue and Jenny were holding eagerly to their lips. In case of bad luck, he let the lighter die then flicked it again to light his own. The three inhaled keenly, their eyebrows raised in anticipation of the comments and observations they were going to make.

Jenny checked to see if anyone could overhear them before saying, 'Bloody hell. Bentley sounded like a saint. Don't think I can go through that again.'

'God, I know. But we have to go. It would be so obvious if we didn't turn up. His poor parents,' Sue said, while taking a drag on her cigarette before adding, 'They're nothing like I expected.'

'Me neither,' Jenny agreed. 'I would've thought they'd be really flash. Upper crusty. The way he talked; you'd think they were lords of the manor.'

'I know. It's weird how they're soooo different. Do you think they knew that Bentley was gay? They look pretty old fashioned,' Sue pondered, flicking the ash from her cigarette at the large metallic ashtray.

'Bentley certainly created another life for himself,' Jenny continued. 'I reckon he was ashamed of his background. Bit sad really.'

'Yeah. Makes you realise that you don't really know what goes on. Secret lives. What you see certainly ain't what you get. What do you think, Bruce?' Sue asked, aware of his silence.

Bruce drew on his cigarette before answering, 'Well, it's bloody difficult being a queer in this environment,' he said, wiggling his index fingers around the derogatory term. 'There's so much prejudice around.'

'Do you mean in the school or Sydney?' Jenny asked.

Bruce sighed. 'Both. It's ingrained. Perhaps Benty created a new persona so that he could build a barrier around himself to resist the hurt he may have been feeling. Also, don't they say that attack is the best form of defence, so maybe his gossip and bitchy comments were a way of protecting himself? I'll attack you so don't attack me.'

The two women listened thoughtfully. If anyone should know it would be Bruce. He'd put his sexuality on hold because of his fear of the prejudice. He didn't pretend to be straight he just didn't want to invest in a relationship because it might cost him his job. And Christians were meant to be loving. Bloody rubbish.

'Is that how you feel, Bruce?' Jenny asked. '*You* certainly don't seem the attacking type. Far too kind and lovely.' She reached out and rubbed his arm. 'But it can't be easy being gay. Actually, it isn't easy being lots of things, including being a woman in this bloody school.'

'Christ. Imagine if you were gay and a female and worked here,' Sue emphasised bitterly. 'Although, you'd probably be a big fantasy for all the guys. Fuck a duck. You can't win!'

Jenny laughed at her friend's emotive outburst but wanted to learn more from Bruce. 'Sorry, Bruce, I seem to be asking lots of questions, but did you like Benty? Or at least have some feeling of unity with him? You were both on the receiving end of dickhead attitudes,' she said, looking at him intently. This was a new conversation for Jenny and Bruce.

Bruce raised his shoulders in contemplation. 'I didn't like him. Just because we're both gay doesn't mean I had to like him or be his friend. Are you friends with every heterosexual person you know?'

The two women shook their heads.

'No. So, I didn't want to be his. He was unpleasant and false. Not qualities I admired. If anything, he did more harm to the gay cause. He perpetuated the stereotype view that all gay men are bitches,' Bruce said despondently.

311

'Yes,' butted in Jenny eagerly. 'In my Friday drama classes, it's unbelievable how many of the boys want to be camp and mince around. It's like they're fixated with being gay. Even the older boys. And yet if you said that it was okay to be a homosexual, they'd all go yuck. Eeeew. The hypocrisy is incredible.'

Bruce shrugged his shoulders again. What could he say?

'How old do you think Bentley's parents are?' Sue asked, changing the subject as she'd sensed a sad anger in Bruce. She didn't want him to feel uncomfortable or for him to think that she and Jenny saw him as some sort of aberration.

'Dunno. Maybe in their late 60s, early 70s. Why?' Jenny asked.

'Silly idea really, but his dad is old enough to have fought in the war. Maybe he fought against the Japanese,' Sue suggested.

'So?' Bruce and Jenny asked together.

'Weeell. Bentley had a thing about collecting Japanese stuff. Perhaps his father didn't like that. All those swords, and paintings, tea services. And he used to wear a kimono.'

'How do you know all that?' Bruce asked surprised. 'I didn't think you'd been in his flat?'

'I haven't, but I've been told. I have my sources,' Sue said, tapping her nose.

'What are you thinking, Miss Marple?' Jenny asked, grinning.

'I'm being silly,' Sue began. 'It just crossed my mind that perhaps his father...,' she stopped.

'That is silly,' Jenny stressed. 'I don't think someone would bump off their son because he wore a Japanese kimono.'

'But what about combining that with being gay? Bentley could certainly stir up intense feelings in people.'

'I can't believe that. Parents don't murder their kids,' Jenny argued. 'Surely not?'

'Don't they?' Sue said, staring from Jenny to Bruce.

'That's crazy,' said Jenny. 'Just look at his parents. Do they look like murderers to you?'

'No. I suppose not. But who does look like a murderer? And don't they say that people are usually murdered by family or someone they know?'

'Well, he knew lots of us,' Jenny said with a tinge of sarcasm.

'He certainly did,' Sue agreed and with that the three threw their butts into the ashtray and walked slowly back into the staffroom.

A RESTORATIVE DRINK

The last of the afternoon light filtered into the headmaster's office. Daphne, Jim, and Pritchard, after seeing Mr and Mrs Shute into a taxi, sank gratefully into the comfort of the armchairs and the sigh of the leather as it melded to their weight mimicked the sighs they had all exhaled once the doors to the taxi had closed.

Thank God they wouldn't have to see the Shutes again till tomorrow afternoon. The day had seemed interminable. The awkward nature of the school assembly for Bentley, the small talk with the parents who were so unforthcoming. And to make it worse, Bentley's real name was Ronald. Ron. Unbelievable. He'd certainly pulled the wool over their eyes. Plus, there was tomorrow to get through. The service and the do. More hypocrisy and obsequious behaviour.

'I think this calls for a restorative drink,' the head said walking towards the drinks' cabinet. 'Daphne, what would you like? Jim?'

'A large gin and tonic if you have it, please,' Daphne requested keenly. She'd meant to leave as soon as her duties were over, but Robert had guided her and Jim back to his office. His need for companionship was obvious.

'Same for me, thanks,' instructed Jim. 'Could definitely do with a drink after today.'

'Bloody hell. I'll say. Oh, sorry about the language, Daphne, but it's been a very stressful day,' Robert excused.

'Don't be silly. Swear away. Wouldn't blame you if you said something stronger,' Daphne said reassuring her boss as he poured the drinks. She accepted hers gratefully. She'd just have the one as tonight she had a date and she wanted to be feeling perky, not tired and end of the weekish.

The three sipped their drinks solemnly, the tension slowly easing out of them, happy to sit quietly.

'Well, that wasn't too bad, was it?' Robert Pritchard asked, staring at the other two for reassurance.

'The service, you mean?' Jim asked.

Robert nodded. 'Yes. I think it went well, don't you?' he pleaded. 'Alistair spoke professionally and with suitable humour and I'm sure that Bentley's parents would have been pleased with what was said. We just have to get through tomorrow.'

'I'm sure it'll be okay,' Jim said, knowing that his answer was what the headmaster wanted to hear.

'I agree with Jim. Today went very well. The boys behaved, and his parents must have loved the pomp and ceremony. And who doesn't like a bit of tradition?' Daphne asked, continuing Jim's positivity. Poor Robert.

'Didn't the parents say anything about his name when you saw them last night?' Daphne couldn't resist asking. It seemed bizarre that they only mentioned it today.

'No. To be honest we didn't stay very long and they seemed overwhelmed by the whole situation,' Pritchard explained. He and Chrissie had found their attempts at making conversation difficult and left the hotel and Mr and Mrs Shute as soon as it were politely possible.

Daphne drained her glass and said her goodbyes. She'd leave Robert in Jim's capable hands while she was looking forward to being in the very capable hands of a strapping policeman.

The two men sat in silence again, neither one in a rush to go anywhere. Robert wanted to delay the thought of tomorrow's agenda and Jim could spare a few extra minutes as Anh was taking the children to MacDonald's for their Friday night treat.

'Another?' the head asked and without waiting for a reply, began pouring a stiffer gin and tonic for Jim and a whisky for himself.

'Do you think the police are any further on with their investigation?' Robert asked as he returned to his seat.

'You mean if they have any idea who killed Bentley, or should I say, Ronald?' Jim couldn't keep the mockery out of his voice. The name Bentley was such an affectation while Ronald or Ron, to use his mother's term, sounded so common.

'God, I know. It's all so ghastly and I know I shouldn't say this, but those ghastly parents. And to have to see them again tomorrow,' Robert groaned.

'I'm very grateful for the support that you and Daphne have given me,' he said raising his glass in Jim's direction.

Jim acknowledged the gratitude with a small smile. 'To be honest, I have no idea who killed him. And I don't think the police do either. There are so many options. Sometimes I wonder if it's a member of the gay community. Someone who has nothing to do with the school. His friends here don't seem to have any real reason to kill him,' He absent-mindedly put the drink up to his lips. 'But then, those whose lives he made a misery, had good cause. It all seems so unlikely. So unbelievable.'

They sipped at their drinks, each wondering what tomorrow would bring.

THE MEMORIAL

The thought of the Saturday memorial service created mixed feelings for the invitees. It soured the weekend for some of those who were attending. A number hoped the time would pass quickly so that they could pay their respects then leave. Others couldn't deny their curiosity. Black articles of clothing were donned, babysitters instructed and dinner left in the fridge for teenage children.

The chapel's pews shone with polish, the school's pennants and patriotic flags had been flicked free of dust. The stone floors were washed, and the In-Memoriam Boards wiped carefully so that the names in gold leaf were easier to read. Despite it being near the end of the rugby season, the weather was warm, although it would turn once the sun had gone.

Guests drove impatiently around the nearby streets searching for a space to park while others were dropped off by spouses, sons, or taxis.

The clusters of mourners had subconsciously divided themselves into their different groups outside the chapel. Old Boys eagerly shook hands with former classmates, parents singled out parents of boys in the same year, teachers huddled together while the guests of honour awkwardly made stilted chit chat. The Prefects and Year 11 and 12 boarders from Bentley Shute's house waited at the front of the chapel, smart in their blazers and grey trousers, to direct the congregation to their pews.

Bentley's parents accepted the condolences from those who had the courage or the curiosity to speak to them. Mr Shute seemed to swell a little in the limelight while his wife deflated into her unflattering jacket. She didn't enjoy being the centre of attention. She just wanted to go home.

Finally, the service began. Each pew was filled with Bentley's admirers and detractors but as Jim Cameron peered around the intimate but cold stone building, he noticed that there were few in attendance who had nothing to do with the school. Even Mr and Mrs Sinclair had come. Where were Bentley's friends from outside the school or extended family members? Seated towards the back, on the end of a pew, Jim spotted Sergeant O'Shea and Detective Stone. Both were dressed in smart suits, dark ties, their faces impassive, seemingly at ease in this place of worship.

Marlene sat with her head bowed, tears dripping onto her black synthetic trousers. Gary tentatively placed his arm around her shoulders in an attempt to comfort her while Rodney Addington stared glumly ahead.

After the eulogy, given by an Old Boy who had been taught by Bentley, a Year 12 student walked to

319

the front and positioned himself at the organ. *Abide with me* emerged from the pipes and the congregation sang a spirited version and even the least religious staff members found themselves singing the hymn lustfully.

As the President of the Old Boys Association drew the service to a close, thoughts were brought back to the present. Sue had been thinking about her brother's untimely death. Jenny stopped reminiscing about the large Italian gathering when her grandfather had died and Graham Russell, who had quietly entered the chapel once the service had started, his mother's passing.

He stood at the back away from the congregation, his eyes drawn to the coffin covered in flowers. He couldn't equate the coffin placed near the altar with Bentley. Perhaps if he'd seen the body, it would have made his death more real. But his heart ached. He'd never experienced such a sense of loss before. It was unbelievable that he would never see Bentley again. As he fought back tears, the journalist in him struggled to the fore; there were so many unanswered questions.

The service over, the crowd of mourners eased their way from the pews into the aisle and out of the Chapel, again to gather in groups murmuring platitudes to each other. Daphne, with School Sergeant MacGregor and Jim, smiled their greetings at parents or Old Boys they recognised while Mr Pritchard, accompanied by his wife, vigorously shook hands with anyone who thrust theirs at him. Detective Stone and Sergeant O'Shea, waiting their turn, filed past the headmaster and his supporters. O'Shea paused slightly in front of Daphne, then moved on. Stone nodding at the headmaster and Jim, kept walking.

Most of the congregation had left the chapel but Jim noticed a man he didn't recognise hovering at the chapel doors. He could see the man wiping at his eyes as he peered at the remembrance plaques and war memorabilia near the doors. The man didn't seem in a hurry to join the others. Perhaps he didn't want to be seen crying. He didn't look like the other members of the congregation, being more casually dressed, with longish hair unlike a businessman or a teacher. Finally, the man walked out from the Chapel and made his way across the grass distancing himself from the crowd to light a cigarette.

The Sinclairs waited until the throng had thinned and stopped in front of Mr Pritchard. Mrs Sinclair, with her husband's arm linked protectively through hers, smiled weakly at the headmaster as he clutched at her hand with both of his. She had obviously been crying, her mascara smudged under the bottom lashes and her nose was shiny from rubbing.

'Thank you so much for coming, Mrs Sinclair,' Mr Pritchard said quietly and then included Mr Sinclair in his gaze. 'You too of course, Mr Sinclair. Such a sad time.' Mr Sinclair reached out his hand to Mr Pritchard who disengaged himself from the grieving mother and shook it firmly.

'I do hope you'll be joining us for refreshments in the dining room,' Mr Pritchard urged.

'Yes, of course,' Sinclair agreed and placing his arm around his wife's shoulder, led her across the lawn to the school dining room.

Groups started to dissipate and wander towards the Boarders' Dining room where trestle tables were covered with white tablecloths laden with plates of sandwiches, pastries, sausage rolls and cakes. Piles of napkins in the school's colours were placed around the plates of food, and by the servery hatch, on separate trestle tables, casks of wine and bottles of beer were lined up with collections of plasticware.

'After all that outpouring, I need a bloody drink,' Rodney Addington muttered to Marlene and Gary and made a beeline for the beverage table where a queue was already forming. He grabbed a bottle of beer and expertly flicked the cap off with a bottle opener.

As he turned to re-join his colleagues, his elbow banged against a guest's chest. He began to apologise but stopped once he saw who it was. Sue Armstrong opened her mouth to speak then changed her mind. She smiled forgivingly at him while he flustered his way back to Marlene and Gary who had been joined by Bentley's clique.

What a sad case, Sue thought with pity. He can't let go of his grudge. Pathetic. She pressed the plastic tap on the cask and poured two glasses of white wine, aware of the other guests waiting impatiently in line to pour a wine or grab a beer.

'There you go,' Sue said as she handed over the glass to Jenny. 'God knows what it'll be like. You'd think the school could afford something a bit flasher than Chateau Cardboard.'

'Yeah. They spend a fortune on cricket pitches but won't fork out for decent wine. Anyway, better than nothing. I need something to anaesthetise the hypocrisy of today's proceedings,' Jenny declared while gulping down a couple of mouthfuls.

The two friends cradled their drinks and gazed around the room. The noise was already changing from respectfully subdued to that of a party. Old Boys who hadn't seen each other for a while were catching up on past events or boasting about their successes. The parents attending discussed sporting fixtures or whether their sons were coping with academic stress and the declining teaching standards. When a teacher wandered past they would call out greetings in slightly guilty voices.

Daphne had found Mrs Shute a chair and sat her near the door in case she needed a breath of air or a quick getaway. Mrs Shute placed her black plastic handbag next to the chair leg and sipped at her tea. No, she hadn't wanted anything stronger.

Mr Shute, however, with Jim's help, found the beer table and the two helped themselves. Mr Shute threw the first one down in well-rehearsed gulps and quickly picked up another. The whole day had been excruciating. He hadn't wanted to come and neither had his wife but how would it have appeared if they didn't attend their son's memorial service? He knew that Ron, or rather, for God's sake, Bentley, would be squirming at the sight of them in this environment. What had he done to deserve a son like Ron?

He sucked at his beer as two middle-aged men and a younger, but matronly looking woman came and stood next to him.

The first man with military stiffness, put out his hand. 'Mr Shute. Rodney Addington, a friend of Bentley's.'

He indicated with his other hand, Gary, and Marlene. 'We'd like to offer you and your wife our sincere condolences. Bentley will be very much missed. He was a fine man. A great teacher and a good friend.' The other two nodded in agreement and they too held out their hands. Mr Shute awkwardly took Marlene's proffered hand and quickly turned to shake Gary's.

'Ah. Thanks. Been a good turnout. Can tell that Ron-um-Bentley... had some good mates. At least he had a decent send off,' Mr Shute said in their general direction, his eyes not making contact. He'd never been one to make small talk unless it was about the League.

'Your son was well liked. No doubt about that,' Gary reassured him. Mr Shute was surprised at hearing how fond the three were of Bentley. They didn't look up to much. Rodney, whatever his name was, seemed a little snootier than the other two.

More Bentley's sort, but the woman and Gary seemed a bit shabby. He struggled for the correct description as he doubted whether they were as close to his son as they made out.

Daphne's sudden arrival was a relief. 'Can I get you another beer?' she asked Mr Shute and reached over to the table to pick one up. While she was prising off the cap, the three teachers made their excuses and took the opportunity to move away, inwardly thanking Daphne for saving them.

Handing Mr Shute his beer which he swigged it in relief, she asked, 'How are you and your wife bearing up?' she asked. 'It's a terrible tragedy for you both. And the school,' she added as an afterthought.

Daphne blushed. Why on earth had she mentioned the school? The parents couldn't care less about the school. They'd lost their son. Mr Shute didn't seem to have noticed Daphne's faux pas and answered that it was. The unease of the conversation finally proved too much and she too excused herself giving him the chance to return to his wife.

The noise level continued rising, and laughter was pervading the smokey atmosphere. Sue, taking emotional shelter with her close colleagues, asked how they'd found the service. Bruce shrugged nonchalantly. What could he say? The whole event had been a travesty of hypocrisy. The teachers stared from one to the other. Bruce was right. Their silence ignited Sue's desire to leave.

'Think I'll make a move soon,' she stated. No-one argued against her. They wouldn't be far behind.

'I'd better make sympathetic noises to Mrs Shute before I go,' Sue said after saying goodbye to Jenny and Bruce and walked towards the door where Bentley's mother was still sitting with an empty cup and saucer placed under her chair.

Mrs Shute looked up as Sue stood before her. Sue was about to offer her condolences when she noticed a student standing in the shadows just outside the entrance.

'I'm so sorry, Mrs Shute, but could you excuse me for a minute?' Sue asked and without waiting for a reply, hurried towards the open doors.

Students had not been included in this part of the function and the boarders had been given early dinner. Standing in the entrance, she stared into the dark and down at the terraced area and steps at the front of the dining room which were partly in shadow. She could make out a figure sitting on the bottom step. It was definitely a student judging by the blazer and grey trousers. Sue walked down the steps. George stood as she neared

'Why are you still here?' Sue asked.

'I came to see you,' he whispered in reply. 'I got interviewed by the police.'

Sue frowned. 'Everyone is. You know you're not meant to be here. No students are.'

George leaned into Sue as if to touch her, but she pulled away. 'Don't be silly. You'd better go before someone comes out. You could get into trouble.'

George looked up at the dining hall then at Sue.

'Well, if that's what you want? I'll piss off. Enjoy your night.' He sighed defiantly and strode away.

Sue watched until he'd vanished into the darkness covering the Oval and she walked wearily back up the steps to rejoin Mrs Shute.

GEORGE SPIES ON SUE

George walked angrily into the dark of the Oval. Fuck, fuck, fuck. Why did she have to sound so dismissive, so teachery? He kicked at the grass, annoyed with himself for being upset.

What had happened to the cool old George who felt no qualms about dumping a girl after a quickie? Sue had really got under his skin. She was in his thoughts constantly and if he didn't see her at least once during the school day, he'd drive past her house or where he thought she might be in the hope of a glimpse. Even the jealousy he felt when he watched her with friends and family, was worth it. At least on Saturdays he was able to talk to her at the school sporting events, but Sundays were the worst.

He knew the chances of their being together in the future were impossible but he fantasised about waking up with her in the morning after a night of fucking.

The shit would hit the fan if his mother ever found out that he was infatuated with an 'Aussie' girl. Her constant nagging about his marrying a good Greek girl drove him mad. And of course, Sue wasn't a girl. She was a married woman with two children.

His temper cooled. It wasn't her fault that students were not allowed to attend the function for Benty. Maybe if he went around to the back of the building, he might be able to watch through a window and see what she was up to. See who she talked to.

Skirting around the outside of the dining hall, George made his way towards the kitchen and stood on one of the many produce boxes placed outside for collection. Mrs Withers and one of the mothers were tidying up at the large sink. Mrs Withers was hot, but not as hot as Sue.

He moved further round the building to the other side where windows opened from the dining hall. It was risky to stand looking in, but they probably couldn't see him as it was so bright inside. Guests were holding drinks and talking. He could make out Sue on her way through the crowd to Miss Bartoli. The two stood intimately, sharing something they didn't want others to hear. George imagined himself in bed with the two of them. That would be bloody awesome, he thought, unable to stop himself from becoming instantly aroused. He pushed down hard on his erection as he ducked down in case he was seen.

He peeked again. He could see Mr Cameron talking to some bloke he didn't recognise. Looked like a bit of a wanker and Mr Cameron didn't seem to be too impressed either, judging by the expression on his face. Sue and Miss Bartoli now stood at the edge of a large group of people who were standing in a huddle staring down at someone. George stood on tiptoe; his eyes peering through the opened window. Fuck. There was someone lying on the floor.

Can't hold their grog, George laughed to himself. And neither can old Benty's father. Sitting on a chair by himself. He watched Miss Bates join him. Poor bugger having to talk to her. Sorry about your son, blah blah blah. She seemed a bit pissed. Was she crying?

George looked back to circle surrounding the person on the ground. Was it Benty's mother? Big fat thing. The two policemen had joined the action, although it was a bit hard to tell if it was them as they weren't wearing uniforms.

Where was Sue now? She wasn't with Miss Bartoli. There was no point in hanging around if she'd gone. Maybe she was outside having a cigarette? She'd seemed a bit miserable and stressed before.

George stepped away from the window and retraced his steps around the back of the building.

JIM CONFRONTS GRAHAM RUSSELL

While George had peered through the windows into the boarders' dining room, Sue was smoking urgently outside on the steps. Why on earth am I still hanging around? she asked herself. Bloody George. Bloody Bentley. Bloody school.

'Everything alright, Sue?' Jim asked as he came through the doors onto the steps. He'd needed a breather from the mindless chatter.

'Oh. Yes. I'm okay. Thanks. I've just got to say my goodbyes to Mr and Mrs Shute, then head home.'

Sue forcefully stubbed out her cigarette and walked back into the dining room with Jim following. She appeared out of sorts, but he doubted if it would be about Bentley. He'd seen her talking to someone outside and whoever it was seemed to be in a bad mood judging by the pace of departure.

Jim wandered over to the makeshift bar and picked up a beer. He looked around the crowd to see where Anh was and if she had a drink. She was deep in conversation with Mrs Sinclair and held a full plastic glass of wine. Although functions like this were not easy for Anh, as frequently she was the only Asian, she made an effort to mingle and support

Jim in his role. She was a good listener, always an endearing quality.

Near the servery hatch, the man who'd been crying in the Chapel was leaning against the wall sipping on a beer, his eyes taking in the action of the room. Jim thought for a couple of seconds about approaching the man. How did he get an invitation to the do and how did he know about the memorial service?

Jim took the plunge and walked over introducing himself. 'Jim Cameron. Deputy head. And you are?'

'Graham Russell. I'm a mate of Bentley's. Wanted to pay my respects,' Graham explained, his equanimity was now restored.

'Ah. That's understandable,' Jim responded, wondering if Graham Russell had gate-crashed the function. 'Known Bentley for long?'

Graham grinned grimly. 'Quite a while. We were good friends.'

Jim smiled sympathetically, acknowledging the information but he could sense a hint of sarcasm in the man's voice. 'Did you go to this school?' he asked.

'No. I went to Danehurst. Very similar. We used to play against St Cuthbert's.'

Jim nodded and then it dawned on him. This was the man who'd been asking questions at the school. He must be the reporter Daphne had mentioned and no doubt had his ways of finding out what was going on.

'What do you do for a living?' Jim asked, thinking that he may as well be in for a penny. Graham looked slightly surprised at the sudden question, but he quickly pulled his face into line. 'Journalist. I write for *The Sydney Times*.'

Jim raised his eyebrows to show he was impressed. 'That must be interesting. Are you busy with anything exciting now?'

Graham's eyes scanned Jim's face and then the room. He bent his head and whispered into Jim's ear, 'Why are the two cops here? They weren't friends of Bentley's.' Graham folded his arms as if to challenge Jim. 'The school seems to be making a big fuss for a teacher.'

Jim could sense the man's anger or was it grief? He was sure Russell had been crying before. Mentally, he was fumbling how to reply. Then it occurred to him. How did he know O'Shea and Stone were police? Had they interviewed him? Was he a person of interest? This chap doesn't look like a murderer, nor particularly gay. Is he just after a good story?

Stepping back to distance himself from the journalist and to regain control of the situation, Jim said firmly, 'I don't agree. Bentley was a respected member of the school community and his work was really appreciated by staff and boys.'

Graham's expression showed his scepticism. 'Maybe you're right, but it does seem a lot of show for a lowly teacher.' He stepped closer to Jim, saying, 'I spoke to Des Campbell after my visit from the police and he told me that Bentley had died. But the school wouldn't. Funny that. You know Des, don't you?'

Jim tried to hide his shock at the question and the change of direction Graham Russell had taken.

'Yes. I do. How did you know?'

'Don't panic, Mr…?' Graham reassured smugly.

'Cameron, James Cameron,' Jim repeated.

'As I said, don't panic, Mr Cameron. I just asked if Des knew Bentley was dead and he said yes and that was all. He knew that I'd find out soon enough. Bentley told me that you had contacts with the media.' His face softened. 'I used to say to him that he should've been a journo' rather than a teacher. He could sniff out anything.'

Jim didn't respond to this observation. The thought of Bentley knowing about his private life made him uncomfortable. He also didn't like the thought that Bentley had shared information with this man.

Both men stood silently until Jim broke his own rule and said, 'Des and I have professional connections. We don't really mix in the same social circles.'

Graham stared carefully at him, detecting his discomfort. Jim's irritation was increasing at the knowledge Des and this man had been discussing him.

'And that's all Des said?' Jim couldn't resist asking. It would be good to know if there were more disclosures.

'Yes. Unfortunately.'

Cameron's negative view of Des' lack of loyalty shifted slightly.

'You know, Mr Cameron, Bentley talked a lot about you. He liked you.'

Jim couldn't disguise his surprise at hearing this. Although Bentley had treated him courteously, he'd never felt that the teacher had given him much thought and as he wasn't prone to gossip, Bentley wouldn't have had much use for him. He'd only collected those who had information or could be manipulated to do his bidding.

'Thank you. Well, Mr Russell, I won't hold you up anymore.' Jim put out his hand and was intrigued by the strength Russell had in his grasp. 'But there is one more thing, if I may ask. How do you know the police were at the service?'

Graham laughed self-deprecatingly. 'You've caught me out, Mr Cameron,' he said continuing to clutch Jim's hand. 'They came to see me for a chat. Wondered if I was responsible for Bentley's death but I convinced them I didn't do it.' Russell again leaned his face close to Mr Cameron's. 'You sure there's nothing you can tell me, Mr Cameron, as I know Bentley was murdered.'

Jim removed his hand from the tight grip and said, 'Honestly, there is nothing to tell you other than Bentley died. I'm very sorry. I do have to go. Please excuse me.'

Jim walked away, his heart beating madly. Graham Russell had been almost threatening in his manner. Wending his way through the groups of guests, he found the headmaster in conversation with an Old Boy who'd left the school a couple of years ago.

'Could I have a word, Mr Pritchard? Sorry to interrupt,' Jim excused.

Robert, glad to be relieved, made his excuses to the Old Boy and the two men found a corner away from the crowd.

'What's the matter, Jim?' Pritchard asked. 'Was it the memorial service?'

'No. No. Not that,' Jim began. 'I've just been talking to that Russell fellow. The man, you know, the journalist, who came to the school asking for Bentley. Just after he died. He was trying to find out from me how Bentley died. He knew he was murdered. He even mentioned my mate Des. He actually admitted that the police have questioned him.'

'Well, aren't they questioning everyone? Settle down, Jim,' Robert soothed. 'Perhaps he just used Des's name to make you want to talk to him? Remember, he is a journalist, even if he knew Bentley.'

'Yes. Yes,' Jim replied impatiently. 'But, apparently it was Bentley who told him that I'm friends with Des. What was there that bloody Bentley didn't know?' he asked rhetorically.

Robert patted him on the shoulder. 'Look, Jim. Let's forget about all this for the moment. Come and help me chat to the parents.' He bent his head towards Jim's and said quietly, 'With luck they'll be going soon. Talk about hard work.'

Jim shrugged his agreement and trailed after the headmaster to Shute's parents who were sitting in isolation by the door wishing they could leave.

SUE AND MARLENE HAVE A CHAT

Sue Armstrong stood by the door, waiting for her chance to say goodbye to the Shutes once the Head and Jim had finished their attempt to make small talk with the parents. Would they even care if she spoke to them?

As she watched the four of them making awkward conversation, George's words kept repeating in her head. He'd sounded upset. Why had she reacted so school-marmishly? There was no-one else outside to have witnessed his presence and he'd obviously stayed on after the service in the hope of talking to her. She should have had a quick chat if nothing else. Now he was angry with her. George was becoming demanding.

It was hard to tell how long Mr Pritchard and Jim would take talking to Bentley's parents so Sue edged her way through the crowd to the Ladies room and replenished her lipstick after going to the loo. She didn't want to stay at the function but she didn't want to go home either. The children would be or rather should be in bed, and the thought of sitting silently in front of the television with Brian for the rest of the evening did not appeal. It all seemed too boring for words.

As she was gazing at her reflection and idly contemplating a change of hairstyle, Marlene pushed open the door and rushed to an empty cubicle, fumbling to lock the door. Sue could hear the sound of sheets of toilet paper being yanked from the holder and a flurry of nose blowing. Despite Sue's dislike of Marlene, her instinct for sympathy overtook her antipathy as she hovered outside the cubicle.

'Marlene. Are you okay?' Sue said to the door.

There was silence from the cubicle. The sniffing stopped.

'You sure you're okay?' Sue persisted.

Marlene flushed the toilet and Sue could hear her picking up her handbag. A few seconds later, Marlene emerged, ignoring Sue as she made her way over to the hand basins where she rummaged through her handbag for makeup.

Sue dithered. Part of her did not want to have any sympathy for this woman but she didn't like seeing anyone in distress. And if she were honest, she couldn't resist nosing into the cause of Marlene's tears.

'Must have been hard for you today?' Sue proffered.

Marlene slid her eyes across the mirror to catch Sue's. She was about to speak then the tears welled up again and she ran back into the cubicle grabbing handfuls of paper to wipe her eyes. Her sobs gathered momentum as she pawed at her face with the cruel toilet paper.

'What's the matter?' Sue asked while putting her arm around Marlene, who continued to weep noisily in obvious despair.

Between the gulps of anguish, she kept muttering, 'I didn't want him to die.' Sue didn't need to ask who and waited till the sobbing stopped.

Whether it was the cheap wine or the unexpected sympathy, Marlene couldn't hold back. Her pent-up emotions exploded. She stared at Sue searching her face as if she had the answer to Bentley's death.

'He shouldn't have died. I could have been with him. We could have lived together.'

Sue tried to keep the shock out of her voice. 'But Bentley was gay? How could you have been together as a...?'

Marlene shrugged her off. 'Of course I knew he was gay, but we could have been together as companions. His reputation would have been safe.'

'But what about...?' Sue began.

'I could live without *that* if I could be with him,' Marlene snapped back.

'Oh dear. You poor thing,' Sue sympathised.

She'd known that Marlene was very caught up with Bentley. He was definitely charismatic even if a negative force but to be in love with someone who was gay and to make it worse, for him to be murdered. She couldn't help feeling sorry for Marlene despite her cynicism at the possibility of such a relationship actually occurring. There was

341

nothing worse than unrequited love. No wonder Marlene was such a bitter woman.

Marlene threw a scathing look at her sympathizer. 'Why do you care? You didn't like him.'

'Can you blame me?' Sue asked, unable to keep the self-righteousness out of her voice. 'He said horrible things about me.'

Marlene shrugged. The moment of connection was over.

Sue waited till Marlene left the bathroom. There was no point in trying to continue the conversation. Marlene had been sufficiently indoctrinated against her and no show of sympathy could bridge the gap between them. Sue took one last look in the mirror and returned to the dining hall. She'd give the do another few minutes, then make a move.

Marlene had disappeared into the crowd, but the two policemen could be seen chatting to Jim. He must have finished with the parents. The policemen's eyes stared over their stubbies at the gathering, appraising who was there and why they had attended the event. Sue could understand Jim and Anh attending the funeral and the party or wake or whatever such a function was called but it seemed strange that the police had come. They didn't know Bentley and listening to eulogies about someone they'd never met must have been boring. Perhaps it was police protocol.

Seeing that Stone and O'Shea were smoking, Sue wandered over, lighting a cigarette once she'd joined the trio.

'Hello, Sue,' Jim said. 'Do join us.'

'Yes, please do,' Stone encouraged. 'Have you recovered from the service?'

'I have,' Sue replied, somewhat taken aback by the question. It was as if he'd heard what she was thinking, and with as much sincerity as she could muster, said, 'It was very moving. His poor parents. I do hope they're okay.'

The three men twirled the beer in their bottles. It crossed her mind that most men, including her husband, appeared uncomfortable whenever feelings were mentioned.

Bugger it, she thought, I don't care what they think, and asked abruptly if they were any further on in their investigations.

O'Shea and Stone muttered something about progress being made but too early to say. Jim thought he'd detected a slight glance from the detective at the sergeant. Perhaps a hint not to say too much. The four stood silently with cigarette smoke swirling around them. Jim sensed Sue's stress. Was it caused by the service, the police questioning or what he had witnessed outside?

'It was a good service,' Jim said, breaking the silence. 'His parents must be happy with the accolades Bentley received. Not that they

343

compensate in any way for his death,' he quickly added.

He wasn't sure why Sue had joined them. It was as if she wanted to draw attention to herself. Perhaps she was trying to tell Stone that she had nothing to fear. He'd noticed that the policemen had reacted to her in a positive way. Not that they'd said much but their expressions admitted they found her attractive. It was difficult to disguise admiration even if they may think that she, or her lover, could have murdered Bentley.

Sue crushed her cigarette in the ashtray on the table behind them and excused herself.

Jim watched her walk away then returned his attention to the detective and sergeant. 'Has any of this socialising helped with your investigation? Or do you find it boring? I have to admit it is for me and Anh. But she's much better at making conversation than I am,' he said, in praise of his wife.

'Wife? I'd like to meet her, Jim,' Stone said. 'Weren't you single when we were in Rarotonga?'

'No, but I hadn't been married long then.'

'Oh. For some reason I thought you were a commitment phobic,' Stone said laughing. 'Most men are.'

'Oh. Really? Well, Anh certainly won me over.'

'Her name sounds Vietnamese,' Stone stated. Jim said it was. 'Nothing to do with the war?'

'Well, it suppose it was in a way. Anh was a refugee after the war and I met her in Sydney. She was one of the boat people. We met at a charity fund-raiser and after what she'd been through and my being in Vietnam, we had a lot in common,' Jim reminisced. His mind swung back to the days of the intensive bombing by the Americans and their use of napalm. Anh had been lucky to survive.

'I'll introduce you. She probably needs saving,' Jim said as he led the two policemen towards Anh, who was politely listening to an older Old Boy venting his views about Australia's involvement in the Vietnam War.

'Sorry to interrupt, but I'd like to introduce my wife to Detective Stone and Sergeant O'Shea,' Jim excused to the Old Boy.

'Ah, well,' the Old Boy grunted. 'Mustn't get in the way of the law. Eh?' he said, sniggering at his own joke as he wandered off to find another audience.

As the policemen were chatting to Anh, Jim surveyed the room. Sue was standing by the open door to the dining room again, lighting yet another cigarette. The fierce dragging on her cigarette reflected her mood.

The whole day and evening had been a strain for all of them: Bentley's parents, Old Boys, staff whose allegiances were either for or against Bentley, the police, parents, the journalist, the headmaster and Daphne. The combination was a volatile mix, and he wished that everyone would just go home. Was it the free alcohol that made them stay or were they waiting for something to happen?

'I'm sorry, but could you excuse me for a minute?' Jim asked the group. 'Just want to have a quick word with Sue before she leaves.'

'Sorry to keep asking, but are you alright?' Jim asked as he joined her by the door.

Sue turned to look at him and fluttered the hand holding the cigarette, and it was obvious to him she was struggling not to cry. He placed his hand on her arm and as sympathy does, it set off her tears.

Jim steered her outside. He knew that if anyone saw her crying, tongues would start to wag immediately. She groped through her bag for a tissue and after blowing her nose, calmed down enough to voice her thanks.

'It's quite alright, Sue,' Jim responded. 'I don't like to see you upset. And,' he stressed, 'this whole situation is very awkward and uncomfortable.' Sue nodded vigorously, wiping her nose.

'What really pisses me off is the hypocrisy of the whole thing. I feel bad that Bentley's dead. No one would want that to happen to anyone, but I don't feel sorry about him. He was a nasty piece of work and he got us all suspicious of each other. The police are actually going to ask my husband if I was at home on the night Bentley was killed. It's come to that. As if I would murder anyone,' she protested while taking a deep drag of her cigarette. 'And what about Marlene? She told me tonight that she was in love with Bentley,' Sue stated in disbelief, staring at Jim as if to challenge him to dispute the information she had revealed.

Jim's face couldn't conceal his surprise. 'But she must have known he was….' He left his statement hanging.

'Yes, she did know but it seems that she was happy to have him no matter what.'

'Takes all sorts,' Jim volunteered.

'It sure does,' Sue said as she ground her butt into the grout between the row of bricks. 'And why are the police here?'

'The decision was made to invite them,' Jim justified.

'Well, I wish they weren't. It's creepy having two men hanging around pretending to feel sympathy for someone they didn't know.'

'Did anyone really know Bentley?' Jim asked after a short pause. Sue was really working herself up. She wasn't normally so, how could he put it, out of control.

'No. Probably not.' Sue picked up her bag from the wall and wearily hung it over her shoulder.

'Suppose I'd better go back in before they start thinking that you and I are having an affair.' She laughed sadly, and Jim smiled in sympathy. Why didn't she go home?

'It'll all be sorted out soon. Don't worry about the police. They're talking to everybody. Not just you. You've got nothing to worry about.'

Sue looked at him and he could see the doubt in her eyes. She blinked slowly, turned, and walked back into the noisy dining hall.

MRS SHUTE COLLAPSES

Daphne, busying herself, picked up discarded paper plates and empty plastic glasses, and made her way to the large rubbish bin immediately inside the door to the dining room kitchen. She threw the detritus into the bin and as she rinsed her fingers under the cold tap at the sink, a hand placed itself on her bottom. She continued to let the water wash over her hands then picked up a tea towel that had been left on the bench and slowly dried her wet fingers. The hand continued to run its palm down the back of her thigh, pausing to outline the loops and catches of her suspender belt.

The hand stopped suddenly at the top of her stocking. The door to the kitchen had swooshed open and the mother of one of the prefects in Year 12 blustered in carrying used paper plates. Sergeant O'Shea stepped back while Daphne casually put down the tea towel and turned around.

'That's good of you, Mrs Taylor,' Daphne choked, attempting to put authority into her voice as the intruder dumped the rubbish into the bin along with the other discarded plates and plastic glasses.

O'Shea picked up a paper plate off the kitchen bench, threw it on top of Mrs Taylor's pile in the bin and casually wandered out.

'No problem. Less to do later,' Mrs Taylor justified as she watched the sergeant leave the room.

'He's one of the policemen, isn't he? Saw him at the service. Nothing like a man in uniform, eh? Not that he's wearing his uniform now,' she continued, smiling at Daphne.

Daphne agreed, hoping that her colour had faded. He'd taken such an exciting risk. Thank God it hadn't been anyone important walking in. Imagine if it had been Mr Pritchard or Jim. Mind you, Mrs Taylor could talk under wet concrete.

As Daphne and the chatty mother tidied up the kitchen, she tried to push the groin twitches for Sergeant O'Shea aside. Forcing herself to think about Mr Pritchard would deflect any amorous thoughts.

Robert was proving to be a bit stronger than she'd previously given him credit for. He seemed to be dealing with Bentley's death and the enquiry fairly well. Of course, they would all be glad when whomever had done it was caught and life could get back to some semblance of normality if a school could ever be described as normal.

Once some time had passed she'd be able to go out more openly with Ray. But was that what she wanted? Once a relationship like theirs became socially acceptable it could lose much of its zest. Forbidden fruit, the fear of being caught, the excitement of breaking society's mores. Well, she'd just have to see how she felt when the mystery was solved.

'Thanks for your help,' Daphne reiterated to Mrs Taylor, while she wiped down the stainless-steel benches and the stovetop. As soon as she felt it was appropriate, she told Mrs Taylor that she'd catch her later, and went out to join those still drinking and chatting.

Hardly anyone had left. Usually by now there would only be the stayers; the ones who didn't want to go home or the ones who liked the free drinks. And, of course, the ones who couldn't bear to miss out on the gossip.

Ray O'Shea quickly joined his colleague who was wearily listening to a story of the past glory of a rugby win by the same Old Boy who'd button-holed Anh. He'd had his fair share of the school's Chateau Cardboard.

The Old Boy, enjoying the audience, also felt it was his duty to comment on the current role of the police. 'Don't know how you buggers deal with all the riff raff. In my day we'd have given them a bit of biffo. Kept them in their place.' The Old Boy took a swig of his wine and grimaced while complaining, 'Bloody hell this stuff's rubbish. But at least it's free,' and with that he waddled off to replenish his glass.

'Bugger me,' Stone sighed. 'What a pain. Let's get out of here. We've done our duty and you've had your daily dose of Mrs W.'

O'Shea looked at him as if to say, 'I don't know what you mean', when a loud crash could be heard over the laughter and chatter.

The two men turned quickly to see that Mrs Shute had fallen over on to one of the trestle tables and her bulky frame had collapsed it to the floor. A number of guests rushed over to help, crowding around the flattened table, some not sure what to do but wanting to appear concerned.

Alan Stone quickly brushed through the cluster of guests and knelt down next to Mrs Shute. Her face had gone waxy and perspiration dotted her forehead and above her top lip. Stone deftly pulled down her voluminous skirt, which had flown up in the fall. He was protecting the onlookers as much as Mrs Shute's dignity. Looking up at the eager, peering faces, he instructed them to call an ambulance.

Sergeant O'Shea could see Daphne standing in the circle surrounding Mrs Shute and with a hand gesture, signalled for her to ring for help. Daphne gave a thumbs-up and dashed off to the kitchen.

Sergeant O'Shea bent over his boss. 'Mouth to mouth?' he asked. 'Maybe,' Stone answered reluctantly. 'She's breathing, but she doesn't look too good. Her colour is terrible.'

Stone turned his face up to the circle of guests again instructing, 'Can you open all the doors and windows. Let some air in.' He felt for her pulse.

Suddenly, Mrs Shute emitted a gurgling sound and froth bubbled up from her throat. The audience collectively stepped back in horror. Her body convulsed and much to everyone's embarrassment, she farted loudly. O'Shea had to stop himself from laughing out loud and he could hear the odd guffaw which was quickly stifled.

Her breathing had become erratic. Was it an epileptic fit? Stone stood to take off his jacket and hurriedly placed it over her chest. He kept his hands on her shoulders in an attempt to keep her still but the tilt of the tabletop on the floor wasn't making it easy.

A guest, watching the detective's efforts at calming Mrs Shute, could be heard chuckling to a neighbour, 'Rather him than me.'

Jim frowned, shaking his head. Sometimes these snobby parents were so, so, up themselves. That was the only way he could think of describing them. Who the hell did they think they were?

O'Shea, seeing Stone's difficulty, indicated to him that they should move Mrs Shute off the table and onto the floor. It would be easier to apply mouth to mouth if still required. A couple of men moved forward and lifted a leg each and after much puffing, the four managed to place Mrs Shute onto the wooden floor. Another guest removed his jacket and placed it under Mrs Shute's head.

Mr Shute, who had forced his way through the throng with the assistance of Jim and the headmaster, bent over his wife and attempted to kneel down, but his legs had difficulty manoeuvring.

'Bloody arthritis,' he grumbled to Jim. He remained standing, awkward and powerless. Jim rushed off to find him a chair and he begrudgingly sat down at the back of the circle of onlookers, all watching his wife writhe on the floor as Stone tried his best to save her.

The spectators were grimacing at the undignified thrashing and Mr Pritchard and Jim averted their eyes from the horror of her indignity.

Gulping for air, it became apparent that Mrs Shute was able to breathe unaided, but her jerky movements and the constant bubbles blowing out of her mouth like a clown at a child's party unnerved the gathering and some moved away to replenish their drinks.

The crowd parted when two ambulance men, led by a puffing Daphne, briskly strode towards the body on the floor. Stone calmly informed the paramedics about the situation and they efficiently set up a respirator and attached the regulation paraphernalia required at the scene of an accident.

The detective directed the curious guests to stand back so that the paramedics could hoist Mrs Shute on to the waiting stretcher and carry her out to the ambulance parked on the Oval near the steps to the dining hall. Its doors were left open in anticipation.

Stone, after he'd watched the stretcher with its cumbersome cargo being carried out to the ambulance, stared around the room to note who was still there, and seeing that it was virtually everyone, called out for them to stay in the building.

'It looks like Mrs Shute may have had an epileptic fit but in case it wasn't we'll have to take the names of everyone present,' he instructed his sergeant.

353

'And get the list of those who attended the service from Mr Pritchard or Daphne.'

ANOTHER MURDER?

Sue too was appalled by the sight of Mrs Shute lying on the floor, her dress hoiked up to her waist and the ghastly bubbling from her mouth. What on earth could have made her collapse like that? Bentley's mother didn't seem like the sort of woman to be overcome with grief.

Topping up her wine to help calm her nerves, Sue took her drink and walked out to the top of the steps and watched the paramedics struggle their way down the steps to the ambulance, its headlights shining over the empty Oval.

Sue could see Daphne waiting by the ambulance and she was soon joined by the policemen followed by Jim and the headmaster. The group huddled around the open door at the back of the van watching Mrs Shute being slid inside and then the doors were slammed shut. The ambulance drove off, its siren blaring once it had crossed the Oval and was onto the road.

Those outside walked slowly back to the boarders' dining room, all asking themselves questions. Was it another attempted murder? Was Mrs Shute unwell before she came to Sydney? Was it merely a coincidence that she became unwell at her son's wake? Had someone poisoned her tea?

When everyone had returned to the dining room, conversation dimmed, and the guests faced the detective and his entourage. Their faces showed concern but also curiosity. Detective Stone stood silently in front of the audience, holding up his hands to indicate he wanted their attention.

'Ladies and gentlemen. Mrs Shute has been taken to hospital,' he began. 'She's in good hands and doesn't appear to be in any danger. I ask that you all remain here for the time being so we can talk to anyone who may have any information in relation to Mrs Shute that may aid us in our enquiries.'

A voice called out, 'But you said she's not in any danger. Why do we have to stay?'

'The circumstances are somewhat unusual. Mr Bentley Shute has died and now his mother has been taken ill. We just want to make sure that nothing untoward has happened. If you could give your name to Mr Pritchard, Mr Cameron or Mrs Withers and anything you may feel is relevant to our investigation. Then you'll be free to go.'

'Do you think someone tried to murder Mrs Shute?' a woman asked importantly.

'As I said, the circumstances of Mrs Shute's illness are unusual. We must take every step necessary,' Stone stated, unwilling to expose further information.

Shit. Bentley's father, Stone suddenly remembered, and turning to Sergeant O'Shea, urgently asked him to see if Mr Shute was okay. In the drama of the awkward situation with Mrs Shute, both he and O'Shea had forgotten about her husband. It was too late for him to accompany his wife in the ambulance. The sergeant hurried over to Mr Shute who was still sitting despondently, but now accompanied by Marlene, who was crouched at his feet talking earnestly.

O'Shea leant over Mr Shute, who stared up at him anxiously, clutching his stubby of beer. 'How's my wife? She's done this before. I feel bloody useless sitting here. Can I go with her?'

'I'm sorry, Mr Shute. She's already gone in the ambulance. But of course, you can visit her. I'll organise for someone to take you home and you can visit her tomorrow. Or tonight, if that's what you want. Mrs Shute is going to St Vincent's so she's in good hands,' O'Shea reassured him.

He couldn't help but feel sorry for the man. Shute was probably someone who in his own environment had clout, but in this environment was out of his depth. His passivity was indicative of his unease.

Marlene, struggled to her feet, holding onto the back of Shute's chair. Ignoring the policeman, she stared at Mr Shute. Her face was mottled. She tugged at her hair and pulled at her lips, forcing them into grotesque shapes. 'Will you be alright, Mr Shute?'

Bentley's father mumbled that he would be. Sergeant O'Shea couldn't tell if Marlene's presence was annoying him or whether he was upset about his wife. Marlene's behaviour was odd. Maybe, she'd had too much to drink.

'Would you be able to call Mr Shute a taxi, Miss Bates? If that suits you, Mr Shute?' O'Shea asked, looking from Marlene to Bentley's father. Mr Shute sighed his agreement and Marlene pushed her way through the crowd to the kitchen. O'Shea waited and a few minutes later, Marlene was back, saying a taxi was on its way. The sergeant thanked her and made his excuses to the two of them.

The policeman hoped he'd done the right thing asking for her assistance. She seemed different to when he and Alan had interviewed her. Perhaps it was the effect of the memorial service and a few drinks.

'I got Marlene to ring a taxi for Mr Shute,' O'Shea informed Stone. 'And I told him where Mrs Shute had been taken.'

Stone nodded. He felt guilty that he'd forgotten Mr Shute but the man was easy to overlook.

'This can't be easy for him,' Stone said. 'We need to do the room and see if anyone has noticed anything unusual. Mrs Shute may just have had a fit or a gastric attack but we need to make sure that's all it is. After what happened to her son, someone may be attacking the parents.'

'Fuck, there are so many people here. How are we going to talk to them all?' O'Shea questioned.

'We can't. But we'll know who was here and can interview them later. Just see if anyone has anything that might be of interest. Keep your eyes peeled. The person may still be here. That's if Mrs Shute *didn't* have a medical incident.' Stone raised his eyebrows to intimate the possibility of more foul play.

O'Shea grunted his agreement and went in search of Daphne. Perhaps she'd been given some info by the guests. He could see her with Mr Cameron.

As he walked towards Daphne, Marlene escorted Mr Shute to the entrance of the dining hall. A number of guests stood watching. Mrs Sinclair whispered to her husband that Miss Bates seemed more upset than Mr Shute's father. It was understandable that she'd be sad about her friend's death, but judging by her face, she appeared to be in a state of shock.

Bill MacGregor noting the same, quickly approached Marlene and offered to see Mr Shute to the taxi. The School Sergeant's offer was ignored. Marlene grabbed Mr Shute's arm and forcefully led him out of the room. It crossed Bill's mind that she was drunk.

The Sarge peered around the room. Where was Jim? Daphne? He'd have a word with them and they could help him make sure Marlene got home safely. What on earth was she doing looking after Bentley's dad in her state?

'Daphne, I'm a bit concerned about Marlene. She doesn't seem herself,' Bill said, once he'd found her.

'She doesn't, does she?' Daphne agreed. 'Has she had too much to drink? Hope she doesn't drive

359

home. We'll have to call her a taxi,' Daphne suggested as Sergeant O'Shea joined them.

Seeing their concerned faces, O'Shea asked what was wrong. Both started to reply but Bill was determined to be heard. 'Marlene. She's very upset. She shouldn't drive home. Too much to drink.'

O'Shea agreed, inwardly groaning at the pomposity of the man.

'Can I ask if either of you have noticed anything unusual tonight? Or overheard any comments or seen something that could be useful to our investigation?'

'Like someone admitting to the murder?' Bill asked sarcastically.

'No, Bill. But some of the guests have been drinking quite heavily and something may have been said inadvertently,' Sergeant O'Shea replied firmly.

'Well, that bloke over there might be of interest,' Bill said, pointing at Graham Russell. 'Might be a poofter friend of Shute's.'

Sergeant O'Shea was about to tell him that they'd already interviewed Russell but changed his mind. Bill wasn't someone he wanted to share information with.

He turned to Daphne saying, 'Mrs Withers, did you notice anyone hanging around Mrs Shute? Anyone who was paying her a lot of attention?'

Daphne tried not to smile at Ray O'Shea. His tone of authority was sexy. 'I didn't, Sergeant. Most of the guests just seemed intent on catching up with each other. And having free food and drink. Do you think there is something suspicious about Mrs Shute being taken ill?'

O'Shea delayed answering. If it were just Daphne, he would have told her about Stone's concern, but as MacGregor was present, he didn't want to share.

'Probably just gastric. Or maybe some type of fit.'

Bill couldn't put his finger on the feeling, but his intuition was to leave the two of them alone. He felt in the way.

'I'll go and find Mr Pritchard. Maybe he can help you.' He looked at Daphne who seemed preoccupied with a loose thread on her jacket.

MacGregor walked off, shaking his head. Nowt so queer as folk.

AN APOLOGY

Marlene stumbled Mr Shute to the cab. She hugged him tightly before he got in. 'I'm so sorry. So sorry.'

Shute uncomfortably acknowledged her words with a grimace and a slight shrug before slamming the door shut. Thank God he was out of there. Bunch of bloody idiots and how come the missus got sick now? Typical. Visit the hospital tonight or in the morning?

As the taxi drove away, Marlene leant against the wall in front of the Old Block. She felt dizzy. It would be so nice to lie down. To sleep, perchance to dream. Where the hell did that come from? Better get back to the do. Oh God, to face all those people.

She carefully trod her way back towards the dining hall and stopped on the stairs to the entrance. Could she bear to go back in? She saw that Sue was on the steps smoking and peering into the darkness of the Oval.

'You alright, Sue?' Marlene asked.

'Me? Yes. Why do you ask?' For Marlene to be concerned about her was very unexpected. Was Marlene drunk? She sounded a bit slurry.

'Just wondered. I haven't always been supp...supportive of you. 'Sorry 'bout that.'

Sue was gob smacked. Where had this come from? Marlene must be really pissed.

'Are *you* okay?' Sue asked, trying to ascertain Marlene's state of mind. Her face was mottled and blotchy.

Marlene ignored the question and grabbed Sue's arm. 'I mean it. I'm sooooo sorry 'bout everything.'

Sue looked down at Marlene's hand clutching her arm. 'It's alright. It's been hard for all of us.'

She put her other arm around Marlene and hugged her. This was so strange. Poor girl, losing such a close friend.

Marlene leant into Sue and she could feel tears and mucus wetting her top. They stood for a minute then Marlene pulled herself away muttering about having to leave. She steadied herself by holding onto the wall then hurried down the steps into the gloom of the Oval.

My God. That was weird, Sue thought. She walked slowly back up the steps. Something wasn't right. Marlene's behaviour was so out of character.

Only a few of the guests had finally left and there was still a large crowd surrounding the policemen. Jim stood on the periphery of the circle with his wife, both worried as they listened to Stone's questions and comments.

Sue quickly made her way over to the deputy head. 'Jim. Jim. Can I have a word?' she whispered, indicating for them to move away from the others.

Jim and Anh followed as Sue walked to edge of the room.

'It's Marlene. Something is very wrong with her. She apologised to me about not being supportive,' Sue explained unable to keep the shock out of her voice.

Anh frowned at Jim as if to say, so what?

'Really? That is unusual. Where is she now? I hope she's not driving,' Jim said. Turning to Anh he added quietly, 'Marlene and Sue haven't exactly got on with each other. A bit of jealousy on Marlene's part.'

Anh's eyebrows rose in understanding.

'She went onto the Oval. I should have gone with her, but she just dashed off,' Sue explained.

'I think we'd better have a word with Alan. We don't want her to do anything silly,' Jim said, his face crinkled with worry. 'It's been a trying day for everyone and after a few drinks she may be feeling very....' he couldn't think of the word.

The three walked back to the group surrounding the detective and his sergeant. Jim manoeuvred his way into the circle. 'Alan, a word, please.'

Stone detecting Jim's urgency, left the group and followed the trio. O'Shea quickly joined them, and the two policemen listened intently to Jim's concern about Marlene.

Stone turned to Sue. 'Do you think that she may do something stupid?'

'God, I hope not, but she's definitely not herself. We've never got on so for her to apologise to me is very odd. She sounded really sad and desperate.'

'Do you know where she is?' the detective asked.

'She went onto the Oval,' Sue told him.

Stone stared thoughtfully at the floor then said, 'We need to get the Oval lights on again. Ray, can you ask Daphne to turn them on. Also, we need to check if she has driven home. Sue, do you know her car? Can you see if it's still here? Jim, can you get some of the guests who haven't had too many drinks and ask them to check around the school and on the Oval? Mrs Cameron, would you mind looking in the women's toilets and the kitchen? Anywhere around here. Just in case Miss Bates has come back into the hall.'

Everyone nodded vigorously.

'Come back here as soon as you have any information,' Stone instructed. The area of the school was enormous. With luck she may have just gone home in a taxi.

'Also Ray, can you ask Daphne if she has a phone number for Miss Bates? She may have gone home.'

Ray's eagerness to have an excuse to talk to Daphne was not lost on Stone nor Jim and Anh smiled as they watched him rush off.

'Right, let's get cracking,' Stone commanded, almost clapping his hands. He'd been at the school too long.

Jim scanned the room to see who he thought would be helpful. He saw an Old Boy he'd taught a few years ago and remembered him to be a reliable student.

'Hamish, sorry to interrupt, but could I ask for your assistance?'

The Old Boy seeing it was his past teacher, reverted to his student days. 'Yes, Mr Cameron, Sir. How can I help?'

The other Old Boys, some a little put out that they weren't included in the request for assistance, lingered waiting to hear to what Hamish was asked to do.

How much should he tell Hamish? He didn't want to make Marlene appear in a negative light, but she had to be found. 'We're a bit worried about one of the teachers. Miss Bates. She's had a few to drink and we don't want her to be driving home. She's very upset about Mr Shute's death. If you could help us find her, we can make sure she's alright.'

The group gathered around Hamish, all making suggestions about where to look.

'Can you come back here and report to Detective Stone if you do find her? Oh, and bring her with you,' Jim added.

All agreed and dashed off, led by Hamish. It was exciting being part of a police investigation. The lights again flooded the Oval.

Anh cautiously searched the Ladies toilets, the kitchen and every nock and cranny of the boarders' dining room. Nothing.

Sue made her way up to the street where teachers usually parked their cars. Marlene's car might be a Datsun or a Toyota, but she wasn't really sure. Maybe it was cream. There it was, a fairly old cream Toyota and there were none similar in the street. Most were much more expensive.

Sue quickly returned to the dining hall, glad to be back in a brightly lit room with Stone waiting for updates. She informed the detective that the car was still there and there was a good chance it was Marlene's.

'Can you think of anywhere else that she might go? The staffroom? A classroom? The Ladies' toilets?' he asked.

'I'll check. She didn't have an office and none of us has a regular classroom. Anyway, I'll go and see if I can find her,' Sue complied.

Classrooms at night were eerie and although the lights were on in the corridors, it was spooky. Sue sprinted down the hall and peered into the classrooms. This was going to take ages. Marlene could be anywhere. Sue poked her head around the door to the staffroom. It was empty. What about the telephone cubicle? Nothing. She ran upstairs to the toilets and bending down looked under each door. Again, nothing. Where the hell was she?

Jim stood in the centre of the Oval. Would Marlene still be here? Were they making a fuss about nothing and she had just gone home? Was Alan Stone more suspicious about Marlene than he was letting on?

He stared up at the top of the main building which towered over the Oval. There were no lights on the balustrade, but did he detect movement? Was someone up there? A trick of the light? The balustrade was only used on ANZAC Day by the lone piper. Jim wasn't even sure how anyone got up there.

He walked briskly back to the dining room. Stone was listening to Anh's report that she had found nothing. Both stopped their conversation and turned to face Jim. 'Anything?' Stone asked.

'Not sure, but I think I caught sight of some movement on the balustrade. I could be wrong.'

Seeing their puzzled expressions, he explained it was where the piper performed on special occasions. 'It's the little balcony off the top of the main building. The one that overlooks the Oval.'

'How do you get up there?' Stone asked. Jim admitted that he had no idea but maybe Daphne or Mr Pritchard would know.

The three peered around the room at the few people who were still in the dining hall. There was no sign of Daphne or the headmaster.

THE PLOT THICKENS

Sue nervously made her way down the stairs from the Ladies' toilets into the corridor. She paused outside the staffroom. Was it worth another look?

As Sue went to open the door, a hand was placed on her shoulder. Her heart stopped. Oh God. I'm going to die, she screamed inwardly. She couldn't move. The hand was removed. Fearfully, she turned her head slowly. George was standing behind her grinning.

'Oh my God, you gave me such a fright. What on earth are you doing?'

George laughed. 'Sorry.'

'And so you should be. I thought I was the next victim.' Sue ran her hands through her hair and breathed deeply.

George grimaced, seeing how afraid she was. 'I saw you leave and come over here, so I followed you.'

Sue stared at him. For goodness sake.

'We're looking for Marlene. Miss Bates. She's gone missing. Have you seen her?' Sue asked, unable to keep the irritation she felt out of her voice. What on earth was George doing hanging around? Didn't he leave ages ago?

'She went into the assembly hall after she talked to you,' George said, glad that he could assist her in some small way.

'Really? Are you sure?' George nodded. 'We need to go and tell the police. Come with me and you can tell them what you saw.'

George's reluctance was clear. He made no effort to move.

'George. She may do something rash, so you have to come with me. Everyone is looking for her,' Sue said, annoyed with his unwilling attitude.

The boy hesitated. 'But will I get into trouble?'

'Oh, George. Don't worry about that. There's more important things going on. And I'm sure the police will be grateful for your help.'

George didn't reply but followed Sue down the corridor. She was angry with him. Not the outcome he'd hoped for.

'Mr, er, Detective Stone. This is George and he saw Marlene go into the assembly hall,' Sue explained breathlessly as soon as she found the policeman still in the dining hall.

'Hello, George,' Stone greeted with a quizzical rise of an eyebrow. What was the student still doing here? 'We've met before,' he told Sue. 'You have some information?' he asked, turning his attention back to George.

'Um. Yeah. I saw Miss Bates going into the assembly hall after she'd been talking to Mrs Armstrong.'

'How long ago was that?' Stone asked.

'Oh. Um. About half an hour ago.'

'How did she seem?'

'Dunno really. She seemed in a hurry. Kept tripping over.'

Stone thought for a few seconds and looking around for Jim, called out, beckoning him to join them. 'Jim. George here saw Miss Bates go into the assembly hall. We need to get everyone over there immediately.'

Jim and Anh listened closely, eager to hear more instructions.

'Jim, is that balustrade thing near the assembly hall?' Stone asked urgently.

'Yes. Yes it is. It's above the hall. I've never been up there but there must be a way. Bill was the one who took the pipers up.'

Jim looked around for the School Sergeant, but MacGregor was not in the hall. Where the hell was he? And where was Daphne? She'd know.

The deputy was about to ask if anyone had seen her when Daphne and Sergeant O'Shea appeared in the doorway.

'Daphne. Thank God you're here,' Jim said as he ran towards them. 'We need to get up to the little balcony in the tower off the assembly hall.'

Daphne, a tad perplexed, asked, 'Where the piper plays?'

'Yes. Yes. We don't know how to get up there. You know, don't you?'

Everyone stared at Daphne. 'It's normally locked, so I'll have to get the key from my office,' she explained without asking why the key to the tower was needed. All followed as she led the way to her office.

The door to Daphne's office was open and the lights were on. They followed Daphne into the room, shocked to see that drawers had been pulled out and papers thrown onto the floor. Cupboards had been searched and one small door with hooks on the inside had gaps where keys should have been.

Daphne, ignoring the mess in her office, searched through the keys to see which ones were missing.

'The key to the assembly hall isn't there and the one to the piper's balcony isn't either. Others are missing as well.'

All turned to Detective Stone. What was going to happen next?

Stone pointed at Daphne, Sergeant O'Shea, and Jim. 'Daphne, you can lead the way and as a woman, we'd appreciate your gentle touch with Miss Bates.

If it's needed. And if it is her up on the balustrade.'

Daphne nodded.

'Ray. Jim. If you could gather the men and place yourselves below the balcony.'

Both men looked at him questioningly.

'Miss Bates seems very distressed and there is a chance she may do something stupid. We need something to stop a fall. Can you get some large blankets or tarpaulins?'

Sue, who had been hovering in the background with George, asked doubtfully, 'Do you really think she'd jump off the building?'

'We have to be prepared for anything. Miss Bates appears to have been in love with Mr Shute and now he's dead. She may be so distraught that she could do anything,' Stone justified.

No-one said a word. The thought of a teacher jumping off a building was unbelievable. But, Bentley Shute had been murdered, so anything was possible.

Sergeant O'Shea and Jim muttered to each other and left the room. There were tarpaulins in the Art Department and the grounds-men had cover sheets for the cricket pitches. Time was of the essence.

'Sue, Mrs Armstrong. I'd like you to ring an ambulance in case the worst happens. Tell them to come immediately. Warn them that there may be an attempted suicide,' Stone instructed.

Sue opened her mouth, then closed it. She would do as she was told. Marlene had certainly been acting oddly, but would she commit suicide? However, it was better to err on the side of caution rather than assuming she wouldn't do anything extreme.

'Yes of course. I'll ring from the staffroom. Where do you want the ambulance to come?'

'We don't want sirens to frighten her, so tell them to park in the street next to the Oval. And no sirens.'

Sue nodded her head vigorously to show she understood and after picking up her bag, walked to the staffroom to make the call.

Stone and Daphne were about to leave her office when they noticed George hovering near the door.

'George. Still here?' Stone asked.

The boy shrugged his shoulders as if to say where else would he be.

'Well, as you are, I'd like you to go and find Mr Pritchard and Mr MacGregor and ask them to join Mr Cameron and Sergeant O'Shea outside the assembly hall. Tell them to go there immediately. If they ask why you are here, tell them that I gave you permission.'

George hesitated and looked to Daphne for reassurance. She gave him a tight smile and he quickly left the room.

THE HUNT IS ON

'Right, Daphne. It's you and me. We need to go and find Miss Bates,' Stone said, hoping that she would be up to the task. There'd been no point asking Sue to be part of the possible confrontation as there had obviously been too much bad blood between them. Even if Marlene had apologised to her.

'Yes. Yes we do,' Daphne replied nervously. She was proud to be involved but it was an enormous responsibility to try and comfort a distraught woman who may be thinking of jumping off the building.

Marlene had never been a favourite of hers. She'd often treated Daphne differently to the way she was with the teachers. It was as if she wasn't as important, being only a secretary. Also, Daphne had never allowed Bentley to inveigle his way into her life. She knew he only wanted to befriend her because of her position as the headmaster's secretary and her access to the inner workings of the school. No doubt Bentley would have made disparaging remarks about her to his circle, once she realised she wasn't going to play his game.

'Are there duplicate keys to the ones Miss Bates may have taken?' Stone asked, remembering Daphne had told him before that there were master keys in a locked drawer. She pulled out a key fob from her handbag and opened the drawer at the bottom of the desk. 'These should open most of the doors in the building,' she said as she retrieved the set.

'Good. Marlene may not have bothered to lock the doors behind her, but just in case.'

The two looked at each other. What on earth was going to happen next? Stone, sensing her concern, put his hand on her arm. 'We can only do what we can.'

Daphne grinned weakly and followed the detective as he led the way out of her office.

Their footsteps echoed down the empty corridor. The eyes in the photos of past and present students and teachers seemed to be watching them as they tiptoed towards the assembly hall.

The doors to the assembly hall were open, the key still in the lock, but the hall was in darkness. Stone and Daphne stood in the doorway. The cavernous room seemed threatening without students.

Stone turned to Daphne. 'Where's the entrance to the piper's balcony?'

'It's off the stage, at the back.'

'If we turn on the lights, will every light go on? Including the one on the balustrade?' Stone asked quietly. He didn't want light to let Miss Bates know that they were there.

'I don't think so. But I'm not sure,' Daphne answered uncertainly. The stairs to the balustrade were really only used once a year so it was hard to remember.

'I think we'll have to make our way to the back without light. Will you be alright?' he asked her.

Again, she nodded. She could see the logic. If Marlene knew they were there, she might do something in desperation. But she had left the key in the door. Was this a cry for help?

Stone held out his hand to Daphne and they carefully made their way down the assembly hall to the stage. The exit signs gave a tinge of light as they climbed up the few steps to the stage. Daphne tripped on a chair which hadn't been placed correctly for the next assembly. They stopped. Would Marlene have heard?

Daphne put her finger to her lips and mimed to the detective that the door was off the back of the stage. Every footstep they took seemed amplified despite their attempts at being quiet. The door was behind a black curtain that hung covering the whole of the back wall.

Daphne stopped, dropping Stone's hand, thinking, Where was the door? She groped her way along the curtain and coming to the end of the heavy material, walked behind it fumbling for the door.

Stone waited, feeling helpless. Suddenly, the curtain bulged out and he could detect where Daphne was from the shape. He walked as quickly as he could around to the back of the curtain and felt his way to where she was standing. He could just make out Daphne's body in the darkness. She felt for him and holding his hand, she lifted it up and held it against the door. The squeeze told her that he understood.

This time, there was no key left in the door.

Daphne fumbled in her handbag and pulled out the set of master keys. The set fell to the floor. Both scrambled to find them in the darkness. Every noise might warn Marlene of their presence. Stone rubbed his hands over the floor. A clink told him he'd found them. Grasping the keys, he stood and with his other hand, felt for the keyhole. Daphne held her breath as he inserted the key. It was the wrong one. He tried another. This one opened the door. Both held their breath. Stone pushed the door open a little. The stairwell was black. He reached out to Daphne. His touch told her to stay back until he had gone first. Daphne's heart was pumping. The situation was almost erotic. Stop it.

Stone stepped out in front of her then fumbled for her hand. Daphne grabbed his and allowed herself to be led cautiously up the stairs. The steps wound their way in medieval style. This part of the school had been built in the late 1800s and were fashioned on the 'public' educational institutions of Britain.

Being careful not bump into each other, they slowly ascended. Moonlight, shining through a tiny window, revealed a small area at the top of the stairs and to the side of this was a door. Both stopped still.

Would this door lead to the balcony? Was the door locked?

Stone tentatively pushed at the door. It creaked slightly. It wasn't locked. They could hear breathing, or was it crying? Marlene must be out there. Stone was aware that they had to be delicate in their movements. Anything sudden or threatening could literally drive Marlene over the edge.

He signalled to Daphne for her to whisper to Marlene that she was there. He also silently hoped that Jim had found something that would break her fall. If she did jump.

Daphne gulped. The enormity of what she had to do was frightening. She knew she couldn't sound anxious or challenging.

Pushing the door open a little, Daphne said quietly through the gap, 'Is that you, Marlene?'

There was no reply except for sniffing.

'Marlene. It's Daphne. How are you?'

Daphne peeked around the door and in the moonlight, she could see Marlene turn her head towards the question. The sniffing had stopped but she said nothing.

'I hope you're okay. Can I come and talk to you?'

Marlene gave a slight shrug. Did it mean yes or no? Should she go out onto the balcony now?

Daphne swivelled her head to the detective for confirmation. Stone mouthed 'yes' while pointing at himself and shaking his head.

'Marlene, please don't be frightened. I just want to make sure you're okay.'

As Marlene didn't make any objections, Daphne opened the door just enough so she could pass through without revealing Detective Stone. Marlene was sitting on the stone floor with her back to the balustrade, her knees hugged to her chest.

Daphne stepped delicately towards her. She wished she hadn't worn such inappropriate shoes. Vanity had played a part, especially as she knew she'd be seeing Ray at the memorial service.

'Do you mind if I take my shoes off?' Daphne asked.

Marlene obviously taken aback by the question muttered, 'No.'

Daphne sat on the floor, not too close to Marlene. She pulled off her shoes with a sigh and placed them neatly beside her. 'That's better. They were killing me.'

The two sat in silence. Daphne desperately tried to think of what to say. She thought of hostage movies and how the negotiator charmed the hostage takers into releasing their captives. But they were unrealistic American films with unconvincing dialogue.

Marlene stared straight ahead. She flinched slightly when Daphne reached out and put her hand on her arm but remained silent. At least she hadn't pushed Daphne's hand away.

'I've never been up here before,' Daphne said lightly.

Marlene turned her head. 'Oh?'

'It's a bit too high for me. I don't like heights.'

'I don't either.'

Daphne was in a quandary. Was this the right moment to ask Marlene what she was doing?

'As neither of us like heights why don't we go down?'

Marlene shook her head vigorously. 'No!'

Daphne removed her hand. Silence returned.

Stone stood hidden at the doorway listening. He hoped that Jim and others had found a tarpaulin by now. They should be waiting down below, but after hearing how Marlene responded to Daphne, he thought that perhaps she was not going to do anything drastic. Better to be on the safe side though. If only she'd open up to Daphne. How long to wait?

Daphne too, was wondering how long she'd have to sit there. Marlene must have been incredibly fond of Bentley to be acting in such an extreme way.

'Did you talk much to Bentley's parents?' she eventually asked. 'They seemed nice.'

Marlene sniggered. 'Nice? Do you *really* think so?'

'Well, I don't know them, but they seemed pleasant enough,' Daphne answered. Had she hit a raw nerve with Marlene? Better change the subject.

'The service went well, didn't it? A good turn out.' Daphne stopped. She was talking platitudinous rubbish.

'Why don't you go? I want to be on my own. I don't need you feeling sorry for me,' Marlene whined.

'I don't feel sorry for you. I really didn't mean to make you feel that way,' Daphne said, hoping that she sounded genuine. Marlene was a difficult woman to warm to. Too defensive and bitter. And if she were honest, she found Marlene's fascination with Bentley and his group, unhealthy and a bit creepy.

'Marlene, I don't want to leave you like this. You're obviously very upset by this whole situation. It's upsetting for all of us.'

'Really? Really? You didn't like him. You didn't know him the way I did.' Marlene's voice had risen in anguish.

How could Daphne respond? It was true, she hadn't liked Bentley at all.

'Yes, you're right. I didn't know him the way you did, but I'm sorry that he died.'

Marlene hummed in disbelief. She wiped her nose on the sleeve of her jacket; her face a mixture of grief and anger. 'I loved him. Really loved him.'

How could Daphne respond to such a revelation? Bentley was gay. Surely Marlene knew that? 'I'm so sorry,' she said and reached out again with her hand to comfort the woman.

'I don't need your pity. It's all over. I can't take any more,' Marlene cried out as she began to prise herself to her feet.

Daphne watching, worried, asked, 'Are you going down now?'

'Yes. I am,' Marlene said.

'I'll come with you,' Daphne said desperately. Was Detective Stone still there?

As Daphne clumsily clambered to her feet, Marlene placed both hands on the railing of the balustrade and with a spring lifted one leg on to the top of the railing. A second leg soon followed. She sat swaying on top of the concrete parapet.

'Help. Help. Alan. Mr Stone,' Daphne cried out as she saw what Marlene was doing.

'Marlene. Don't. Stop. Please get down.'

Stone rushed out from behind the door, but it was too late. Although the balcony was not large, in the few seconds it took him to reach her, Marlene had lent over and let herself fall off the balustrade.

He stood at the edge peering down, hoping to God that Jim was prepared while Daphne covered her eyes in horror.

While Daphne and Stone were preoccupied with Marlene, the group of men were waiting below, staring upwards in anticipation. They stood on the grass at the bottom of the building, holding the edges of a large tarpaulin like flag bearers at the opening of an international rugby match.

Anh was standing to the side of the men with her arm around a teary Mrs Sinclair who watched her husband nervously clutch the tarp. The other women, including Sue, stood holding their breath. All they could think of was, Will she? Won't she?

Graham Russell had pushed his way into the group of men so he too could assist. Despite his grief he couldn't help but think what a great story this would make. Rodney Addington looked on miserably, feeling helpless. There was very little room for him. Gary had dragged Brian and Ian with him to join the square around the tarpaulin. Even George was holding a corner.

Matthews and the boys in Churchill watched the activity from the upstairs windows of the boarding house. Peter Charteris, feigning disapproval, stood with his charges. The proximity of the boarding house offered a great view. This was better than watching a rugby final.

As Marlene's body dropped heavily through the air, Jim shouted directions for the men to move slightly one way, then another. The tarpaulin was not to be pulled too taut as the last thing Jim wanted was for Marlene to bounce off as if on a trampoline.

Her body thwacked onto the tarp and the men slowly lowered it to the ground. Jim carefully stepped onto the tarpaulin and walked towards her. She was not dead, nor did she appear to be badly injured.

'Marlene. Are you okay?' Jim asked as he knelt down beside her. She lay on her back sobbing, her arms crossed over her head in humiliation.

Stone and Daphne arrived panting from their run down the winding stairs. Detective Stone stood over Marlene and stated for all to hear, 'Miss Marlene Bates. You are under arrest for the murder of Mr Bentley Shute.'

DETECTIVE STONE EXPLAINS

Jim Cameron and Daphne sat silently but expectantly with Mr Pritchard in his office waiting for the police to arrive. A full explanation of events was due although they had attempted to put together the pieces of the puzzle by themselves over the last few days.

A knock brought the three of them to their feet. Detective Stone and Sergeant O'Shea were at the door. All would soon be revealed.

Daphne smoothed her skirt and flicked a glance at the sergeant. Ray O'Shea caught her eye and his face softened from his usual professional police passivity.

He smiled, then quickly included Cameron and Pritchard in his welcome. Stone shook hands with the two men and nodded his hello to Daphne.

'Let's sit down, shall we?' Mr Pritchard suggested tentatively, indicating the couch and armchairs with a slight wave of his hand.

O'Shea and Stone waited till the others returned to their seats. Their eagerness to hear the outcome couldn't be disguised.

The detective cleared his throat to begin. They watched him eagerly.

Alan's certainly a lot more handsome than Hercules Poirot, Jim thought and couldn't help but smile at the familiarity of the scene, the denouement, the solution to so many whodunnits and television crime series. His mind wandered back to the incident in Rarotonga. Stone had proved himself well then.

'Miss Bates has been arrested for the murder of Bentley Shute,' Stone began in a formal tone. 'She hasn't been granted bail as it was believed she may try suicide again.'

Everyone nodded with understanding at the decision.

'When did you know it was her?' Daphne asked eagerly.

The detective took his time before answering.

'We contacted the neighbour Miss Bates used as her alibi. She did in fact go home after the game on Saturday and she knew that her neighbour had seen her. Miss Bates called out as she drove into the driveway. Mrs Sidoti usually sat on her balcony in the early evening. She also knew that as Mrs Sidoti is elderly, she retires early to watch television. Miss Bates could hear the TV in her unit because Mrs Sidoti is quite deaf and has the volume up high. Therefore, the car probably wouldn't be heard leaving again. Miss Bates left the unit to return to the school about quarter past six. She knew Mr Shute was meant to meet Mr Russell around half past seven so she had to visit him early enough to stop him leaving.'

'Did she set up this alibi?' Jim asked.

'No, she didn't. But later she realised that it was useful for her to have Mrs Sidoti as a witness.'

The detective paused giving Jim the opportunity to ask, 'Alan, why wasn't Marlene arrested before?'

Stone embarrassed, nodded his head to indicate he understood why he was being asked the question.

'Ye-es Jim. You did tell me about your conversation with Miss Bates but unfortunately we focused more on other suspects.'

'What conversation?' Daphne asked, her eyes narrowing at Jim then Detective Stone.

'I'll hand that over to you, Jim,' Stone said.

Jim's face indicated surprise at being asked to explain. He felt uncomfortable as he realised that what he was about to say could make the detective appear unprofessional.

'Well. It was something and nothing. I was chatting to Marlene in the staffroom soon after Bentley was killed. She was, how can I put it? A bit distracted and upset. I asked her how she was and she started to tell me but we got interrupted.'

Jim rubbed his chin as if it would help him remember the incident. 'She said something about Bentley and about feeling guilty. She seemed a bit teary. I wondered if she wanted to tell me something important but then Rodney joined us and she stopped. When he'd finally gone, I asked her what she meant about feeling guilty but she just shrugged it off and wouldn't say anything else,' Jim paused and turned his attention to Daphne. 'I felt a bit like Mrs Armstrong did when Marlene apologised to her. It was so unusual for her to be emotional. I mentioned it to Alan as I thought it may be useful.'

Stone abashed, said, 'I'm ashamed to say that I was being somewhat sexist. I thought it seemed unlikely that a woman would have the strength to do what she did....'

His explanation was interrupted by Sergeant O'Shea who couldn't resist reminding him that he'd wondered the same thing.

'Yes. Yes. I know. I was being hypocritical, but as Marlene seemed so devoted to Mr Shute, I thought it was unlikely that she had a motive.'

Pritchard could be heard muttering in agreement. He found it hard to believe that a woman had the inclination or strength to perform such an act.

'Anyway, Alan. That's understandable,' Jim quickly said, to save the detective from any more embarrassment. 'What about Marlene's neighbour? Did she provide her with an alibi?'

Stone couldn't disguise his relief at changing the subject. 'Yes she did. When we talked to Mrs Sidoti previously she convinced us that she'd seen Miss Bates drive home and enter her unit and hadn't left home again. We didn't realise how deaf she was as she had her hearing aids in when we spoke to her.'

Seeing the doubt on Mr Pritchard's face Sergeant O'Shea hurriedly explained, 'Her hair covered her ears. She had a Princess Leia type of hairstyle.' His audience couldn't help but smile at the analogy.

'She seemed a reliable witness and had no reason to lie,' Detective Stone justified.

There was a mutter of understanding. Why would a nice old lady not be believed?

Stone gave everyone time to absorb his words then continued. 'We believed that Miss Bates was at home on the night Mr Shute was killed,' the detective stressed. Again there was murmuring of understanding at the explanation.

Stone waited until there was silence then said, 'However, as there was no sign of a struggle in Mr Shute's rooms, it seemed that he willingly let the perpetrator into his apartment. That made me think he knew the person or persons well.'

'Persons?' Mr Pritchard asked. 'Oh my God. How many were involved?'

'We'd had our suspicions about some of the boys and a couple of the teachers but it turned out their alibis were sound.'

'But how on earth would a big chap like Bentley allow himself to be killed?' Mr Pritchard asked. 'Surely, he'd put up a fight?'

'I'll come to that,' Stone said reasserting his authority then continued his story. 'According to Miss Bates, that night she asked him to marry her. She suggested marriage as a way for him to cover up his homosexuality but mainly because she was besotted by him.'

'Yes. Yes. She told me she loved him,' Daphne agreed, looking at the others with excitement.

'She also told Mrs Armstrong the same thing,' Sergeant O'Shea said, reinforcing Daphne's observation.

'Yes. And as we know on the night of the memorial function she apologised to Mrs Armstrong for not being supportive of her. That struck Sue as very odd because they had never been close. The opposite in fact. It was as if Marlene knew what she was going to do and wanted to make amends,' Stone surmised.

Jim, still puzzled as to why a strong man like Bentley did not fight back, asked, 'But Alan, how did she manage to actually kill him? It seems almost impossible. She's not a weak woman but I can't believe he'd be so passive.'

'She put tranquilizers in his drink,' Stone answered bluntly.

'Bloody hell. So she planned it,' Jim stated in disbelief.

'Yes and no. She already had the tranquilizers in her handbag. There's the possibility that she may have taken them herself. She believed that asking Bentley to marry her was her last chance at some form of happiness.'

'Are you saying that Marlene was contemplating suicide?' Jim asked.

'It appears so. Seeing that the other women on the staff were being paid attention by the male teachers and she wasn't, reinforced her belief that she was no longer attractive to the opposite sex. A relationship with Mr Shute was better than nothing. And she did love him.'

Stone's audience tutted at the enormity of the woman's desperation.

'But using her neighbour as an alibi seems to indicate that she had murder on her mind,' Mr Pritchard suggested.

'That's what I mean by yes and no. She thought of that later. Miss Bates was going to ask Shute to marry her and if he said no, then she planned to take her own life. She *was* very depressed,' Stone stressed. 'But when he declined her offer so vehemently, cruelly, Marlene snapped. She couldn't take any more humiliation.'

Silence dominated the room. It was a Shakespearean tragedy. They waited for the detective to keep talking.

'Miss Bates went to his apartment with a couple of bottles of wine and although he was meant to meet Graham Russell that night, he couldn't leave as she became very distraught.'

'So, by being kind and not leaving, he was killed,' Jim said.

'Yes! Miss Bates said that she knew he was meant to go out but because she was so upset she thought he wouldn't leave. She made sure that he had a number of drinks, thinking that would soften him up but then she started to put the tranquilizers in his wine after he told her that he wouldn't and couldn't possibly marry her.'

Mr Pritchard shook his head. 'This is incredible. Why would Miss Bates want to marry a homosexual?'

Daphne sighed then stressed, 'Marlene was lonely. She had no boyfriend and Bentley was a dynamic man. She probably felt that a life with him was better than being a clichéd spinster high school teacher.'

The men, other than Stone, seemed dubious.

'Come on,' Daphne argued, unable to keep the cynicism out of her voice. 'Marlene teaches at a boys' school where the decent men are already taken. She hasn't met anyone and has got to a certain age when her chances of meeting someone are diminishing. Everything is starting to look a bit bleak and having children seems out of the question. But marrying Bentley would give her companionship and kudos as he was, in her eyes, a great catch. Also, she might have believed that she was doing him a favour. A lot of men marry to cover up the fact that they're gay.'

This time, the men couldn't help but agree with Daphne's reasoning.

Stone, reinforcing Daphne's argument, explained, 'Once Mr Shute had said no to her suggestion, Marlene saw all her hopes of future happiness go down the drain. Also, as I said, it sounded as if he got rather nasty in his rejection of her. Apparently, he didn't think she was in his league.' Stone raised his eyebrows at the implication of Shute's reaction.

They all felt a degree of sympathy for Miss Bates.

'At first we thought that Bentley was prone to taking tranquilizers especially as we'd gathered that he had sometimes taken recreational drugs. He'd need to calm down after a big night. Get some sleep. Large traces of them were found in his blood,' he added. 'She kept pouring him drinks and adding the pills a few at a time.'

'That's so calculating,' Mr Pritchard said despairingly. 'Normal people don't do that sort of thing.'

'When it comes to matters of the heart, there is no logic,' Jim justified. 'What did Shakespeare say? Love is a form of madness.'

Sergeant O'Shea glanced at Daphne. Would he do something crazy for her? Definitely.

'So, after a few more drinks and the pills had taken their effect, Miss Bates led Mr Shute into his bedroom and after he'd gone to sleep, she attacked him with the samurai sword and then kicked it under the bed. It seems that she didn't really care if she was caught, although she did wipe the handle to get rid of fingerprints.'

'What about the broken cup?' Jim asked.

'I guess it was anger or humiliation,' Stone replied. 'She knew how fastidious he was, so to destroy his… how can I put it? His neatness. It was another emotional nail in the coffin.'

All agreed. Bentley was renowned for his tidiness. To some it was verging on obsessive.

'I can't help but feel sorry for Marlene,' Daphne said, catching the sergeant's eye. The things we do for love.

'She murdered a colleague,' Mr Pritchard exploded.

'I know. But she must have felt absolutely desperate to have done something so ghastly,' Daphne argued.

Mr Pritchard said nothing. He couldn't think of sympathetic words. The school was more important than a forlorn, rejected woman. What was going to happen to the school's reputation? A murder committed by a teacher against another teacher. What would happen to enrolments?

'Do you think that when Marlene saw Bentley's parents she realised the devastating effects of her actions?' Jim asked the detective.

'Perhaps. She managed to carry on as normal before the memorial service with the help of tranquilizers but being confronted by his parents drove her over the edge. Especially seeing Bentley's mother collapse. The full force of what she had done became too much.'

'But when I asked her about the parents she sounded… How can I put it? Quite critical. As if they were beneath Bentley,' Daphne said.

'She may have been repeating Bentley's attitude to his parents but at the same time she did feel sorry for them. Losing a son, even if they didn't get on, must have made her regret her actions,' Stone analysed.

'Jumping off a building seems a pretty old fashioned way of killing yourself,' Jim wondered aloud. 'There must be other more efficient methods. An overdose.'

The others turned their heads in surprise at his practical suggestion.

'Maybe it was a spur of the moment decision?' Daphne wondered. Jim was sounding rather hard-hearted. It wasn't like him to be so brutal.

'It was,' Stone confirmed. 'Miss Bates has admitted that she'd planned to resign at the end of the term and leave Sydney. She thought it would look suspicious if she left immediately after his death.'

'My God!' Daphne exclaimed. 'She has been calculating.'

'So, the journalist chap...?' Jim began, keen to lighten the atmosphere as he was aware that he had come across as insensitive.

'Graham Russell,' Daphne supplied quickly.

'Ah. Yes. Yes. Graham Russell. So he had nothing to do with anything?'

'It appears not, Mr Cameron. He was Mr Shute's partner. If that's the term these days? He was merely trying to find out what had happened to Bentley as he didn't turn up for their date,' O'Shea explained self-consciously. The thought of men having a date with each other was a little challenging.

Pritchard jumped in. 'The atmosphere around the school ever since Bentley died has been ghastly. Sue

Armstrong told me the other day she felt like resigning. Family trouble as well. Luckily, I talked her out of it.'

Daphne exchanged a look with Jim. What a tangled web we weave.

'Well, at least Mrs Shute has made a full recovery,' Mr Pritchard said with relief in his voice. 'It turns out that she is prone to epileptic fits. The stress of everything brought on her collapse.'

'Have they gone back to the country?' Jim asked.

'Yes,' replied Sergeant O'Shea, 'but they'll be back for Miss Bates's trial. That won't be for a few months.'

'I suppose we'll all have to give evidence?' Jim asked again, directing his question at Alan Stone.

'Bit like the old days, eh?'

'You could say that, Jim. But I think this time, it's a bit more straightforward.'

No-one said anything. At least for now the school's dust could settle.

9 780646 822761